PRIVATE
MONACO

James Patterson is one of the best-known and biggest-selling writers of all time. Among his creations are some of the world's most popular series including Alex Cross, the Women's Murder Club, Michael Bennett and the Private novels. He has written many other number one bestsellers including collaborations with President Bill Clinton, Dolly Parton and Michael Crichton, stand-alone thrillers and non-fiction. James has donated millions in grants to independent bookshops and has been the most borrowed adult author in UK libraries for the past fourteen years in a row. He lives in Florida with his family.

Adam Hamdy is a bestselling author and screenwriter. His most recent novel, *The Other Side of Night*, was an NPR best book of 2022 and a *New York Times* best thriller of the year, and has been described as ingenious and deeply moving. He is the author of the Scott Pearce series of modern spy thrillers, *Black 13*, *Red Wolves* and *White Fire*, and the Pendulum trilogy. Keep up to date with his latest books and news at www.adamhamdy.com.

THE PRIVATE NOVELS

Private (*with Maxine Paetro*)
Private London (*with Mark Pearson*)
Private Games (*with Mark Sullivan*)
Private: No. 1 Suspect (*with Maxine Paetro*)
Private Berlin (*with Mark Sullivan*)
Private Down Under (*with Michael White*)
Private L. A. (*with Mark Sullivan*)
Private India (*with Ashwin Sanghi*)
Private Vegas (*with Maxine Paetro*)
Private Sydney (*with Kathryn Fox*)
Private Paris (*with Mark Sullivan*)
The Games (*with Mark Sullivan*)
Private Delhi (*with Ashwin Sanghi*)
Private Princess (*with Rees Jones*)
Private Moscow (*with Adam Hamdy*)
Private Rogue (*with Adam Hamdy*)
Private Beijing (*with Adam Hamdy*)
Private Rome (*with Adam Hamdy*)

A list of more titles by James Patterson appears at the back of this book

WHY EVERYONE **LOVES** JAMES PATTERSON **AND** THE **PRIVATE SERIES**

'Great action sequences...
breathtaking twists and turns'
ANTHONY HOROWITZ

'An **unmissable**, breakneck ride'
JAMES SWALLOW

'**Exhilarating**, high-stakes action'
LESLEY KARA

'An exhilarating and **totally satisfying read**' *NB MAGAZINE*

'A **breakneck fast**, brutally good page-turner' *DAILY MAIL*

'Hits the ground running and the **pace never misses a beat**'
DAILY EXPRESS

'Yet another fine outing from the **master of thrillers**' *CITY A.M.*

JAMES PATTERSON
& ADAM HAMDY

PRIVATE MONACO

PENGUIN BOOKS

PENGUIN BOOKS

UK | USA | Canada | Ireland | Australia
India | New Zealand | South Africa

Penguin Books is part of the Penguin Random House group of companies
whose addresses can be found at global.penguinrandomhouse.com

Penguin Random House UK,
One Embassy Gardens, 8 Viaduct Gardens, London SW11 7BW

penguin.co.uk
global.penguinrandomhouse.com

Penguin
Random House
UK

First published by Century in 2024
Published in Penguin Books 2025
001

Typeset in 10.9/16.31pt ITC Berkeley Oldstyle Std by Jouve (UK), Milton Keynes
Printed and bound in Great Britain by Clays Ltd, Elcograf S.p.A.

The authorised representative in the EEA is Penguin Random House Ireland,
Morrison Chambers, 32 Nassau Street, Dublin D02 YH68

A CIP catalogue record for this book is available from the British Library

ISBN: 978–1–804–94618–3

For everyone who pursues excellence

CHAPTER 1

LIFE HADN'T BEEN this easy for a long time.

Justine and I had lingered over breakfast at the Hôtel de Paris in Monte Carlo. Our suite there was an extravagance for this leg of our European tour. It was opulent, bordering on decadent, but exactly the luxurious retreat we needed.

I had kept my promise to bring her back to Europe for a vacation. In the past two weeks, I hadn't regretted for a moment the commitment I'd made earlier in the year, when we'd been investigating the murder of Father Ignacio Brambilla, the priest who was shot dead at the launch of Private Rome. We'd spent days battling the forces of evil on the streets of the Eternal City, exposing a conspiracy that extended from a deadly criminal gang known as the Dark Fates as far as the ancient corridors of power in the Vatican itself. We'd discovered the Dark Fates were the street, verging on paramilitary, arm of a secret society known

1

as Propaganda Tre, which had infiltrated almost every part of Italian society. We'd uncovered a conspiracy to seize power in the Vatican, and the conspirators, including Milan Verde, leader of the Dark Fates, had been imprisoned.

As accustomed as I was to the challenges of running the world's biggest private detective agency, I had to admit I was enjoying the languid pace of our first proper vacation in a very long time. Late breakfasts, endless lunches, sights, beaches and award-winning dinners and shows had replaced crime-scene photos, fights and chases, and given me and Justine the time and space we needed to enjoy each other's company.

She looked amazing today in a lightweight green summer dress. The bright sunshine picked up the highlights in her brown hair and made her eyes sparkle. She'd caught the sun during the weekend we'd spent on the beach in Antibes, and seemed relaxed and revitalized.

We crossed Avenue des Citronniers and headed for a row of two-story buildings constructed in the French Empire style, with ornate colonnaded façades. They evoked past grandeur but were dwarfed by the contemporary apartment blocks surrounding them.

This was our only work appointment of the entire trip and was one of the reasons we'd come to Monaco. Philippe Duval, Monaco's former Minister of the Interior, had reached out via Eli Carver, the US Secretary of Defense and a man I now considered a friend, to see if I'd be interested in establishing a Private office in Monaco with him. I'd done my homework and Duval had impeccable credentials. He'd had a reputation for being a tough but fair minister and a track record of meeting threats head on. He was exactly the sort of partner I liked to work with, and I appreciated Carver's introduction.

With Monaco's wealthy population and connections to France, Italy, Spain and North Africa, this location was an interesting proposition, and the timing of our trip meant I could also take Justine to the Monaco Grand Prix. I hoped a couple of days attending one of the world's most iconic motor races would make up for this work meeting intruding on our vacation.

Duval's office was above the storefront of an independent financial advisor in one of the most impressive buildings overlooking the tree-lined avenue. Monaco was a hub for the super-rich. A tiny principality on France's southern border, it had taken a bite out of the French Mediterranean coastline and, in addition to the premium beachfront, offered both high-end gambling and wealth protection, which was the polite term for tax avoidance.

"It's a beautiful part of the world," Justine remarked as we neared Duval's building. "I could cope with coming here once or twice a year."

"I bet you could," I replied, taking her hand. "So could I."

I stopped and pulled her in for a kiss.

"I wish we could have stayed longer in bed," she whispered as we parted.

I was tempted to suggest we skip the meeting and return to the hotel, but I never got the chance to utter the words.

There was the roar of an engine, the squeal of tires, and a white van screeched to a halt beside us. The rear doors opened and three men in ski masks jumped out and ran toward us, brandishing pistols.

"Get in the van!" the tallest of the trio yelled, waving his gun at me.

Justine caught my eye and nodded.

Neither of us had any intention of complying.

CHAPTER 2

I RUSHED AT the man training his gun on me and could tell from the way he froze that he was shocked by my split-second reaction. Years of facing danger and violence had trained me to respond to threats without hesitation. I acted decisively, barreling into him, grabbing his wrists and forcing his arms up before his first shot cracked from the muzzle and whipped into the air a few inches left of my head. I was no stranger to firefights, but no matter how familiar I was with the experience, I couldn't control my physical response. The volume and pressure of the gunshot caused a stabbing sensation in my ears, which started ringing. I didn't let that slow me down but slammed the man's head hard against the side of the van. I saw his eyes roll back. In the instant it took him to recover his senses, I wrested the Glock 19 from his limp fingers.

I turned the gun on his two startled accomplices, but they'd had a chance to regroup after the shock of seeing me go on the attack. They darted around the far side of the vehicle, taking cover as I tried to get a clear and safe shot.

Sounds of panic filled the air. Pedestrians in the background were scattering into the boutiques and cafes that lined the avenue. I heard shouts and screams from every direction. There was movement to my left and a masked driver emerged from the vehicle carrying some kind of club in his hand.

Justine barged into the door, slamming it hard and wedging him between it and the chassis. I took advantage of his confusion and pain to drive my fist into his nose through the open driver's window. Bone cracked and he yelped and tried to stagger back, but was unable to move. He dropped the club—a police baton—and clutched his face. I grabbed the discarded weapon before it reached the sidewalk and drove it tip first into his chin. His head snapped back and he went limp, crumpling in a heap on the driver's seat.

"Jack!" Justine yelled, and I turned to see one of the other assailants round the van, gun leveled at us.

"Drop your weapons," he yelled, his Italian accent unmistakable.

But there was a hesitant note in his voice, and he hadn't opened fire, so I seized the chance to grab Justine's arm and spin her around. We started running.

CHAPTER 3

WE SPRINTED TOWARD some raised flowerbeds in the median and jumped the low wall that separated them from a narrow sidewalk.

"Stop!" the man with the gun yelled. When I glanced over my shoulder, I saw him fire twice, high and wide.

My gamble had paid off. They wanted us alive.

"Halt!" he shouted before discharging another pair of shots.

Justine and I raced through some shrubs and dwarf palms before jumping the wall on the far side of the bed. We turned right, veering away from a towering apartment block that loomed ahead of us on the opposite side of the street.

A masked man ran down some steps next to the building's entrance, making it clear we faced more assailants.

We sprinted left at a small roundabout and took a road that curled down toward the sea. To our right lay a park. Through the black-and-white railings surrounding it I saw another van and a motorcycle on the far side, racing in our direction, recognizable as hostiles by the ski masks worn by the rider and driver.

The bike shot ahead of the slower-moving van as they reached the sweeping turn that would bring them level with us.

Ahead I could see an extremely sharp turn, the famous Fairmont Hairpin Curve that formed part of the Grand Prix course. There was a low wall to our left with beyond it a steep drop down a bare rockface to where the road bent back on itself, heading south, some fifteen feet further down the hillside.

I heard the roar of the motorcycle behind us.

"Come on," I yelled, and grabbed Justine's wrist, urging her to the left.

We hurdled the barrier and slid down the retaining wall onto the street below, landing on the sidewalk so heavily I almost rolled into the path of an oncoming car. Justine yanked me back and the driver swerved clear.

Above us, I heard the bike kick down a gear with behind it the growl of the van's engine. Both vehicles sped down the sloping road to the sharp hairpin turn, which would bring them directly to us.

I jumped to my feet and Justine and I sprinted toward the sea, a couple of hundred yards away, beyond a busy overpass.

My lungs burned and I could hear Justine gasping for breath as we raced along the busy road toward the overpass. Here cars slowed to join a one-way system that took them round a tree-covered island feeding branch roads in every direction.

I glanced back to see the motorbike accelerate away from the hairpin, zipping down the median, weaving to avoid oncoming traffic. It would be on us imminently, and the van containing an unknown number of assailants would not be far behind. In fact, as the thought flashed through my mind, the large white vehicle fishtailed around the bend, before the driver managed to bring it under control and stepped on the gas.

I hated doing anything illegal, but our situation was desperate. I ran up to a silver saloon car at the end of the short line of slow-moving traffic idling around the tree-covered island.

"Out!" I yelled at the startled driver, a middle-aged woman, who froze instantly. She went pale, and I suspect her heart started thumping at 200 beats per minute.

I felt sorry for her and guilty about involving an innocent civilian, but it was this or be captured by persons unknown.

The motorcyclist started firing from a machine pistol. Bullets sprayed the trunk of the silver Mercedes E-Class. It was a clear attempt at intimidation. These people might not be trying to kill us, but that would not stop them from doing so by accident.

I smashed the driver's window of the Mercedes with my gun and reached for the lock as the terrified woman finally reacted and stepped on the gas. I was dragged forward for a few yards before the vehicle crashed into the one in front. The impact seemed to bring the fearful driver to her senses. I managed to get the door open and pull her from the vehicle.

I got behind the wheel and Justine jumped in beside me. I put the Mercedes in reverse, accelerated and swung the wheel, so the car whipped around to face the approaching biker. The rider sprayed bullets at the road ahead of us as I accelerated, heading straight for him.

He stopped shooting when he realized I wasn't slowing down, making it abundantly clear these people wanted us alive. I was under no such constraint and fired back at him through the smashed window as we neared his bike.

He reacted instinctively, swerving toward the sidewalk and crashing into the rear of a vehicle that had pulled over in response to the approaching mayhem.

I floored the accelerator as the rider recovered his senses and fired off several rounds after us. The road ahead was clear as far as the hairpin turn, but the driver of the second pursuit vehicle wasn't about to let us get away so easily. The van swerved out of the flow of oncoming traffic and raced toward us on the wrong side of the road.

I stepped on the gas, and the powerful E-Class leaped toward the van and its driver. In the distance I could hear sirens, adding to the chaos that had engulfed our once-peaceful day.

When the van was a few meters away, I mounted the side-walk, smashing through a bus stop and narrowly avoiding a collision.

As we bounced off the curb and rejoined the road, I heard tires screech behind us and glanced in the rear-view mirror to see the van's brake lights flare bright red, like a pair of angry suns.

I accelerated into the hairpin, not realizing my mistake until it was too late. I heard the roar of an engine close by and felt the impact before I realized the first van had reappeared. It slammed into the rear wing of the Mercedes and sent Justine and me into a wild spin. I smashed my head against the windshield and the world was swallowed up in a burst of blinding light.

I must have blacked out momentarily because the next thing I knew was the car was stationary and masked men were dragging Justine out through the passenger door.

CHAPTER 4

"JACK!" SHE CRIED as she struggled against the men holding her.

She looked unsteady, movements uncertain and poorly coordinated. I knew she'd been injured in the crash but she still put up a good fight, scratching, punching and trying to bite the men who were restraining her, until one of them slapped her face, dazing her.

Seeing that, I felt anger course though my body like electricity. I glanced around to get my bearings. The Mercedes had smashed against the bollards outside the Fairmont Hotel, a luxurious low-rise residence overlooking the bay. The van that had rammed us, engine smoking, was wedged against the rear driver's-side door. The second vehicle, a white Fiat van, came racing toward us, and behind that came the motorcycle.

Feeling dizzy, I forced open the door and looked around,

hoping to see the Glock I'd confiscated. There was no sign of it. My knees felt weak and my steps faltering. The world spun and I could feel liquid running down the side of my face. When I put up one hand, my sticky red fingers told me I was bleeding heavily, but I didn't care. My eyes were fixed on Justine, who was being dragged toward the approaching van. She was conscious but looked stunned.

I sucked in air, snapped out of my daze and forced my feet, one in front of the other, until I was running toward the kidnappers.

Justine's eyes met mine. As if revived by the sight of me, she renewed her struggles against her captors.

"Jack!" she cried, clawing at the face of the man closest to her.

"Put her down!" I yelled, feeling my strength return as I dashed toward them.

They ignored me, and the man who'd just been scratched by Justine punched her, knocking her unconscious. Fire burned within me at the sight of further violence against the woman I loved. No amount of pain or injury would deter me. I ran on, aware of the sound of sirens as the Fiat van screeched to a halt.

Another masked man slid open the side panel and the gang manhandled Justine inside before jumping onto the flatbed beside her. They moved with speed and precision, not exchanging any words. I had no doubt they had trained for this.

I was very close now, and the last man had the misfortune to face my fury when his accomplices sacrificed him. The van accelerated away before he could jump inside. I barreled into him and his head glanced off the side of vehicle as it sped past.

Confused and knocked off balance, he stumbled. He tried to draw a pistol, but I parried his arm and the gun discharged into the ground before I clapped my fists over his ears and head-butted him, my forehead cracking his nose.

He crumpled. I grabbed the pistol from his limp hand and wheeled around to fire two shots into the motorcyclist's back as he slowed for the hairpin. He lost control of the bike and skidded wildly before toppling into a slide that came to a crashing halt when he collided with the wreckage of the Mercedes.

As the white Fiat van raced away up the steep incline, weaving around vehicles whose drivers had stopped to watch or video the carnage, I ran over to the bike. I removed the unconscious rider's mask and quickly searched him, finding a wallet and phone tucked into the inside of his jacket. I took both. I also discovered the guy was wearing a bulletproof vest, which had taken the impact of my shots, and was already starting to stir.

I punched him, knocking him out completely, then yanked him away from the bike and lifted it upright. I deactivated the emergency kill switch, turned the ignition, and was relieved when the Suzuki R600 roared to life.

CHAPTER 5

THE MOTORCYCLE ENGINE snarled as I overrevved it to accelerate up the incline in pursuit of the van, already making a left turn near the flowerbeds where the men had originally tried to abduct us. The large vehicle slewed dangerously as it wove between slower-moving or stationary traffic. Roaring engines and burning rubber were regular features of the Monaco Grand Prix, but gunfire, crashes and speeding vehicles were out of the ordinary for this quiet district, and the commotion had brought people out onto their apartment balconies and had stopped traffic. The rest of the world seemed to be on pause as I roared by.

I kicked up a gear and the angry buzz of the engine became a deep drone as the bike gobbled up the road, closing the distance to the van.

Tall trees lining the edge of the small park flashed by to my left; to my right was a blur of boutiques and restaurants. Patrons were open-mouthed on seeing the mayhem disrupting their otherwise peaceful day. Some of them had their phones out and were trying to capture the action racing past.

Ahead, the van approached an intersection. The driver hit his horn with a heavy hand, blaring an alert to any vehicle ahead to stay out of his way as he shot up the center of the road, grinding between cars on both sides, knocking off wing mirrors and smashing up bodywork. The stench of burning diesel filled the air as I followed, catching my first glimpse of flashing blue lights as I sped across the intersection. There was a police car racing toward us, heading south along the avenue lined with palms.

Ahead, the van was speeding toward Place du Casino, a grand square of historic buildings, including the iconic Casino de Monte Carlo, which resembled an Ottoman palace.

The buildings to my right gave way to the lush greenery of the Casino gardens and then a road. Down this, fast heading toward me, I saw a motorcycle ridden by another masked man. He was brandishing a sub machine gun and was on an intercept course. I swerved left around the outside of the square, trying to avoid him while still keeping one eye on the Fiat, which had continued straight ahead on the road crossing the broad square, heading west.

I heard the rattle of gunfire over the roar of the bike's engine and glanced behind to see the gunman directly to my rear, lighting up the road around my back tire. He was trying to unseat me.

I cut right, mounting the sidewalk for a moment before the tires bit into the beautifully manicured lawn of the Casino gardens. Passersby cried out and scurried clear as I shot across the green space.

I heard more gunfire and felt the rear tire burst. I stepped on the brake and slowed the bike sufficiently, so that when the rim of the wheel hit earth, and I lost control, I wasn't moving fast enough for the impact to injure me seriously. The bike went south, in a slide, while momentum carried me north, rolling and tumbling over the grass.

Winded, I forced myself to my feet and saw the gunman stop on the north side of the square to reload his weapon. Terrified bystanders scattered, running into buildings, side streets and alleyways. Beside me, a taxi driver started the engine of his BMW 5-Series and made ready to move.

I caught sight of the van ahead, rounding a corner to disappear down a narrow street running alongside an imposing building that looked like a museum or art gallery.

I sprinted over to the taxi, opened the driver's door, and pulled the startled cabbie from his seat. He was a heavyset man who looked like he wasn't afraid of trouble, but I think the scale of the violence he'd just witnessed in this peaceful, privileged enclave had momentarily converted him to pacifism. It didn't last. He started to object and struggle against me. I dragged him away from his vehicle and jumped inside. I shut the door and locked it while the cabbie pounded against the windscreen, cursing me.

Ignoring his protests, I looked back at the motorcyclist, who began to spray the wheels of the BMW with bullets. The gunfire terrified the cabbie, who ran for cover. He just cleared the danger zone moments before bullets thudded into the tires, puncturing them. Satisfied he'd immobilized me, the motorcyclist twisted his throttle and took the same course as the van.

I floored the accelerator, fighting for control of the car, which now had two flat tires and was running on wheel rims. But unlike a bike, it was possible to steer it on flats, and I didn't need to go far.

I aimed for the shortest point between me and the gallery, judging it perfectly so that the gun-toting motorcyclist would have no time to react when he figured out we were on a collision course. I swung the wheel at the last minute and the BMW lurched into a sharp turn and sideswiped the bike, knocking the rider clean off the saddle. The bike hit a low stone wall in front of the gallery and fell onto its fairing as I stamped on the brakes.

I jumped out of the BMW and ran toward the fallen cycle. The masked rider was stirring nearby but I kicked him in the head, knocking him cold, my eyes hardly leaving the white van, now almost at the end of the long straight road directly ahead of me.

The sirens were growing louder. I became aware of increased activity: roaring engines, screeching tires, and shouts of protest when I lifted the bike.

There were vehicles around me, men and women yelling, but I paid no attention. I mounted the bike, resetting the engine kill switch and pressing the ignition. Nothing happened. I looked down to see oil everywhere. The bike had been totaled by the impact.

Up ahead, I saw the van make a right turn and disappear from view.

My focus shifted abruptly as I registered the cops were out of their vehicles now, aiming pistols at me, yelling instructions for me to get off the bike and lie down with my hands behind my back.

Reluctantly, and with a sick feeling of loss swelling in my stomach, I complied.

I had failed the most important person in my life. I had lost Justine.

CHAPTER 6

MONACO POLICE HEADQUARTERS was located in a modern concrete building with a red-tile fascia. It stood directly west of Port Hercules, the city state's principal harbor, which was crowded with luxury yachts in town for the Grand Prix.

I wasn't under arrest, but Valerie Chevalier, the inspector in charge of the investigation, had made it clear I wasn't free to leave either. She was a tall, slim woman with sharp eyes and a no-nonsense demeanor, honed during years working with the force's Criminal Investigation Division.

After being given the all clear by a police doctor, I'd sat in an interview room on the first floor of the five-story building and tried to hide my mounting frustration as I recounted what had just happened. Monaco was a society in which rank still mattered, and I could tell Duval's name carried weight as a former minister of the principality. I wasn't looking for special favor by revealing who we were going to meet, just explaining what Justine and I had been doing on Avenue des Citronniers that fine May morning.

My account of events stacked up with those of eyewitnesses, and Valerie told me my story was supported by city surveillance and police video footage from vehicles and body-cams. Her team had also been deluged with phone footage shot by members of the public after an appeal went out on television and radio. The attack was big news in this normally law-abiding city state.

I'd asked the inspector to call Jean-Luc Leterrier, Private's lawyer in Paris, to request him to recommend a local attorney. However, it seemed I might not need representation because she was prepared to accept my actions were proportionate to the crimes that had been committed against me, and that no one other than the perpetrators had been injured.

The first man I'd knocked off his bike near the Fairmont Hairpin had apparently fled the scene, but the guy I'd taken down in Place du Casino was in custody and refusing to talk. Valerie said he had a phone and wallet on him, but that they contained no identifying data or materials and he was refusing to give his name.

I suspected the wallet and phone I'd taken from the first motorcyclist would also be anonymized. I'd signed them over to the booking sergeant when the police had taken my belongings. I'd told him they belonged to me and he'd slipped them into a custody bag along with my own stuff. I hoped Maureen 'Mobot' Roth, Private's head of technology and resident hacker, would be able to work her magic on the biker's phone, and do it faster than the police.

Inspector Chevalier kept leaving me alone, disappearing to attend to new aspects of the unfolding investigation. The room's whitewashed walls were stained yellow by time, its chrome chairs and steel table were unforgiving, and its strip lighting emitted a slight flicker that was certain to induce a headache sooner or later. I guessed her most recent absence could be explained by the fact she was off conferring with her superiors.

She returned after twenty minutes and told me, "You may go."

And with those simple words, the ambiguity about my custody status ended. I was free.

"I can't imagine you will leave Monaco without Ms. Smith," the investigating officer said. "But please ensure you make yourself available to us for follow-up. We may have more questions, and hopefully some positive news. We would like to put a tap on your phone in case the kidnappers make contact."

I shook my head. "That won't be possible. My phone receives confidential calls and information from clients. If the kidnappers make contact, we will record everything and run our own traces."

Chevalier's face puckered as though she'd encountered a bad smell. "I thought you would say as much. Please make sure you tell us if contact is made. Ransom demands are the best way to recover kidnapping victims." She smiled. "But I probably don't need to tell you that given your expertise in this area, Mr. Morgan."

I stood. "Is there anything else?"

She shook her head. "We will do everything we can to find Ms. Smith."

"Thank you," I replied.

I appreciated her words but knew I would do more. I would tear the city apart if need be. I was terrified of what might be happening to Justine and felt terrible guilt for failing her. I planned to devote all the expertise the inspector had mentioned, along with Private's considerable resources, to tracing and rescuing the most important person in my life.

"I suspect you will make your own efforts to find Ms. Smith," she remarked. "But don't impede our investigation, and please share anything useful and observe the laws of Monaco at all times."

I nodded, but those men, those hateful men, had crossed a line in targeting Justine. I couldn't make any promises that might affect my capacity to act. If laws needed to be broken, so be it.

And the first law I broke was tampering with evidence and impeding an investigation by pretending the first biker's phone was my local cell and his wallet my travelling billfold for emergencies. After some paperwork, I left the station with both items and all my own belongings.

I had my phone out and was about to call Mo-bot when I saw a face that I recognized across the busy lobby. Looking immaculate in a tailored gray suit was the familiar elegant figure of the man we'd come to Monaco to see: Philippe Duval.

CHAPTER 7

"MR. MORGAN . . . Jack, I'm so sorry to hear about what happened," Duval said, offering me his hand. "Based on news reports and information from my friends in the police, this was no street robbery gone wrong."

I shook my head. "No. It was targeted. They tried to abduct us both. And when that failed, they took Justine."

"I'm so sorry," he repeated.

I considered myself a good judge of character, and he seemed genuinely concerned and shaken.

"Such things don't happen in Monaco, and the fact it took place outside my office when you were on your way to meet me . . ."

He didn't need to finish the sentence because we both understood the implication. He was demonstrating intelligence as well as empathy. If he hadn't shown up at police headquarters, he would have been the second person I spoke to after being released.

"I need to know who you told about our meeting," I said.

There was no point in choosing my words more tactfully. There were a limited number of ways the kidnap gang could have known where we'd be. An operation like that took careful planning. It wasn't a spur-of-the-moment thing.

"It is natural for you to be cautious in your dealings with me," Duval said. "We don't really know each other—only by recommendation of Eli Carver, and by reputation. But I can assure you, I told no one of our meeting. I didn't even record it in writing, a security habit from my days as Interior Minister. And I can assure you, I never record any sensitive information on a computer. My time in government impressed upon me the need for vigilance, and since I retired my ministerial post, my diary is not so busy that I cannot commit significant events to memory."

He smiled.

"I feel personally responsible for the disappearance of Ms. Smith and would like to offer you all the assistance I can. I still have friends here and in government in Monaco and France. I will place all my resources at your disposal."

He seemed genuine and I was prepared to take him at face value—for now. One of the many things I planned to request from Mo-bot was a thorough examination of every aspect of Philippe Duval's life.

I shook his hand. "I'm grateful for your support, Monsieur Duval."

"Philippe, please," he corrected me. "I was eager for us to work together, but not under such circumstances."

"I appreciate that, and I would like your help," I told him. "I'm going to need someone local to steer me around the hazards of Monégasque politics, someone who can name people with the capacity to pull off this sort of thing in broad daylight."

He nodded. "We should go to my office then and discuss—"

I cut him off. I wouldn't put him on the inside of any investigation until I heard the outcome of Mo-bot's review. "First I need to call my team and set certain things in motion."

"Of course," he said. "I understand. Tomorrow then?"

I nodded.

"Shall we say eight?"

"See you there," I replied, and we shook hands again before he left.

I paused before discreetly following him out of the lobby. Much like police headquarters in Rome, this building featured an archway that connected the street with a parking lot filled with liveried police vehicles.

I turned away from the lot and stepped onto the street that ran alongside. To my left at the other end of the street lay the main port. I could see the bristling forest of yacht masts. Opposite me was a ramp leading to an underground parking garage and next to it a narrow street with an ice-cream parlor on one corner.

I stood beneath the awning as I took out my phone and

dialed. It was a little after 3 p.m. in Monaco, which meant it was 7 a.m. in Los Angeles, but I knew Mo-bot would already be up.

"Jack," she said enthusiastically when she answered. "How's the honeymoon . . . I mean, vacation?"

"Very funny," I replied.

She and Sci had been cracking wise about a secret European wedding ever since Justine and I had told them about our vacation plans.

"It's over," I said. "Justine has been kidnapped."

I heard a sharp intake of breath and felt Mo-bot's shock.

"You're not—" she began.

"No," I interrupted. "I'm not kidding. Justine has been taken. I want you to alert the entire Private organization. I want everyone on this. We have to find her."

CHAPTER 8

JUSTINE HAD NEVER known such fear. She lay trembling, her mind racing, aware of the masked men lying either side of her. A scent of stale cheap aftershave wafted from one, while the other smelled like a musty, overused towel. The sound of their breathing was so close, so intimate, and so unwelcome.

She could hardly stand to think about what had happened. Jack had tried his best to stop these evil men, but they'd taken her, forced her into the van and then pushed her into a secret compartment beneath the flatbed. Almost the width of the vehicle, as deep as a coffin and long enough for a tall man to lie down, this smuggler's box held her and two of her captors while the van made its escape through Monte Carlo. And escape was the right word because she'd been tossed around early on, thrown against first one man and then the other, as the driver raced through the streets. She'd heard roaring engines, gunfire, sirens, and knew Jack hadn't given up on her. And even now that the engine had settled, the gunfire had stopped and the sirens had faded to nothing, Justine knew Jack would never give up on her.

There wasn't so much as a crack of light in the confined space. She drifted on a sea of darkness. The van slowed down and she heard a man she assumed was a police officer quiz the driver in French. Justine was about to scream when a gloved hand forced itself over her mouth and pressed down so hard she could barely breathe. She wanted to fight these two men, to rebel and make them suffer, but there wasn't the space, and her captors were bigger and stronger than her. She was one of the world's leading forensic profilers and an expert in human psychology, but it was always easier to understand and analyze the emotions of another than to master one's own. She wanted to vent her anger, to sate her thirst for justice, but she couldn't and so she tried to find a calmer center, reminding herself of her training, which reinforced action from a position of strength.

She was in a position of weakness now, confined and outnumbered. There would be better opportunities to escape, and the very fact she was being held told her these people did not want her dead. They wanted something else, but that unknown quantity concerned Justine. It was sufficiently valuable to them that they would be prepared to use any leverage at their disposal to win it, and that might include hurting or eventually killing her. She pushed such dark thoughts from her mind. She had to stay positive.

Justine heard the van's side panel open, and footsteps above her as someone jumped in and checked the rear compartment. She felt the second man pin her arms and wrap a leg over hers to prevent her from flailing out to draw attention to herself. She felt violated by such intimate contact, but there was nothing she could do, and so she lay in impotent silence as the person above her completed their search, jumped out of the vehicle, and slid the side door shut.

Moments later, the heavy hand and restraining limbs were removed as the van accelerated away. Justine was relieved to be able to breathe freely again.

She lost track of time in the darkness, but it could not have been more than an hour later when she felt a shift in gravity toward her feet as the van began to climb a steep incline. Then there were a series of sharp turns that made her feel queasy in the confined space. The winding climb seemed to go on and on, which meant they were on a hill or mountain, probably somewhere in the southern ranges of France, north of Monaco.

With each passing moment Justine was drawing further and further away from Jack. She struggled to control mounting fear as she tried not to anticipate what lay ahead.

CHAPTER 9

OUR SUITE AT the Hôtel de Paris was alive with the buzz of activity, but in the most important way it felt lifeless to me.

Justine's empty suitcase was set on a stand at the foot of our king-size bed, the contents distributed between the closet, antique dresser and shining ebonized chest of drawers. I couldn't believe she was gone and still half expected her to come through the door, smiling.

I was on a video call with Mo-bot, who had mobilized the Los Angeles office, and Seymour Kloppenberg, our resident forensics expert, who wore the same worried expression as I did.

My landline kept ringing with calls from international offices who'd been alerted by the company-wide bulletin Mo-bot and I had drafted, giving details of Justine's abduction. I spoke briefly to each and every country manager and thanked them for their offers of practical or emotional support. My experience of running large teams was that people needed to feel invested in an idea, personally connected to it in some way. Each one of these leaders would convey that to their team, so I knew it was important for me to take the time to talk, listen and instill in them the conviction that there was no higher priority than finding Justine Smith.

I had no idea who had taken her or what I was up against, so I wanted everyone to be ready. Better to overreact and scale down as the nature of the crisis became clear, than try and play catch up when things were in motion.

I answered my hotel line. "Morgan."

"Jack, I'm so sorry to hear about Justine."

It was Dinara Orlova, the head of Private Moscow. We'd become close after smashing a Russian intelligence operation that had almost claimed the life of Secretary of Defense Eli Carver and put US geopolitical superiority at risk.

"I know you are busy, but I just wanted to let you know we will do whatever you need from us to get Justine back. Our thoughts are with you, but we also stand ready to act," Dinara said.

"I appreciate it. I'll keep you posted," I replied, before hanging up.

"Busy," Mo-bot observed.

"It's good to feel the love," her colleague remarked.

On the video call, I could see both of them in Private LA's fourth-floor server room. They were surrounded by members of Mo-bot's team, all focused on screens full of information on Justine's abduction.

Mo-bot was a formidable white-hat hacker. A digital genius

who used her skills for good. Fifty-something, she was the embodiment of the unexpected. Her tattoos and spiky hair suggested a cold, hard rebel, but she had the warmest heart and was thought of by many at Private as their second mom, someone they could go to with any problems. The only thing that hinted at a softer side were the bifocals she wore, which I always said looked as though she'd lifted them from a Boca Raton grandmother.

Seymour Kloppenberg, nicknamed 'Dr. Science'—'Sci' for short—ran a team of twelve forensic scientists who worked out of a lab in the basement of the Los Angeles building. He was an international expert on criminology, and when time allowed, would consult for law-enforcement agencies all over the world, ensuring Private stayed current with the very latest scientific thinking. A slight man, Sci dressed like a Hells Angel, which was where I think his heart lay because he was always restoring old muscle bikes.

Diligent and brilliant, I'd known them both long enough to consider them good friends, but I wasn't about to tell them the other reason I was glad of all the calls: distraction. By taking Justine from me those men had torn out my heart. If I allowed myself a moment to reflect on what had happened, it might break me. The steady stream of people expressing concern and offering support was all that enabled me to keep my composure.

I was grateful when my landline rang again. I picked up the receiver without hesitation.

"Morgan," I said.

"Jack, it's Eli Carver," the US Defense Secretary said. "Philippe

Duval told me what happened. I'm so sorry. I'm sure you're being pulled in every direction, but I want you to know that if there's anything I can do, you are to call me. I'm in London right now, so we're almost in the same time zone. You need something, you pick up the phone anytime, day or night."

I had seen news reports on the London summit Carver had organized, which aimed to bring lasting peace to Eastern Europe. War had spread instability throughout the region, and Carver had made it his mission to ensure lasting peace and American geopolitical security by negotiating a multilateral non-aggression pact, with the tacit threat of US military intervention in the event of a breach. I'd saved his life during the Moscow investigation, when he'd been taken hostage at Fallon Airbase by a deep-cover Russian operative who'd tried to murder him, and since then our paths had crossed enough times for us to become friends.

"Thanks," I replied. "I appreciate the call."

As a senior member of the government, he knew what it was to face a crisis, and he didn't linger.

"Anytime, Jack, you hear me? And anything," he reiterated.

"I hear you, sir," I replied.

"Good. And cut the 'sir' stuff. Keep me posted," he said, before hanging up.

"I've pulled the data from the SIM," Mo-bot announced as I replaced the receiver.

I could see her peering at her screen.

"It's encrypted, but I can handle that. Once I break it, we'll know where the guy you took it from has been."

She was talking about the data from the SIM card in the

phone I'd taken from the first motorcyclist. I'd downloaded the contents and sent the file to her through Private's secure server, along with images of fingerprints I'd taken from the wallet and phone. Sci was working on those to see if he could come up with a match.

I was impatient and eager for a breakthrough that would lead me to Justine, but experience had taught me these things took time.

Burning with nervous energy, I almost jumped when there was a knock at the door of my suite.

"Careful, Jack," Sci cautioned, glancing at the web camera that was picking up their end of the video call.

He needn't have worried. When I glanced through the spyhole, I saw a skinny uniformed bellhop. The young guy was peering into a mirror opposite my suite and fixing his hair. He held a brown envelope.

I reached into my pocket for a five-euro note as I opened the door.

"Package for you, Mr. Morgan," he said, turning away from the mirror.

"Thanks," I replied, taking the envelope and handing him the tip.

I closed the door and tore open the package to find a cell phone inside. The device rang almost immediately, and the screen displayed the words "unknown number."

"Hello," I said when I answered.

"Mr. Morgan," a distorted voice replied, "we are the people who have Justine Smith. Listen carefully."

CHAPTER 10

"IF YOU PAY attention to what I say and do exactly what we tell you, both you and your woman will be unharmed," said the machine-altered voice.

I swallowed my anger at the dehumanizing description of Justine as my "woman," and the fact that this coward was using intimidation and threats of violence against her to coerce me. I focused on remaining as dispassionate as possible and applying my experience as a detective to the situation.

Their choice of phone was the second indication we were dealing with professionals. Mo-bot had tapped my cell and the hotel line, and her team was ready to run a trace at a moment's notice. If the police were in any way competent, they would have at least covered the hotel switchboard, but here was an unexpected element, and like the scale and discipline of Justine's abduction, it suggested we were facing people with a high degree of experience in serious crime.

"No," I said, gesturing at the phone expressively, so I would be seen by Sci and Mo-bot via my computer webcam.

On-screen, I saw their reactions as they registered who I was talking to. Sci shrugged in frustration, and Mo-bot threw up her arms in exasperation. They realized the kidnappers had circumvented our plans to trace them.

"No?" the machine voice answered. The growling distortion was so effective, it masked whether the speaker was a man or a woman, but even through the vocal disguise, I could hear hesitation.

Good.

"No," I repeated. "I'm not new to this and neither are you. Professional to professional, let's show each other proper respect. You know what I need from you next."

I'd spun that out for as long as I could because every second gained meant further grounds for hope. Mo-bot was marshaling all the means at her disposal, poised to act upon any slip-up, phone log, mast relay or data packet she could trace while I was on the line to the kidnappers.

"Proof of life," I continued after stretching out the pause. "I need to know you have Justine and that she's safe and unharmed."

I didn't bother with macho threats uttered to serve my own ego. We both knew what would happen if she had been harmed, and I'd already settled on the best way to deal with this person when I got my hands on them. I didn't need to broadcast it. They would find out soon enough.

"Proof of life?" the voice sneered.

"Proof of life," I reiterated coolly.

"Okay," the voice said before hanging up.

I lowered the phone.

"Is it over?" Sci asked.

I nodded.

"You give me the number of that phone you're holding, Jack. Right now," Mo-bot instructed. "And I want all the data off the SIM."

"And when you're through with it, you'd better tell the Monaco police," Sci suggested.

I nodded again and walked to my computer. I picked up the SIM card-reader and prayed Mo-bot would be able to work her magic.

CHAPTER 11

JUSTINE HAD FOUND it increasingly difficult to breathe in the stuffy, cramped space, and was suppressing waves of panic at the idea that she might die next to these unknown, silent men. She tried to control her rising anxiety, telling herself the compartment had to be ventilated otherwise she'd be dead already. But panic couldn't be reasoned away and it was made worse by the combined body heat of three people squeezed into a metal coffin.

Justine's legs tingled with the desire to kick out, and her stomach churned with the nausea that resulted from feeling out of control. She tried to focus on the journey, but it was hard to tune out the physical manifestations of stress.

She'd been aware of the van continuing to climb, of more twists and turns, which exacerbated her queasy feeling, but kept being drawn back into the storm inside her mind until she lost track of how long they drove or their direction of travel.

When they finally stopped, Justine experienced a surge of relief. She heard the engine fall silent. Then came footsteps and the sound of the rear doors being opened. More footsteps on the flatbed above her, and then a catch being drawn back and the concealed panel opened to allow soft light to fill the compartment. Justine found it dazzling and squinted as her eyes took a moment to adjust. In that time, arms closed around her and she was lifted from the compartment and pushed out of the vehicle.

Forcing her eyes open, Justine saw a red sun, partially obscured by a nearby mountain. The terrain, rustic architecture and notices printed on sacks of grain leaning against an old barn, told her they were in the south of France. She could see a stone building further down the mountainside, and bare brown fields either waiting to be sown or recently seeded.

There were six men around her, all masked, wearing combat trousers and dark T-shirts, light jackets and protective vests. The two men who'd been in the compartment with her were walking off their stiffness. Justine tried to record any distinctive features. Four of the men were tattooed, but she couldn't see the full patterns, just the beginnings and ends, rising from their collars or peeking from their cuffs. She focused on trying to remember their unique gaits, which was a reliable way of identifying people. There was a bulky man who lumbered, one who walked with a limp, another who moved fluidly, and one with a confident strut. The two who'd been in the van with her weren't sufficiently limber yet for her to receive any impression of them.

She was pushed across a cobblestone yard, away from a large two-story sandstone farmhouse, and taken to a small outbuilding made of the same stone. It looked as though it might have once been a stable or livestock pen because there was an old stone trough by the steel door, which was secured with a padlock.

Justine didn't resist but allowed herself to be steered across the shiny cobblestones. One of the men, the lumberer, fiddled with the padlock and opened the door, and Justine saw her cell. Twelve feet long, twenty wide, there was an army surplus cot, a simple table and a single chair. A partially screened toilet and a wash basin beneath a barred window completed her new accommodation. Justine could feel the remains of the baking heat that had filled the space during the day. It was unventilated and would be extremely uncomfortable when the sun was high, but she could already see the advantages to this place. She was alive, and the cell they had prepared was a sign her captors intended to keep her that way. At least for now.

"Inside," Strutter said, giving her a shove.

She didn't resist or complain and allowed the momentum to carry her in. The door shut and she heard the padlock being secured on the other side. As she stood in the center of her cell, surveying it in the fading light of the day, her mind turned to thoughts of escape.

CHAPTER 12

I HARDLY SLEPT.

I couldn't.

Every time I closed my eyes, I was haunted by the events of the day and returned to them over and over, torturing myself with what would have happened if I'd been half a beat faster, a little stronger, more aggressive in my response. There were a hundred ways I could have saved Justine and I hadn't been able to deliver on a single one. I'd failed, and she was now in the hands of dangerous people who were going to use her to get something from me. Money would be the obvious option, but I'd made a lot of enemies over the years, all of whom had different ideas about their preferred means of retribution.

Instead of sleep, I'd kept the LA team company on a video call and exchanged information and theories with them. Sci and Mo-bot were on a flight to Paris that was scheduled to arrive first thing. They would travel on to Monaco as soon as they landed.

Mo-bot hadn't been able to pull anything useful from either of the SIM card packets I'd sent her. The phone I'd taken from the motorcyclist was proving hard to crack. Mo-bot believed the men who'd assaulted us and taken Justine had been using proxy servers and encryption that spoofed data sources to stop anyone identifying which cell towers their phones had connected to, preventing us from tracking where the motorcyclist had been. Mo-bot was working on ways around the problem but said it would take time.

The phone the bellhop had delivered had never been used prior to the call I'd received. Mo-bot had traced the device to a consignment stolen from a container that had gone missing soon after leaving the factory in China. It could have been bought on the street anywhere in the world. It hadn't been switched on until it had been given to me, and when I went to reception to quiz the bellhop on how it had come into his possession, he said the package had been delivered by a DHL courier. Once he'd given me the original plastic bag it had come in, Mo-bot had used the tracking number to learn it had been sent from a drop-off point the previous day. A convenience store in Toulouse, deposited by someone who'd paid cash and given the French Ministry of the Interior as their contact address and phone number, which suggested a dark sense of humor if nothing else.

Mo-bot messaged me from somewhere over the Atlantic. She was working on tracing the incoming call but had encountered the same digital subterfuge.

So, we hadn't had any breakthroughs yet, but I'd bought us some time by refusing to cooperate with Justine's captors until I had proof of life.

When morning finally came, and the May sun rose over the city, making everything blush, I forced myself to eat the continental breakfast I'd ordered to my room. Without proper sleep, I'd need to gain energy from somewhere. The last thing I wanted was to let Justine down again by being unable to perform at my best.

I showered and dressed, choosing the lightweight blue suit and white shirt I'd bought in Rome.

I walked across the city, taking in the early-morning sea breeze, the cawing of the gulls, the building traffic and all the pre-race activity.

The Grand Prix was organized by the Automobile Club of Monaco, which had staged the event so many times it was now a well-oiled operation. The city became a giant racecourse every May, and to make that happen there were rigging teams and cranes everywhere, preparing barriers, stands, pedestrian walkways and other crowd-control measures. The prefabricated buildings and elevated bridge tunnels had been installed weeks previously, bringing a contemporary touch to the waterfront and other spots around the city.

I avoided the Fairmont Hairpin and approached Avenue des Citronniers from the east. I didn't want to revisit the scene of yesterday's struggle, though couldn't help but spy it from a distance as I neared Philippe Duval's building. There was a team of people setting up race barriers, hoardings and stands at the bend, making it almost unrecognizable as the place Justine had been taken the previous day. I tried to suppress the memory of seeing her being hauled into the van, but couldn't shake off the desperation I'd felt when she was taken from me. I hoped she was okay.

I hurried along the broad sidewalk, past the boutiques, the sweet-smelling flowerbeds, and a cafe that filled the air with the scent of coffee and fresh pastries.

Duval's office was accessed through a colonnaded entrance at the end of the terrace. I stepped through the baby-blue double doors, presented myself to the security guard who sat behind a plywood desk in a cramped lobby, and was directed to the second floor.

A broad marble staircase doubled back on itself to take me to the upper story, and I found Duval's suite marked by a sign on the second door to the left. I could see an expansive reception area through the part-glazed door, and a woman in her late thirties sitting at a large desk.

"*Bonjour, Monsieur,*" she said, when I entered.

"I'm here to meet Philippe Duval," I replied.

"One moment," she said, before disappearing into another part of the office hidden from view behind a partition.

The reception area was bright thanks to the large windows overlooking the street. I could see trees in the park opposite, their branches swaying lazily in the breeze.

"Good morning, Mr. Morgan," Duval greeted me when he appeared from behind the partition moments later.

He approached and shook my hand enthusiastically.

Mo-bot's team had declared him clean as a whistle, with no question marks over his integrity, and none of our European offices could find so much as a whisper of criminality or corruption. He was a vanilla former minister from a tiny wealthy principality who was figuring out what to do after a lifetime in state politics.

"Any news?" he asked, but before I could answer my phone rang.

"Excuse me," I said, glancing at the screen and seeing Mo-bot's name. "I have to take this."

"Of course," he said, and I stepped away to answer the call.

"Sci and I just arrived in Paris. I've got a location from the phone you took from the biker," Mo-bot said without so much as a hello. "It's a hotel in a place called Menton, just along the coast from Monte Carlo."

"You're a genius," I replied.

"I'm in the mood for compliments," she said. "It's been a long day. Let me know what you find."

"Will do," I assured her, before hanging up. I turned to Duval. "Do you have a car?"

CHAPTER 13

MONACO WAS WELL known as a wealthy city state, but the roads still needed to be cleaned, hotels staffed, utilities provided and the wheels of society kept running. The wealthy residents weren't going to waste their time on such menial tasks, so they drew their workforce from less affluent neighborhoods across the invisible border with France.

Known for its pastel-colored medieval buildings, Menton was a few miles from Monte Carlo. Away from the beaches and gardens, the bell tower and museums, back toward the northern reaches of the town where the sea breeze was rarely felt and fewer tourists ventured, there were post-war apartment blocks and social housing that spoke of poverty.

The Hôtel Athos was a two-star dive located in one of these poorer neighborhoods. Duval's classic black Mercedes G-Wagen looked completely out of place when he parked it a short way down the street from the hotel, at the end of a line of rusted, dented and tired old automobiles that couldn't have cost more than a couple thousand each.

Duval didn't speak much during the drive, focused on getting us to the address as quickly as possible. But as we left the car, he said, "You know, the law obliges me to inform my former colleagues at the Monaco police of anything relevant to an ongoing criminal investigation."

I tensed, very aware I was walking alongside a former government minister.

"However, if I do, there will be administrative delays notifying the French authorities, and anyone who knows anything about kidnapping realizes time is of the essence. So we will pretend you didn't tell me why we came here and that I thought you were looking up an old friend."

I smiled. "Thank you."

"With pleasure. I can't imagine what I would do if my wife or children were taken from me."

I looked at Duval with new eyes and saw a loving father, a human being trying to do his best.

"How old are your kids?" I asked as we neared the entrance to the hotel.

"Ten and twelve. Monique and Charles. They are terrors," he said. "Amazing terrors whom I love with all my heart."

I smiled, touched by his sentiment.

The metal canopy outside the Athos was rusting and letters were missing from the hotel's name. One of the double doors had been boarded up, making it look like the kind of place that

48

rented out misery and bedbugs by the hour. Inside, the lobby did nothing to counter that impression. The floor tiles were cracked and filthy. Two leather couches were brittle and worn through to the hessian webbing, and the walls were grimy.

A large man in a straining white shirt and limp black tie stood in a reception kiosk. He took a sip from a large mug as we approached, and foamy liquid collected on his thick mustache and beard. He wiped it off with the back of his hand.

"*Bonjour, Messieurs*," he said. "*Comment puis-je vous aider?*"

"We will speak English for the benefit of my friend," Duval said, nodding at me.

"Of course," the receptionist replied.

"We're looking for a man," Duval revealed.

"Police?" the receptionist asked nervously.

"Private investigators," I said. "This man is believed to have been involved in a kidnapping."

"In Monaco?" The receptionist took another sip of his milky drink and wiped his mouth. "I saw it on the news."

I nodded.

"Wow," he said. "We get troublemakers here, but never some-one like that. Who are you looking for?"

"Those things work?" I asked, pointing at the surveillance cameras in the corners of the lobby.

He nodded, and minutes later we were in a cramped, messy office behind the kiosk, reviewing footage from the previous morning.

I saw the biker emerge from the solitary elevator just before 7 a.m. He smiled when he was met by a man at the hotel entrance.

His confederate kept his back to the cameras and stayed at the very edge of the frame.

"That's him," I said.

"Room twenty-one," the receptionist replied. "On the second floor."

"Did he come back after this?" I asked, pointing at the man leaving the building.

"I don't think so," the receptionist replied. "Not unless he returned when the night shift was on."

"Can we take a look at the room?" Duval asked.

The receptionist led us upstairs and took us into a musty single room, which contained a bed, rickety wardrobe and cracked bureau.

There was no luggage, litter or any sign that the room had ever been occupied, and the bed was perfectly made.

"Tidy," Duval observed.

"Or careful," I suggested. "Someone with something to hide."

I opened the wardrobe and found a pair of jeans and a shirt hanging inside.

"How did he pay?" I asked.

"Cash." The receptionist's reply didn't surprise me.

"Passport?" Duval asked.

"Spanish ID in the name of Pablo Cortez."

"We'll need a copy," Duval told him. "The police will too."

The receptionist looked exasperated. I imagined a lot of his clients wouldn't want cops sniffing around the place, but he had the wisdom not to share any such thought with us. My tolerance for people who took cash and looked away from wrongdoing was extremely low.

I focused instead on searching the room. The bureau and bedside cabinet drawers were empty, but when I got down on my hands and knees and checked under the bed, I saw something flat and gray just beyond the edge of the frame.

A keycard.

It was blank and could have belonged to the biker or a prior guest, but it was all I had, so I feigned a close search under the bed. As I was patting around, I palmed the card and slipped it into my pocket as I stood up.

"Anything?" Duval asked.

I shook my head. "We should notify Monaco police. See if they can identify the guy from his photo or pull anything useful off those clothes."

CHAPTER 14

THE ANCIENT STONE was already starting to bake, and Justine was sweating as she used a broken chair leg to gouge a gap out the mortar between two of the big stones forming part of the outer wall. She'd chosen a stone roughly the diameter of her shoulders and had moved the table against the wall to obscure what she was doing. The angle of the tabletop to the door meant her work wouldn't be seen by a guard performing a casual check on her.

And such checks had happened every couple of hours. A masked man would unlock the door, poke his head inside and leave quickly, satisfied all was as it should be. What they didn't see was the growing mound of mortar dust beneath the table and the deep groove around the stone. She prayed the wall was only a single course thick. The thought of moving even this one stone was daunting, but she pushed that problem from her mind and focused on the task at hand: removing every inch of ancient mortar, one millimeter at a time. She was grateful that age and the long hot summers had made it brittle and relatively easy to erode.

Justine had been working on one spot and had dug about twelve inches deep, creating a sharp, narrow dip in the binding around the stone. She could feel a change in the composition of the mortar as she worked, hunched under the table. She crouched forward and when she'd removed the chair leg from the depression, she peered into it and saw glints of light shining through a thin mesh of mortar. One more push and she'd be on the other side. She now knew how thick the wall was and that she wouldn't have to dig through another layer of stone, and that lifted her spirits. She started on the mortar immediately next to the deep grove, but her excavation didn't last long. She heard the sound of the padlock on the other side of the door.

She'd been disturbed in the night and had immediately leaped into bed and pretended to be asleep, but she was drenched in sweat and if they saw her sleeping during the day, they might become suspicious, so she decided on another approach.

She scurried out from beneath the table and strode toward the door. The moment it opened, she said, "I can't take it in here! It's like an oven. I need a fan or a cooling unit. Fresh clothes too."

She stopped when she saw the face of the man who'd stepped into her cell. He was lean, with short black hair and about a week's stubble. He had piercing eyes that looked devoid of pity, and his scowling face suggested a festering, ever-present rage, but the most concerning thing about him wasn't his features, it was the fact he wasn't wearing a mask. She'd seen his face and she knew from experience working abduction cases that being able to identify the perpetrator wasn't a good thing. Her chances of survival had just dropped. The need to escape was now even more pressing.

"I will see what I can do, Ms. Smith," the man said, glancing around.

Justine noticed he was carrying a newspaper.

The chair was propped against the wall on the far side of the table. The missing leg would not have been immediately apparent but he was walking closer to it.

"What do I call you?" she asked, trying to distract him.

"Roman," he replied, casting his eyes over her. "You may call me Roman. We shall get you clothes and washing supplies. The fan may be more challenging, but we will see what we can do. In the meantime, I need something from you."

"What?" she asked, trying to conceal her anxiety.

"Proof of life," he replied. He tossed the newspaper at her feet and pulled a phone from his pocket. "Mr. Morgan wants to know you are alive and unharmed."

Justine's heart leaped at the mention of Jack's name. She stooped to pick up the paper, and Roman held the phone in front of him.

"Please send Mr. Morgan a message telling him you are in good health," he said, before he started to record.

CHAPTER 15

INSPECTOR CHEVALIER ARRIVED at the Hôtel Athos an hour after Duval had made the call. She said that we weren't permitted to search the room without permission from the French authorities, and that the Police Nationale were obtaining the necessary clearance.

A folded fifty-euro note had convinced the receptionist to play along with the story Duval and I had agreed: that we had never been in the biker's room. It staved off any bothersome questions about contamination and removal of evidence.

I'd placed the keycard I'd found in my wallet and would claim it was for the Private building in LA if I was searched. Technically, I was interfering with an investigation, but I knew I'd be quicker than the cops and that no one could analyze and trace the card faster than Mo-bot. If I'd left it to the police, the card would still be on the floor of the biker's hotel room, waiting for a search warrant.

"Are you sure you can't just go in?" Duval asked the inspector between calls. She seemed to spend most of her time on the phone. "The receptionist is most eager to cooperate."

We'd learned his name was Guillaume. Hearing Duval speak, he nodded enthusiastically. I think he was keen to let the cops do their stuff then vacate the premises. The assortment of guests who'd shuffled through the lobby didn't look like people who stayed on the right side of the law.

"And if this is an innocent man? Or the case goes to trial?" Chevalier asked.

She was being very conscientious and thorough, perhaps beyond what was reasonable, I thought, but my experience of the European judicial system was limited.

"You gentlemen can go," she told us. "I thank you for the lead, but we'll take it from here. I will have official approval and a forensics team on site before midnight."

I had to resist the urge to smile wryly. It was currently a little after 1 p.m. She was allowing herself almost twelve hours.

"Thank you, Valerie," Duval said.

I couldn't bring myself to respond and joined the former minister outside.

"What now?" he asked.

"Could you take me back to my hotel?" I replied. "Or I can get a cab if it's out of your way."

"Nonsense," he replied. "Monaco is a small place. It is no problem to me at all."

Forty minutes later, I was walking along the wide corridor to the suite Justine and I had shared. As I approached, I heard music playing through an open door to my left. It was the sort of heavy metal I'd come to associate with one man. I knocked before pushing open the door to see Sci and Mo-bot on their feet, heading toward me.

"It's good to see you, Jack," Mo-bot said. She gave me a warm hug. "I'm so sorry. It must have been . . . I mean it must be . . . I'm sorry, I just don't know what to say."

I stepped back and saw tears in her eyes. It was a rare event that left Mo-bot speechless and tearful, and her emotions moved me. I swallowed the hard lump in my throat.

"It's okay," I assured her. "They say she's well and unharmed. I'm waiting for proof of life."

Sci shook my hand. "Come in, Jack." He patted my shoulder as he led me into their suite. "We asked for a room near yours. They gave us this two-bedroom suite. Said it was the last one available. Something about the Grand Prix."

"Only the biggest and busiest week of the year. You're lucky they had anything left," I replied. "You guys got here quickly."

They had already started transforming their living room into an operations center. Mo-bot had her computer workstations on the dining table and Sci was unpacking surveillance and analytic gear from a collection of large flight cases.

"LAX to Charles de Gaulle," Mo-bot replied. "Then a connection to Nice. Pretty smooth. You get anything from the Hôtel Athos?"

I nodded and took the keycard from my wallet. Nondescript, gray, with no distinctive markings.

"I found this under the bed in the suspect's room."

I produced a color photocopy of the passport he'd presented at the hotel and gave it to Sci. "Passport is in the name of Pablo Cortez. I'm guessing it's fake, but worth running."

Sci nodded and went to a laptop on the dining table.

Mo-bot studied the keycard briefly before reaching into a flight case and producing a card-reader, which she connected to her workstation. She inserted the card into the reader. Moments later, a prompt appeared on-screen. Mo-bot typed a series of commands to interrogate the reader.

"Some keycards are anonymized, but law enforcement asks manufacturers to make identifiers where possible," she explained. "It's like metadata and can be used to identify people or locations in an emergency. Some manufacturers comply, others . . ." Her voice trailed away and then resumed with a note of excitement in it. "Automobile Club of Monaco! This card opens something at the Automobile Club."

I was familiar with the organization, one of the world's oldest and most prestigious motoring clubs. It was famed for hosting the Formula One Monaco Grand Prix, the event that currently had the city abuzz.

What would a violent criminal have to do with one of Monaco's most revered institutions?

CHAPTER 16

I'D ASKED DUVAL to meet me at the Automobile Club head-quarters, located on Boulevard Albert 1er, a block down from the swimming stadium where the large prefabricated race center and stands had been constructed. The iconic six-story head-quarters was a mix of classical and contemporary architecture, with Neo-classical columns and façades rising from a marble and glass floor. The place was the hub of the pre-race activity that stretched citywide as preparations intensified in the run-up to the weekend.

I had guessed I wouldn't get access to the people I needed to talk to, not on the busiest week of the year, and not without help from someone well connected. In this respect, Duval didn't disappoint.

"I managed to secure ten minutes with Miriam Lambert, the head of personnel," he said as we met outside the entrance.

"Thanks," I replied, following him inside.

Anyone who has watched coverage of the Monaco Grand Prix will be familiar with this striking building, and the interior didn't disappoint. It was opulent and full of luxurious touches that accentuated the celebration of motorsport history. There was a restaurant and club facilities for members of the exclusive association, founded in 1890. Rich in marble, leather, gilt and fine art, it was a wonderful environment with every comfort provided, from the inviting deep couches to the tables set with the finest crystal and porcelain. There was a museum next door, a chronicle of the history of the club and the race, and paintings and photos of automobiles adorned every wall of the Club.

"One of the jewels of Monaco," Duval said, as we walked through the building. "Ah, Miriam."

He made a beeline for a woman dressed in a pair of gray linen slacks and a cream blouse. She had wavy chestnut hair and a smile like a 1980s soap star: almost perfect except for the faintest glimmer of insincerity in her eyes. She said something in French to the two suited and booted men with her and stepped toward Duval.

"Philippe, it's been a long time. How are Christelle and the children?"

"Very well," Duval replied. "This is my associate, Jack Morgan. His partner, Justine Smith, is the woman who was abducted yesterday."

Miriam gasped and gave me an apologetic look.

"I'm so sorry, Mr. Morgan."

"Thank you," I replied. "We'd like to ask you about this man."

I produced a copy of the photo we'd obtained from the Hôtel Athos. Mo-bot had established the passport was false. The real passport had belonged to a man who had died five years ago.

Miriam studied the image and shook her head slowly.

"I've never seen him," she said. "Or if I have, I don't recall. Why do you think he has something to do with the club?"

"We found one of your keycards in his hotel room," I replied. There didn't seem to be any point in concealing the truth.

"I see. Come with me."

She led us outside and we walked a short distance down the street to a staging area near the race center. A group of riggers were being briefed by a man who wore a high-visibility vest over his black suit jacket. He had the air of someone who was carrying the world on his shoulders. After a minute or so, he dismissed the rigging team and Miriam led us toward him, saying, "Marc Leroy is our operations director. Marc," she called to him.

He turned and tried to conceal his preoccupation beneath a forced smile.

"Miriam," he replied, walking over.

He looked to be about forty-five, with a neatly groomed black beard and wearing a suit that was tailored to his athletic frame. He nodded to Duval, who responded in kind with a familiar if not particularly warm greeting.

"Marc supports the opposition," Duval remarked. "We're consorting with my political enemy."

"Monaco is too small to have real enemies," Marc scoffed. "What can I do for you?"

"This gentleman is a friend of Philippe's. He wants to know about someone who may work for the race," Miriam explained.

"We think he could be connected to the Automobile Club in some way," I replied, holding out the photo of the biker. "He was involved in the kidnapping yesterday."

"Mr. . . ." Marc began.

"Morgan."

"Mr. Morgan, we employ hundreds of riggers and marshals for the race," he went on. "And I make sure I meet them all."

"Marc is very thorough," Miriam put in.

I was grateful the world was blessed with people like this man. Those with a natural attention to detail, whose work ethic meant exceptional wasn't just a dream but, on their watch, became a reality.

"He is one of our marshals," Leroy said decisively. "We hire them a few weeks before the event to help with crowd control during the race and qualifying day. I can't recall his name, but we will have his records on file."

I suspected we'd find the same fake passport used as ID, and a fraudulent address and employment history, but it was a real lead.

"Would a marshal have access to secure areas?" I asked, producing the keycard.

"Not legitimately," he replied. "May I?"

I gave him the card.

"Can you help us understand why this card would be in his possession?" Duval asked.

"Of course, Minister," Leroy replied.

I detected a hint of sarcasm in his tone. These two really were political adversaries, and despite what Marc had said, experience told me rivalries ran deep in a small place like Monaco.

"I can find out who this keycard belonged to, what it opens, and arrange for you to access this man's personnel records," Marc told us.

"Thank you," I replied, wondering why a violent thug would have gone to the trouble of securing a job at one of the world's most famous motor races.

CHAPTER 17

WHEN MO-BOT THOUGHT of the French Riviera, she never imagined a place like the Promenade Val du Carei, the street on which the Hôtel Athos stood. She and Sci had taken a cab to Menton, the town a few miles east of Monaco. The driver had taken the scenic route to show them the pastel-painted buildings that had lined the seafront for centuries, before heading inland past car dealerships, mini-marts and simple apartment buildings until they reached the rundown neighborhood that was home to the seedy hotel.

Sci and Mo-bot stood on the corner directly opposite the Athos. A trio of police cars had parked out front, and the French uniformed officer at the entrance suggested the cops were in the process of examining the biker's room, or at least preparing to. Jack had told them Valerie Chevalier was hoping to have a forensics team in place by midnight, which meant she and Sci wouldn't be able to access the room for a long time, but based on Jack's account they would be unlikely to find anything useful anyway, and Mo-bot wasn't keen to waste time duplicating the same work as the cops.

"Thoughts?" she asked Sci, who shrugged as he looked around.

They were off the beaten track here. The only tourists who would visit a place like this would either be passing through on their way to someplace else, or they'd be in search of the less salubrious goods and services the neighborhood offered.

Mo-bot's attention was drawn to a couple of young guys in jeans and T-shirts, who loitered outside a convenience store a short way down the street. They were watching her and Sci furtively. Pimps? Drug dealers? Or maybe a couple of grad students on a day off, Mo-bot thought, challenging herself to overcome her inclination to put everyone into a criminal pigeonhole.

A moment later, an emaciated woman in a short, dirty sundress emerged from the store and approached the men. She had bruises, scrapes and lesions on her arms and legs and looked in need of medical attention. She gave one of the men a fold of cash and the other slipped something into her hand.

Drug dealers, Mo-bot thought, and she watched the pitiful woman stagger away, wishing there was something she could do to steer her off such a self-destructive path.

As she considered the bleak future that awaited the poor addict, Mo-bot noticed a camera rigged to the exterior of the store. It looked like a cheap, self-installed unit and was pointed away from the two dealers and aimed across the street toward the hotel.

"Come on," Mo-bot said, nudging Sci and nodding to the camera. "We might get lucky."

As they walked along the street, the two dealers shuffled away, keeping their eyes on the strangers as they moved on.

The convenience store was piled high with discount brands, and a bin near the door was full of yellow-stickered cans near their expiry dates.

Mo-bot spied a grubby man emerging from a stock room at the rear of the store. She shuddered when she saw him zip up his fly and adjust his pants.

"Gross," she remarked to Sci, who was oblivious.

"What?" he asked.

"Either I'm judging an innocent man who has just been to the bathroom or we've got someone here who exploits the vulnerable," Mo-bot replied. "Let's find out which."

She reached the checkout counter at the same time as the debauched-looking man.

"Do you speak English?" she asked.

He nodded.

"You having a busy day?" Mo-bot said.

The guy looked puzzled. "You want to buy something?"

"Your surveillance footage for the past week. From the camera out there."

He gave a hollow laugh. "That's very expensive."

"How much is your marriage worth?" Mo-bot had noticed the man's wedding ring as he'd adjusted his fly.

He looked bemused.

"Because we have photos of the young lady who just left this store with more money than she came in with, and your wife might be interested to know how she earned it."

The guy looked as though Mo-bot had hit him. His mouth opened and closed a few times. Finally, whatever he was trying to say fell away and his bluster dissipated, leaving him fearful, compliant.

"USB okay?" he asked.

"USB is fine," Mo-bot told him.

"Last week?" he checked.

"The past seven days," Mo-bot confirmed, and he hurried toward the stock room.

"Wow," Sci said, finally breaking the stern, impassive silence he'd maintained throughout the exchange. "You're something else."

"Never miss an opportunity to teach a scumbag a lesson," she replied, waiting patiently for the footage. She knew she wouldn't have to wait long. The sleazy man would be keen to get them out of his store.

CHAPTER 18

THE DOOR TO Mo-bot and Sci's suite was ajar when I passed it on the way back to my and Justine's room, so I knocked and went inside to find my colleagues sitting at their workstations, reviewing video footage.

"Hey," I said.

Mo-bot started. "Jeez, Jack, don't sneak up on people like that."

Sci looked round coolly. "I knew he was there. Hey, Jack."

"What are you doing?" I asked.

"We scored footage from a camera outside a convenience store. It's pointed at the sidewalk and street, but it catches the hotel, too," Mo-bot revealed. "We've already got photos of two of the biker's accomplices."

She minimized the video footage and clicked open a photo library showing one of the white vans used in the kidnapping. It was parked outside the hotel and there were two men in the front cab. Both had unkempt stubble, one had a shaved head and the other long, dark curly hair. Mo-bot cycled through a series of images, blowing up the originals to pick out the two men more clearly, capturing their faces in the closest possible detail.

"Clear images of both the driver and passenger," she said. "This is from the morning of the attack. We're just checking the rest of the week to see if they show up any other time."

"Got nothing else so far," Sci added, before resuming his review of the footage.

"We need to get these photos to Chevalier," I said.

Mo-bot nodded. "I'll also run them against the databases I can access and see if I can call in a favor at Quantico," she said, referring to the FBI's computer lab.

Just then the cell phone the bellhop had delivered from the kidnappers rang. Mo-bot had wired it to one of her laptops. As I picked up the device, she moved to the connected computer and checked a tracing program. She nodded at me.

"Hello," I said, answering the call.

"You have your proof of life," the distorted voice responded, and the phone vibrated to indicate an incoming message.

I looked at Mo-bot, who was programming commands into a prompt window. She glanced at me and signaled for me to play for more time.

"Let me check," I said, and didn't wait for a reply as I switched from the call to the messages folder, where I found a video sent from a withheld number.

I opened it and pressed play to see Justine in what looked

like a barn. She was standing in front of a stone wall and held a copy of today's newspaper.

"I'm alive and in good health, Jack," she said before the clip ended abruptly.

My eyes filled and I fought the desire to vent my fury at the caller. Expressing my anger would get us nowhere. I tried to calm my thundering heart, which thumped scalding fire through my veins.

Sci was on his feet and had caught sight of the video over my shoulder. He gave me a sympathetic look and put a reassuring hand on my shoulder.

I saw Mo-bot working furiously to trace the call through various private networks, but she was running into complex systems that tested even her.

"I've got it," I said.

"So now you know Ms. Smith is unharmed and that we are professionals who mean business," the machine voice said, "you will do as you are told. You will be sent an address at the end of this call. You have two hours to reach the address and collect a package that is waiting for you."

"What's in the package?" I asked, playing for more time.

My question was met with silence.

"Can I talk to Justine?" I tried.

"You will find out what is in the package when you collect it, Mr. Morgan," the anonymous voice replied. "You will speak to Ms. Smith when you have completed the tasks we set for you."

The phone vibrated to indicate the arrival of another message.

"You have two hours. Do you understand, Mr. Morgan?" the voice asked.

"I understand," I replied, before the line went dead. "Tell me you got something," I said, turning to Mo-bot.

She shook her head forlornly.

"Work your magic, Mo," I implored her. "Do whatever you have to."

I checked the message.

"I need to go to Nice," I said.

"I'm coming with you," Sci announced. "Make sure you don't walk into a trap."

I smiled. "Thanks."

"Let me get my gear," he said.

He ducked into his room and emerged moments later with a large holdall slung over his shoulder.

"Let's go," he said.

"Stay in touch," Mo-bot advised.

"Will do," Sci replied.

He followed me out of the suite, and we started out to find whatever awaited us in Nice.

CHAPTER 19

THE TAXI WOULDN'T take us to the address I'd been sent. It was on Avenue de la Méditerranée in Moulins, which, according to the research Sci and I did in the back of the gray Honda CRV, was one of the most notorious neighborhoods in Nice. The streets oozed disrepute, and every single building exhibited signs of physical decay. The tower blocks and tenements of Moulins were surrounded by major arterial roads, supermarkets and office buildings, penning in the poverty behind a perimeter of commerce and industry, so that the social failure to provide these people with better lives couldn't be seen by the casual observer. And it seemed few visitors had the courage to venture inside the perimeter. Moulins was listed in a number of travel guides as a dangerous part of Nice that should be avoided.

High-rise apartment blocks were interspersed with long low-rise buildings with boarded-up windows, graffiti tags, and communal gardens that had been left to turn to dust and weeds. The few businesses inside the perimeter functioned behind bars and security grilles. They were skewed heavily toward cut-price liquor stores and money shops that provided high-margin loans and wire-transfer services. There were a couple used goods stores that almost certainly sustained a steady trade in stolen merchandise taken from more residential parts of the city. Gangs of young men and women congregated outside brightly lit kebab and burger joints, smoking weed from pipes.

I didn't blame the cab driver, a genial but nervous man in his early fifties, for wanting to drop us just inside the perimeter. He told us that lawlessness was rife in the side streets and alley-ways that lay to our west.

I paid the man and Sci and I headed along the gloomy street toward Avenue de la Méditerranée, at the next major intersection a couple of blocks away.

The cab driver's local knowledge was spot on, because within about half a block, the streetlights vanished and many of the lamp posts were snapped in two. There were a couple of burnt-out cars on bricks in the courtyard of the adjacent tower block, and the building was dilapidated, with many broken windows.

"You're not worried they want to kill you?" Sci asked. He was grinning, but it was a forced smile designed to hide his nerves.

To be fair to the guy, he looked more at home here than me, with his biker boots, jeans, Metallica T-shirt and black leather biker jacket. I was in my blue suit and might have been mistaken for Sci's parole officer.

"They could have killed me when they took Justine. Or at the hotel," I replied. "They want to use me. If this was about money, we'd have had a ransom demand by now. They're planning to force me into something."

Sci nodded and we walked on.

I sensed we were being watched and caught sight of a group of five men standing outside the next apartment block. They eyed us closely, muttering and whispering.

"You feeling limber?" I asked. "We may need to get physical."

Sci followed my eyeline and clocked the group.

"Whatever it takes, right?"

We walked on in silence, prepared for attack. We crossed two intersecting alleyways, venturing further into darkness and deprivation.

I dealt routinely with criminals, viewing them as somehow set apart from the rest of us, but part of me wondered how much influence places like this exerted on the course of a life. Would I be the man I am today if it hadn't been for my early privilege? What would my life be like if I'd been raised on one of these mean streets?

I didn't have any easy answers, but liked to remind myself every now and again that the kids and young people who caused so much crime and fear didn't choose to be born into poverty.

We crossed the last intersecting alleyway and turned right onto Avenue de la Méditerranée. The address I'd been given was a little way north, the third house in a row of eight. The short terrace was flanked to either side by tower blocks. The row houses could not have felt any sunshine in the shadow of such giants. They exuded a stale, neglected atmosphere. As we came closer I saw mold and moss sprouting from the outer walls, which were covered in sprayed tags.

Sci watched me nervously as we walked through a yard filled with scrap metal and rusting appliances. I tensed, my senses alert, ready for anything.

The last thing I expected was for the front door of the house to open and for us to be greeted by a shirtless, muscular man in his early twenties. He wore a pair of shorts, had a thick mop of dark brown hair, a broad smile and hazy, unfocused eyes.

"*Salut, mecs*," he said. "Oh, I forgot, you are English. That's what they tell me."

"American," I corrected him.

"Of course. Yankee doodle. French fries, which you stole from the true land of liberty." He laughed at his own joke. "I've been waiting for you."

He leaned into the hallway and, when he stood straight, he held a package. A padded envelope no more than eighteen inches long and eight wide.

"This is for you," he said. "The man in the suit, they told me."

"How did they tell you?" Sci asked.

"Just now," the shirtless man replied. "On the phone. They knew you were coming."

"They're watching," I said, looking around.

"Do you know these people?" Sci asked.

The man shook his head. "They're not stupid. A friend of a friend of a friend asked if I wanted to make Bitcoin in exchange for giving you a package."

Sci and I shared a look of exasperation. Bitcoin was almost impossible to trace.

"Most people in this place would kill for less than one Bitcoin. Much less. So it was an easy decision. Now you have your parcel, take it."

He thrust it at me and the moment I took it, he shut the door in our faces.

"You think he was on the level?" Sci asked. "You think he's involved?"

I shook my head. "An operation like the one we're facing isn't planned somewhere like this. The people of Moulins are all about survival. Whatever we're up against, it's about a lot more than that."

I tore open the package while Sci switched on his phone torch and shone it inside.

"What the heck is that?" he asked.

I didn't say anything for a moment, my eyes fixed by what I was holding.

"It's a gun," I replied at last. "It's a 3-D printed resin pistol and a dozen matching bullets. It's designed to circumvent metal detection."

I hesitated, finally understanding why they'd taken Justine.

"They want me to kill someone."

CHAPTER 20

SCI AND I sat in stunned silence for the first part of the taxi ride back to Monaco. The package lay on the back seat between us, infusing the air with evil. My every breath was heavy and filled with sorrow for the choice that lay ahead of me.

"You can't know that's what they want," Sci said beneath the racket from the cab's radio, which played a lively pop tune completely out of keeping with our mood.

"Three-D printed, small caliber," I replied, taking care to talk quietly. "Justine as leverage. They will tell me it's a trade, but they will probably kill her after I've done whatever they ask."

Sci nodded slowly, conceding the truth of my words. What else could it be?

"I'll tell you something else," I said. "That guy knew we were coming because someone phoned him, which has to mean they were watching. And if they were, they might have been taking pictures."

"Setting you up?" Sci suggested.

"Yeah. The thought crossed my mind," I said. "Why not deliver the package to the hotel like they did with the phone? Why make me come out here? Could it be to get surveillance photos of me collecting an untraceable weapon from a cutout? Frame me as an assassin?"

Sci pondered what I'd said, but my own thoughts were disturbed by my phone, which displayed an unfamiliar number.

"Hello?" I said.

"Jack Morgan," Eli Carver responded. "You didn't make good."

My mind was so attuned to the kidnapping, I was momentarily confused and thought he was referring to the package and that he might somehow be involved.

"You didn't keep me posted like I asked," he went on.

My brain kicked into gear. "Mr. Secretary, it's been non-stop."

"So I hear," he replied. "Philippe has given me the headlines."

But Duval only knew part of the story.

"Jack, please cut the Mr. Secretary crap and remember what we've been through together. Let me know what's going on. And if you need help, I want you to pick up the phone. I can't speak for you, but I consider us friends."

"Thank you, Mr. . . ." I caught myself. "Sorry, force of habit. Thank you, Eli. I'll check with my team and see if there's anything we need."

"Good," he replied. "Now I've got to go to post-dinner drinks the Brits have organized. See if we can push this peace deal over the line with some champagne and cocktails."

I knew from the news that the London summit was on the verge of a breakthrough, and presumed that, as Secretary of Defense, Carver's job was to project the might of the US military at the negotiating table. The difference between him succeeding or failing to secure a deal was the difference between lasting peace or chaos in Europe.

"Good luck," I said.

"You too," he replied before hanging up.

"Carver?" Sci asked.

I nodded. "He's putting himself at our disposal. If there's anything we need from him, we just have to ask."

"We should send the images and footage from the convenience-store camera. See if the NSA can identify them," Sci suggested.

"Yeah. Let's talk to Mo. See if there's anything else she needs," I replied.

I was careful not to exploit my connection to the US Defense Secretary, but if he wanted to get involved, I wouldn't pass up the offer of support from the most capable intelligence apparatus in the world. I would do whatever it took to get Justine back because I suspected the people who'd taken her had violent endings planned for us both.

CHAPTER 21

MO-BOT WAS DEEP in concentration when Sci and I returned to the hotel. She was comparing a still from the convenience-store footage to a mugshot. She held a deep-fried chicken wing and was nibbling on it absently. When she realized we'd entered the suite, she used the wing to gesture at a room-service tray laden with food.

"I wasn't sure how long you'd be so I went ahead and ordered for you," she said. "It should still be warm."

Sci put down his holdall and went to the bathroom to wash his hands. I pulled up a chair next to Mo-bot, who'd connected her laptops to the large flat-panel screen hanging on the wall opposite. Her eyes were ringed with dark shadows, and she exuded tiredness, but I knew her well enough not to bother advising her to rest. She was obstinate and pushed through exhaustion whenever she was working a case. She'd do anything for Justine, who couldn't have mattered more to her if she'd been a flesh and blood daughter.

"What have you got?" I asked, drawing closer.

"Dinara Orlova ran the stills through a contact in Moscow and got a possible match." Mo-bot gestured to the mugshot on the big screen, which showed a man with a stubbled head who looked like the driver of the white van outside the hotel.

"It's him," Sci said, picking up a chicken wing from the basket on the food tray. "Fried food? It's almost like being back at home."

He took a bite of the chicken.

"I asked for tastes of America," Mo-bot replied. "The waiter actually tutted when I placed the order, but I told him I wanted fried chicken, burgers, pizza."

"I think pizza is Italian," Sci scoffed.

"How do you know it's him?" I asked, diverting them back to the job. "The image from the surveillance footage isn't great quality."

"The shape of the nose, mouth, but mostly it's the eyes," Sci replied. "The eyes always give a person away."

I took another look at the man and understood what Sci meant.

"According to Russian authorities, his name is Nikolai Oborin," Mo-bot revealed. "He's served time for robbery, assault, wounding. Not a nice guy."

"You think this is linked to what happened in Moscow?" Sci asked.

I sighed. I hoped not. "I don't know."

It was an honest answer. I thought I'd finally dealt with the blowback from the Moscow investigation while I was in Beijing, but we'd angered some pretty powerful people, so it wasn't beyond the realms of possibility.

"Eli Carver has said he'll give us whatever we need. I thought he was making a throwaway remark when he first suggested it, but he just called again and told me to use him."

Mo-bot gave a satisfied nod. "Department of Defense has a long reach. It would put our normal capabilities on steroids."

"Right," I responded. "Email these details and anything else you want checked out to this address."

I wrote Carver's secure DOD email address on a sheet of paper. "And send him a message to let him know what you want."

"Speaking of what people want, what did they want with you in Nice?" she asked, gesturing at the package in my hands.

I shot Sci a hesitant glance, and he nodded. I wasn't in the business of keeping secrets from the people I trusted, but I was ashamed of what was in the envelope. Slowly, I took out the resin gun and put it on the table. Mo-bot's eyes widened when she registered what it was.

"I think they want me to kill someone," I told her. "The price of Justine's freedom is someone else's life."

CHAPTER 22

IF MO-BOT SLEPT at all, she must have done so during the two hours I shut my eyes. When I woke, she was still at her workstation, seemingly sustained by fragrant herbal teas and grim determination.

Eli Carver had connected her with someone known only as Weaver, whom he referred to euphemistically as a Department of Defense analyst, which meant he was probably running desk intelligence for one of America's many acronym espionage agencies.

Weaver and Mo-bot traded information and messages, while Sci and I reviewed the huge volume of data submitted by Private offices around the world.

The identification of Nikolai Oborin had opened up numerous avenues of inquiry and additional background on the man himself. Our offices were digging through anything and everything on the Kutsenko Brigade and the Semion Gang, two criminal organizations Oborin had previously been associated with. They were implicated in arms dealing, people smuggling and the international drugs trade, with tentacles on every continent, so we had our work cut out for us.

I'd finally fallen asleep on the couch in their suite a little after 4 a.m. and woke at 6:15 when my alarm sounded.

"I think we might have something," Mo-bot said, glancing round as I stirred. "Our friend Weaver has access to some pretty neat stuff. He's got an AI . . . artificial intelligence—"

I cut her off. "I know what AI is. Thinking computers."

"Well done," she said mockingly. "Whoever he works for has access to an AI that can review video footage and lock onto an object or face."

I sat up and stretched.

"The AI is reviewing traffic-camera footage throughout Monaco on the day of the abduction," Mo-bot revealed.

"How did we get the footage?" I asked. "Monaco police?"

She shook her head. "Assume the NSA can dip into any machine or network anywhere in the world. If they haven't purchased a back-door encryption key from the manufacturer or got access through the root chipset, they'll hack the system."

I rubbed my face, wondering what would happen when that kind of access was combined with the power of artificial intelligence. I suspected it would mean entire populations could be kept under constant surveillance with AI running real-time threat analysis. But the technology was currently working in my favor and being used to help us find the most important person in my life, so I wasn't about to complain.

"He's sent something," Mo-bot said, clicking on a message that had just arrived on our secure server.

She opened the attachment and the screen filled with a map of Monaco, showing the route of a vehicle: the white van that had transported Justine, with timestamps of different locations in the city. There were inset photos of the van taken from traffic cameras and other municipal surveillance sources. Each photo was also timestamped and identified by location and device name. The final photo had been taken by a traffic camera near a police checkpoint at the edge of the city. It showed an officer searching the van, so either they'd hidden Justine somewhere in Monaco or they had a concealed compartment in the vehicle.

The timestamps of the van's journey through the city from the abduction to the police checkpoint ruled out the vehicle stopping anywhere. I'd followed it for a large part of its journey and knew they hadn't removed her, so I guessed she was hidden in a false ceiling or floor when it was searched. I was pained by the thought of a police officer being so close to finding her. I couldn't bear to picture her captive and afraid, surrounded by enemies.

Mo-bot must have sensed my pain because she minimized the map and the photos.

"We've got a time and a location, Jack," she said.

I knew she was deliberately being optimistic and trying to give me reason to hope.

"We can hit the streets and find out if anyone saw where the van went from there. I'll get Weaver working on whether he can pull anything from the French side," Mo-bot said.

I nodded. "I'll ask Duval if he'll partner with me. His local knowledge will be useful when we pound the streets. I want you and Sci to go to Monaco Police Headquarters. Beg, borrow, steal, call in every favor to get Sci access to their forensics lab. See if the biker's clothes from the hotel or anything from the guy they have in custody can help narrow down a location."

Mo-bot nodded and smiled, but it looked a little forced. "She'll be okay, Jack. We'll find her."

I hoped she was right, and as long as there was hope, there was everything to play for.

CHAPTER 23

SCI WAS IN his second-favorite place, a lab. His favorite place was his garage at home where he restored old motorbikes and the smell of grease, metal and two- and four-stroke combustion brought him to life. Labs were a close second though, and even this under-equipped example was a better place to be than the hotel suite, staring at a computer screen.

Sci didn't know how Mo-bot did it. She never seemed to tire of her machines and didn't even have the outlet of a hobby like his bikes to restore her. Mo-bot's entire existence was devoted to the digital world. Sci was pretty sure that when Silicon Valley started to offer implanted computer chips, Mo-bot would be first in line to have one hooked up to her brain.

But he was happy for her. She had a vocation and, like him, had established herself as a world leader in her field.

It was Sci's notoriety as a forensics specialist that had got him in the lab. Jack had phoned Valerie Chevalier and offered her Sci's services as a consultant. He'd pressed hard and Valerie had agreed to ask her head of forensics, Pascal Garnier. She'd called back minutes later, accepting the offer.

Sci had written books, published papers and lectured on crime-scene investigations. He didn't recall Garnier, but the man said they'd met briefly at a conference in Las Vegas. He was mid-fifties, quiet, thoughtful and so eager to please that he treated Sci like a celebrity, offering him free rein of the lab at Monaco police headquarters.

Sci wished he could have added some real value, but the lab was rudimentary, and any specialist work had to be sent to France, so he and Garnier were limited to reviewing the basics.

"Nothing off the guy's prints?" Sci asked about the man they were holding in custody.

Garnier shook his head. "If he's been arrested, we can't find a record. And we're not getting any results from his photo either."

"Send it to me," Sci replied. "We might be able to ID him."

He was thinking about Weaver and the capabilities of the NSA, which would far outperform the resources of the Monaco police and Interpol. He rocked back on his swivel chair and put a supporting hand against a lab bench. They were surrounded by microscopes, chromatographs and spectroscopes but the place was missing things like fuming chambers, and Sci felt sad for Garnier because he would always be limited by his lab.

"Did you scope the guy's clothes?" Sci asked.

Garnier hesitated, before shaking his head. "I didn't," he confessed. "I would only do that to place a murder victim or a—"

"Criminal at a crime scene," Sci interrupted. "And where is the scene of an abduction, right?"

Sci understood why Garnier hadn't examined the suspect's clothes properly. Conventional thinking said they knew where the crime had taken place: over a relatively expansive area of the heart of Monaco. But Sci couldn't rely on conventional thinking to find his colleague and friend.

Garnier hesitated again.

"Is it where the kidnap victim is taken? Or where they are held?" Sci smiled at him, like a professor trying to encourage a student to think outside the box. Clothes could reveal as much of a story as fingerprints. "A kidnapping is an ongoing crime. Scoping the perpetrator's clothes might give us a clue as to the victim's current location."

Sci felt a little strange referring to Justine as a victim, because she was one of the last people he ever thought of in those terms, but it was an accurate word, and it kept his language from becoming personal and emotive in the company of another law-enforcement professional. For now, Justine was the victim of a crime, but hopefully not for much longer.

"You got some gloves?" Sci asked. "And a mask? Let's gear up, get the suspect's clothes and see what we can find."

CHAPTER 24

WE STOOD ON the Avenue Pasteur a few yards from the street sign welcoming people to Cap d'Ail, signaling the almost invisible border between Monaco and France. There was no indication of separate nations, just a welcome to a new district. Monaco was not officially part of the borderless Schengen Area, but it had opened its borders anyway to facilitate frictionless travel. Technically, this spot on a narrow street flanked by terracotta-colored office and apartment buildings, running off a busy roundabout, opposite a small store selling building supplies, marked the point where two countries converged. The checkpoint had been established a short distance from the border, just after the roundabout.

I tried to imagine what Justine must have felt when the van was stopped by the cops at the hastily convened checkpoint. Video footage from a traffic camera mounted on a post on the corner of the street showed a Monaco police car blocking the narrow route and two officers checking vehicles leaving the city state.

Had Justine attempted to signal the cops? Had she even been conscious?

I'd watched the moment over and over again. One young police officer had approached the van and spoken to the driver. Like a football fan who thinks their hopes and prayers might alter the outcome of a slow-motion replay, I longed for the man to discover Justine when he opened the door to search inside. But the van had seemed to be empty. I knew from my own experiences in Moscow that it was relatively easy to conceal someone in a disguised compartment, and I'd put money on there having been a false bed in the van's floor to circumvent any visual inspection.

Looking around the road and roundabout, which was now busy with morning traffic, I saw no immediate clues as to the van's ultimate destination.

"They went west into France," Duval said, sauntering over.

He was somber and apologetic, as though he was ashamed his city had caused me so much pain.

"We can start a canvas along the route," Duval suggested. "Petrol—gas—stations and convenience stores. See if anyone remembers the vehicle. Local post offices. Talk to the delivery drivers. See if they've spotted the van along their routes."

I nodded. These were good suggestions, but my heart wasn't in it. I knew this was the sort of thing the police did to work every lead, but they could throw resources at a search like this, have maybe a couple of dozen officers out working the places

Duval had suggested. With just a few of us it felt too much like looking for a needle in a haystack. A very large haystack.

My phone rang and I stepped away from Duval to take the call from Sci.

"Jack, we may have something," he said without wasting time on a greeting. "We found traces of germinating seeds on the suspect's pants. Most of the land around Monaco is mountainside or scrub, so we can narrow down our search to only a few properties."

My heart soared. "Good work," I replied, trying to contain my excitement.

"What?" Duval asked, but I waved him away as Sci went on speaking.

"Pascal Garnier, the chief forensic scientist here, has told Inspector Chevalier. I tried to persuade him to let us have the jump on the information, but he isn't a malleable guy. Very much by the book. Chevalier says it's going to take her a while to coordinate with the French police and she doesn't want to send an advance party to investigate in case it spooks them. She wants simultaneous raids on all the possible locations."

I could understand her logic, but it was extremely frustrating not to be moving immediately.

"How long?" I asked.

Sci hesitated. "Six, maybe eight hours."

"That's too long," I replied.

"My thoughts exactly."

"Let's meet at the hotel," I said. "Figure out what we do next. I'll be there in fifteen."

"Got it," Sci replied, before hanging up.

"What is it?" Duval asked.

"We might have a lead," I told him. "I need a ride to my hotel. I'll fill you in on the way."

"Of course," he replied, and we headed for his car.

CHAPTER 25

"WHAT HAVE YOU got?" I asked the moment I entered Sci and Mo-bot's suite.

Sci was on his feet, pacing, and a tired-looking Mo-bot was at her workstation checking a satellite image.

Sci nodded a greeting at Duval, who followed me into the room.

"We found traces of germinating sunflower and lavender seeds on the suspect's pants. There was also a chemical fertilizer and a rare mold that favors drystone barns. Most of the land around Monaco won't support those crops, but there are three farms in the Utelle Valley thirty miles away from here that fit the bill," Sci said, leaning against the back of Mo-bot's chair and pointing to the valley on the map.

"Utelle is known for the quality of its lavender," Duval remarked. "They say the mountain soil makes it hardy, and it grows a little closer to the sun for a sweeter fragrance."

"Good locations to keep someone locked up," I remarked, studying the satellite image, which showed a collection of out-buildings around each of the three farmhouses.

One of them was at the foot of the valley, near the main road that connected Utelle with Saint-Jean la Rivière, a small village to the east. The second farm was a couple kilometers up the valley as the crow flies, and the third closer to the summit, a few kilometers higher.

"No prying eyes, hard terrain in the event of an escape, and good visibility in every direction in case of a raid," I said.

I took a few restless paces. "If the cops go in heavy, there's a good chance the bad guys will see them coming and run. If it was me, I'd cross the ridge here." I gestured at a high point where the mountain joined the neighboring valley. "And work my way down, using the countryside for cover, checking each property en route."

"Then why don't we do that?" Duval asked. "I will make some calls to Inspector Chevalier's superiors and see if I can speed up the wheels of justice, but waiting hours for a police operation is unacceptable in these circumstances, surely? Why don't we pay a visit?"

Mo-bot, Sci and I exchanged approving glances.

"Why not?" Duval went on. "You are a tourist, enjoying the sights of southern France. We survey each property, and if we see Ms. Smith or anything suspicious, we notify Inspector Chevalier and she can use the information for a targeted raid. With perhaps more urgency this time."

Mo-bot nodded.

"I bet a crime in progress gets a higher priority," Sci noted.

"Okay," I said. "The prime objective will be to observe and report. We're not equipped to engage an organized enemy."

Mo raised her eyebrows. "If we find Justine, will you be able to resist the urge to attempt a rescue?"

"None of us are any good to her dead or captured," I replied, but my answer lacked conviction. I'd gladly sacrifice myself for Justine and knew there was a chance I would throw logic out of the window if I found her.

Our conversation was cut short by a call on the phone the kidnappers had sent me. I answered after five rings, once Mo-bot had signaled she'd activated her tracking software.

"Mr. Morgan," the machine voice said. "You have the parcel."

It was a statement rather than a question, so I remained silent.

"You will be given instructions soon. You have killed before," the voice remarked, "so this will not be a difficult exchange. One life for Ms. Smith's."

The distorted voice confirmed my worst fears about the 3-D gun. They wanted me to use it to murder someone.

"You understand what will happen to Ms. Smith if you don't do exactly as we say?"

I hesitated. "Yes," I replied at last.

The line went dead and I looked at Mo-bot, who checked her software and shook her head.

"They're going to give me a target for assassination," I told the others. "I'm not killing an innocent. We go to the mountains, we find Justine, and we help the police get her back."

CHAPTER 26

JUSTINE'S FINGERS WERE raw and the muscles in her arms ached. Her clothes—jeans and a T-shirt provided by her captors—were damp with sweat, and more poured out as the sun neared its high point, but she pushed on, driving the chair leg into the gap she'd gouged around the large stone. It had taken hours and hours of near-constant labor, with brief breaks to throw the guards off her trail when they checked her cell or to sleep when she was near to collapse.

The mortar was harder in some places, more impacted, less affected by rain and atmospheric conditions, and her progress had slowed when she'd hit those. She'd wanted to weep at her painstakingly slow progress and at times had wrung her hands and paced the room in frustration, but she always came back and pushed on, driven by a hunger for freedom and a thirst for her normal life. Her life, not the captivity imposed on her by others.

There was about an inch of mortar left to be ground away. The remainder of the join was wafer-thin, ready to crumble the moment she tapped it away, but there was still an inch of almost solid mortar connecting the stone to the rest of the wall. No matter how hard this section was, though, Justine's spirits soared because she knew it wouldn't take her much longer to dig through it.

The chair leg had been ground down to about half its starting length and was now the size of a large chisel, which suited her fine. It was easier to handle, and she'd settled into a steady rhythm, scraping away millimeter after millimeter. The motion was almost automatic now, and her focus on the mortar bordered on meditative, but thankfully she retained enough connection to the outside world to register noise nearby.

"Get everyone set to go."

She recognized the voice of Roman, the man who'd forced her to record the proof-of-life video.

"We're moving out in twenty minutes. Make sure she's ready."

They were moving. Why?

Justine was filled with panic and despair. She was so close! If they took her somewhere else, there was no guarantee she'd get another chance to escape. She had to go now.

She dropped the chair leg and pushed against the stone.

It didn't budge.

She heard movement outside. Footsteps coming closer. She listened, straining to discern what was happening. No, they weren't coming toward her, but there was activity near the building. Footsteps and the sounds of gear being moved. The muffled chatter of multiple voices.

She didn't have long.

Justine lay on her back on the dirty floor and placed her feet on the wall. She put her palms flat against the floor to either side of her and tried to find some sort of purchase before pressing against the selected stone with all her strength.

It didn't budge. She looked up at the underside of the table and took a deep breath. She was running with sweat again and wiped her brow before pushing on the stone with renewed determination.

She felt the slightest movement and heard a cracking sound. A tiny shift in the stone's position sent her heart flying, infusing her with new energy. The stone was moving now. She had no idea what it weighed, but couldn't recall doing anything quite so physically demanding before.

She focused on the fact it was sliding away from her and kept up the pressure, ignoring the burning ache in her thighs. There was a sudden grinding sound and more movement as all the mortar fell away and the stone came completely free. She forced it out and pushed it to one side to create a gap in the wall she thought she could squeeze through.

Outside, there were voices and more footsteps, and these were definitely coming her way.

Her dress and heels had been taken so she was barefoot, but she didn't care. She had to escape.

She moved to her hands and knees and then slid onto her belly to ease herself through the hole. She put her head through it, squinting into the bright sunlight that greeted her.

She heard a key in the padlock behind her, and forced her

shoulders through a gap that was millimeters too small for them. The stone tore at her T-shirt and flesh as she wriggled through, but she didn't care about the pain. The feel of the sun against her skin and the sight of a nearby treeline spurred her on.

She squeezed herself out as she heard the padlock clinking; got to her feet and took her first few free steps as she heard the door swing open and a voice cry out in surprise.

She sprinted across the cobblestone yard, onto dusty, rocky ground beyond, ignoring the stabbing pain of each step as her soft feet found jagged pebbles and shards of cracked stone. She kept her eyes fixed on the bushes beneath the trees and her mind on freedom.

She heard cries and men mustering on the other side of the building as she made it into the nearest undergrowth. She glanced back through the thick foliage and saw a man push his head through the hole in the wall. He scanned the yard but didn't see her. He withdrew and yelled at his accomplices.

"Spread out and search the area. She can't have gone far!"

Justine didn't wait to hear any more. She pressed on through the scrub and, once she'd cleared it, started sprinting through the woodland on the far side.

CHAPTER 27

DUVAL HAD MADE some calls to his contacts in the Monaco police while we'd prepared for the expedition but had no luck pushing them to deploy faster. Cross-border operations took time, he'd told us with an air of frustration, so we took matters into our own hands and set out for Utelle. Duval drove us up the neighboring valley in his G-Wagen, which was more than capable of handling rough trails when the road ran out.

Sci and Mo-bot had brought three gear bags with them, and when the terrain got too steep and rocky for the Mercedes SUV, Duval parked and he, Sci and I each took a backpack before we all set out on foot.

It took us about thirty minutes to cross the ridge and we reached a decent vantage point shortly after midday. We were on a rocky outcrop surrounded by Aleppo pines, overlooking steep, sloping fields of recently churned and sown earth.

Further down the mountain, to the west, was the first farm, and beyond it a forest of pine and cypress. The farmhouse was an early-twentieth-century rustic building constructed of yellow stone. There was a large cobblestone yard and half a dozen barns and outbuildings. It was the highest of the three properties we'd come to investigate, and I knew it was our target the moment I saw armed men in the yard and others fanning out into the surrounding woodland.

"What are they doing?" Duval asked.

I took a pair of field glasses from my backpack and scanned the scene more closely. I noticed a large stone beside an outbuilding that had a hole visible low down in its wall.

"I think Justine escaped," I said, suddenly alive with excitement at the thought of her slipping away from her captors.

Mo-bot held out her hand and I gave her the field glasses.

"They're certainly searching for something," she said as she examined the farm and its surroundings. "I count sixteen men. Most are armed with pistols or sub machine guns. A couple of automatic rifles."

"That seals it," Sci remarked.

"I'm going to call it in," Duval said, stepping away from us to use his phone.

Sci put his backpack on the ground and opened it to remove a collection of small flight cases. While he rooted around them, Mo-bot returned the field glasses, and I surveyed the scene. I spied the shaven-headed man, the driver of the van from the convenience store video, and noticed another man in the center of the farmyard. He was issuing instructions and appeared to be in command. He was slim and muscular with short black hair. He had a downturned mouth and sharp, pitiless eyes in a scowling face. I couldn't shake the feeling that we'd met before or that he was somehow familiar to me. There was a great deal of anger about him and a slight air of panic, which supported my theory that Justine had escaped.

"Let's see what this baby can find," Sci said, and I turned to see him standing over a small drone.

He used a remote control to launch it, and I moved to get a better view of the footage being broadcast by the drone's video camera, which was displayed on the screen of the controller.

He swept round the farmyard at high altitude, and I went over the outbuilding with the hole in the wall. The large stone looked like a perfect fit for the hole in the wall and there were scuffmarks that suggested it had been pushed from the outbuilding. I was thrilled at the possibility Justine had forced her way out, but now we had to find her before her captors did.

I scanned the mountainside with the field glasses, trying to figure out where she would have gone. The other farms weren't visible from up here, but they might have been from further down the mountain. She could have headed south-west toward them, or maybe she'd opted for the more difficult task of going north-east, toward the summit, toward us. There was plenty of cover in the woods that spread across the mountainside in all directions. Justine was tough and resourceful, but I also knew she'd be frightened. Who wouldn't be? These men looked like killers and they were heavily armed. At a guess, we had fifteen square miles to search, unless she had made it to a vehicle, which seemed unlikely given the response of her abductors. Her escape seemed recent because they were searching on foot, hadn't gone far from the farm and weren't making any use of the vans, pick-up trucks or SUV in the yard.

"How do you find someone who doesn't want to be found in a place like this?" Sci mused.

An idea that had been forming in my mind suddenly crystalized. "I think I know," I said.

CHAPTER 28

JUSTINE'S FEET WERE filthy and bleeding. She was exhausted and breathing heavily as her aching legs carried her across the dusty earth between the trees in the ancient woodland. She headed down the mountain as fast as she could, bounding over rutted, uneven ground, ignoring the tilt and roll of her ankles, praying they wouldn't sprain or snap. Even beneath the shade of the trees, the air was hot and close, but Justine didn't care, she was simply glad of the cover they provided, which had kept her safe so far. She had decided to head downhill because there was guaranteed to be a road further down the valley, the one she'd felt the van climb when she was trapped in the tiny compartment. She thought it was her best chance of getting help.

She moved toward a break in the treeline some 600 feet directly beneath her. She had no real idea what lay ahead, but it had to be better than remaining a prisoner of the gang. She couldn't see them, but she could hear the cries and shouts of the men trying to find her. They were speaking in French, German, Spanish and Italian, but the commands were issued in English, which was probably their common language. They had been ordered to spread out and search the woodland methodically, checking every hiding place. This would force them to move more slowly than her, which made speed her only advantage. She intended to make the most of it and sprinted on.

Her heart skipped at the sound of an explosion, and for a moment she thought someone might have fired a sniper rifle at her. But there was a second explosion and a third, and as their echoes died away, Justine heard shouts of panic coming from further up the mountain.

She ran to the edge of the forest and broke cover to see as much of her surroundings as she could. There was a newly ploughed field directly ahead of her, and further up the slope the farm she'd escaped. The main house was on fire and there were men in the yard, guns raised, shooting into the air.

Justine's eyes were drawn to the target, a tiny drone, which dropped from the sky and exploded when it hit the farmhouse roof. The blast was disproportionately large compared to the size of the craft, and Justine guessed it had been rigged with explosives. Not something cops would do, which meant . . .

She cast her eyes over the mountainside, searching for Jack, and knew the moment she saw the flash of a reflection that the attack had been part distraction, part alert to get her to look uphill. Someone was using a mirror to communicate with her, and whoever was sending the signal was about three-quarters of a kilometer uphill, near the summit. She thought about heading back toward the signal but Jack had taught her Morse code one rare, rainy California afternoon. She recalled enough to know the repeated message said, "Go to eagle."

It didn't make sense, at least not to Justine, and for a moment she wondered whether she'd read the message wrong. And then she saw it: a rock formation to the east. Emerging from the bare rockface beneath the trees about half a kilometer away was an outcrop that looked like a giant bird. She calculated it would take her four to five minutes to traverse the rough terrain.

Justine heard gunfire and saw her pursuers further up the slope. They'd spotted the mirror signal and were targeting it. The reflected glare disappeared, and Justine prayed whoever had been sending her the message had managed to get away safely, because some of her captors were closing in fast on the position.

She took advantage of the distraction to break cover and cross the open ground before jumping into the cover of a ravine that led to the rock formation where she hoped to find help.

CHAPTER 29

I WAS MOVING at full tilt, covering the ground between our vantage point and the rock formation I'd spotted a few hundred meters east of the farmhouse. I'd dubbed it the eagle because wind and rain had carved it into the shape of the majestic bird of prey. I just hoped it looked the same from Justine's perspective and that she saw and understood the Morse code message.

One of the benefits of having a leading forensic scientist on the team was his ability to improvise explosive devices from the gear we'd brought with us. Sci had rigged an IED from the spare lithium batteries and electrical gear he'd scavenged from the drones and surveillance electronics we carried with us in backpacks. He had rigged four flying bombs to drones and they caused the distractions that allowed me to break cover and get down into the valley unobserved.

Mo-bot had already gone back to the car with Duval. The moment there was any shooting Sci was under strict instructions to stop sending the Morse code message with the mirror of an SLR camera and to join them.

I could hear shooting directed at the outcrop where I'd left him, and prayed Sci had the good sense to stick to the plan and make a run back for the car.

According to the map, the eagle was almost halfway between the highest farm and the second one further down the valley. My plan was to take Justine to the lower one and wait for Valerie Chevalier and the cops, who, according to Duval, were on their way. He'd told the inspector that we'd located the gang and there was a crime in progress. That information had been the impetus she needed to take immediate action. She'd assured him she would cut through any remaining red tape and arrive imminently with French police in serious numbers.

I sprinted through the trees, heading downhill, taking great care to keep my footing as I gathered momentum. I hoped Justine had seen the message. She would be casting about, looking for a way clear of this situation, and I had to believe the explosions would have caught her attention. The roof of the highest farmhouse was on fire and the flames were visible from some distance away. The sounds of the gang struggling to bring it under control filled the woods.

I ran on, lungs raw, legs aching, and after another few minutes moving at a speed that took me close to tumbling, I broke the treeline and encountered rocky ground around the eagle formation. I slowed to a walk and crouched down to avoid being seen by the men shooting up the mountainside. I surveyed the rocky terrain around the eagle, looking for any sign of Justine.

After a moment, I saw flashes of movement between the rocks to my right and my heart leaped, but joy rapidly turned to horror as I realized it was a man heading in my direction. It was the guy I'd seen in the farmyard issuing commands to the rest of the abductors. He wore a black T-shirt, jeans and heavy boots, but the most notable thing about him was the sub machine gun he carried in his hands. He was about a hundred feet away from me, coming at an angle, but distance and the rock formations separating us didn't impede him. He spotted me and fired wildly in my direction, bullets rattling out of the gun and zinging against the rocks nearby.

"Stop!" he yelled, but I ignored his command and sprinted downhill.

Justine burst from behind some rocks about twenty yards ahead of me, and my momentary joy turned to dismay as I realized I'd led her into harm's way. She had a similar realization when she registered me and then saw the man on my tail.

"Run!" I yelled, and she ducked back under cover.

I did likewise, following her into a narrow gully that twisted and turned across the mountainside. I ran fast, closing the gap between us, until I was only a few feet behind her. She stopped and embraced me.

"Oh, Jack, it's so good to see you," she whispered breathlessly.

"You too," I replied, my heart thundering with a strange mix of fear and relief.

"You think I don't know Morse code?" the man yelled behind us, his Italian accent unmistakable.

I couldn't see him, but he didn't sound too far away, somewhere along the gully. I signaled Justine to climb a small stretch of scree that would take us onto the mountainside and followed her up.

"That's their leader," she revealed. "He says his name is Roman."

"I bet you're thinking you're safe, Mr. Morgan," yelled our pursuer. "That I won't kill you because I need you. But a good general never relies on one plan."

Justine and I reached the top of the gully and exchanged fearful glances. Our pursuer had just revealed we were inessential, that he had an alternative method of accomplishing his objective and we were disposable. We had to get to safety but there was no obvious sanctuary.

There was about fifty feet of open field ahead before a patch of dry scrub and then thick woodland. I could hear Roman scrabbling along the gully behind us. We were in a tight spot and would have to gamble.

CHAPTER 30

"THERE'S A FARM half a mile south-west of here," I whispered. "If you make those trees, I think you'll have cover all the way. I want you to run as fast as you can. Don't stop for anything."

"No," Justine replied. "I'm not leaving you. You have to come with me."

I shook my head. "He'll catch us eventually. We can't outrun bullets. He's going to chase you, and that might give me a chance."

Justine wavered, but a volley of shots startled us both, hitting the scree beside us and forcing us on, over the lip of the gully.

We ran across open ground, sprinting for the treeline. When we were halfway, I slowed and stopped. Justine had tears in her eyes as she glanced back at me, but she kept running. She understood that if we both went, we'd both die. Separately, we might have a chance.

I rapidly retraced my steps the way we'd come, toward the

gully, and saw the top of the shooter's head as he clambered up the scree. I glanced over my shoulder just in time to see Justine disappear into the trees. She was safe. As long as I stopped this man, she would stay that way.

He saw me as he crested the lip of the gully and raised his gun as I sped toward him.

I fell onto my side as the first shots rang around the valley and bullets cut through the air where my head had been. Momentum carried me on. My feet hit Roman's chest, knocking him back down the slope. The last of his shots went high and wide as his arms flailed. He tumbled to the floor of the gully, hit the rocks on the other side, and the impact knocked the wind from his lungs and the gun from his hand. It clattered away to my right, bouncing across the rocky ground. He made a dive for it, but I wasn't going to give up my advantage. I launched myself at him with a cry of pure hatred. This was the man who'd attacked us in the street, who'd taken Justine and held her, and who was now trying to kill us. He meant me and the woman I loved the greatest possible harm. He was the embodiment of everything I stood against.

Rage filled me as we collided. I drove my fists into his gut, his chest, his face. He tried to block my blows, to fight back, but I was determined to protect Justine, to save myself, to make sure we'd be together again and he would pay.

I don't know how he managed to stay upright. Maybe he was driven by a passion that matched my own. Whatever the reason, he didn't go down. His eyes rolled back momentarily, but he recovered and kicked me in the shin before elbowing me in the face. I saw a flash of white and then stars and put my arms up to defend against the flurry of punches he aimed at my head. I stepped back and almost stumbled, but thankfully I fell against the steep rock-face on the other side of the gully. The stones jabbing against my spine were painful but they kept me upright. I dodged and ducked, sidestepping away from his ferocious assault, and as I moved, I swung a left hook at his ear. He cried out when the blow connected, and his right hand went up instinctively, leaving his side undefended. I aimed a couple of short, sharp jabs at his ribs and then hooked in for his kidney. As he buckled and lost his protective stance, I threw a right cross at his face, catching him on the nose. He staggered back, dazed, and I pushed forward, landing punch after punch, wondering what kept him on his feet. Finally, a powerful trio of jabs and a right hook sent his eyes rolling back in his skull. He went limp and collapsed on the floor of the gully.

I stood for a moment, trying to catch my breath as I looked at my fallen opponent. I remembered the gun, but as I turned toward it, the sounds of dozens of shots filled the air and I realized I was under fire. There were two men further down the gully. One was targeting me with an assault rifle and the other was spraying the air with sub machine gunfire, taking care not to go anywhere near his prone leader.

There were other men now, coming from further along the gully, running in our direction.

I turned and scrambled up the scree slope, leaped clear of the lip, and sprinted toward the trees as though Death himself was chasing me.

I was almost at the protective cover when the air around me

erupted with gunfire, and I glanced over my shoulder to see the man with the assault rifle leaning against the lip of the gully, targeting me, while his accomplices ran up the slope to either side of him. He stopped shooting as they neared the line of fire and joined them in their pursuit.

I pushed into the shadow beneath the dry Aleppo pines and quickly cleared the undergrowth to find myself in heavy woodland. I ran south, heading for the next farm down the valley, weaving between the trees, hoping to get enough cover between me and my pursuers. I could hear them barking at each other, their anger and eagerness palpable.

I caught flashes of someone in the forest ahead of me and pushed myself ever faster, until it felt as though I was flying over the twisted roots, fallen branches and bed of tinder-dry needles that covered the ground. My lungs were burning once I finally caught up to Justine, and when she looked back, her relief was clear.

We raced on and crested a rise. A short distance away the trees came to an abrupt halt. As we neared the edge of the forest, we saw a ploughed field beyond, then a fence, another field and the next farmhouse about 300 meters away. My heart sank because I didn't see how we could cover such a distance over open ground without giving our pursuers clear targets.

"Jack!" Justine said, breathlessly, drawing my attention to a farmer who was no more than fifty meters away.

He was working on the fence that separated the two fields, clearly a boundary between the two farms. There was a pickup truck parked on a track a short distance to his left.

More gunfire behind us. I glanced back but couldn't see the

shooter, just the trunks of trees some distance behind us splintering as bullets hit them. It felt like a blind gamble designed to intimidate us.

The man working on the fence looked up at the sound of the shots, puzzled at first and then anxious when he saw us break cover and sprint toward him.

"Get in the truck," I yelled, and Justine added in French, "*Monte dans la voiture!*"

He hesitated momentarily before heading toward the pickup, a red Toyota.

Justine and I sprinted across the open ground and collided with a wooden fence. I helped her over as splinters and chips burst into the air all around us. I looked back to see our pursuers at the treeline, and half climbed, half vaulted over the boundary.

The middle-aged farmworker had the sense to get the engine started. He threw open the passenger door as Justine and I raced along the track with bullets chewing the fence and ground near us.

She dived into the pickup. I followed a split second behind.

"Drive!" I shouted, slamming the door shut, and the farmworker hit the gas. The Toyota sprung forward, fishtailing wildly as it accelerated along the track, the tires fighting for purchase in the dry dirt.

A moment later, the truck got traction and sped away as a hail of bullets hit the tailgate.

Soon, we were well out of range, on the road that would take us down the mountain to safety.

CHAPTER 31

IF YOU'VE EVER experienced trauma, you will understand the way time slips away from you. The world shifts in and out of focus. One moment you're in the cab of a pickup truck, being driven by a French farmer called Marcel, the next you're in a police interview room, giving an account of your extreme experiences, and later you're on a busy boardwalk overlooking a crowded marina, holding the hand of the most important person in the world, wondering how you got there and whether you've just awoken from a nightmare.

And with the slips in time, like a stone skipping across the surface of a lake, comes an unpredictable trajectory of emotion. Raw, volatile rage, spinning into relief, knocking you off balance into guilt, anxiety, fear, your body flushing hot and cold, heart pounding for no apparent reason, then easing only to start racing again.

This was my afternoon and early evening, jumping through

conflicting emotions, buffeted by the aftermath of events, recounting what had happened to Valerie Chevalier and her colleagues, urging them to start a manhunt for Justine's abductors. The inspector had informed me the gang had abandoned their base and seemingly scattered to the wind before the police arrived.

Roman's words played on my mind. He didn't need me anymore, if he ever had. Today he'd been intent on killing Justine and me because he had a backup plan to help him achieve his wider objective. The person he had wanted me to murder in exchange for her life was still out there, and their continued existence was on the line. His words suggested someone else would kill them if I didn't. I needed to know who the intended target was.

Reconnecting with Mo-bot, Sci and Duval outside police headquarters had given me a feeling of transient jubilation, which was amplified by all the congratulatory messages we received when we notified the entire Private organization that we'd recovered Justine, or more accurately that she'd escaped and found us. The contents of our bulletin passed me by— Mo-bot drafted it, and in my disorientated, unsettled state I had to trust she knew what to say.

There had been a drink at Duval's insistence, a cognac to settle our nerves, but I wanted to be alone with Justine and so I made our excuses and we went for a walk along the broad promenade by the Hercules Marina. The sun had fallen over the horizon, but there was still a pink glow in the sky. Reflected port lights danced on the water around the flotilla of boats moored in the harbor. Prefabricated buildings truncated the wide boardwalk here and there, all decorated with the advertising hoardings and team insignias of the Grand Prix.

I held Justine's hand and we strolled wordlessly, finding our center as the heat of the day dissipated on the evening breeze. The hubbub of distant bars, the lick and splash of magnificent boats bobbing on the tide, and the hum of traffic flowing through the city formed a bed of sound that soothed and reassured me as I eased back into reality.

"I love you," I said, stopping to embrace her. "I was afraid I'd lost you."

"You'll never lose me," she replied. "I'll always fight for you and me."

We kissed.

"I love you too," she said.

When we parted, I saw Mo-bot and Sci approaching from the bar we'd left.

"I used a fake Airbnb account to get us a last-minute deal," Mo-bot informed us. She'd got us alternative accommodation because we couldn't risk Roman and his gang turning up at the hotel. "It's an apartment on the Boulevard de Belgique, about twenty minutes' walk from here."

"What about our stuff?" Sci asked.

"We go back to the hotel in the early hours," I replied. "In and out quickly, take only what we can easily carry."

"We don't need much," Justine remarked. "Just enough to get home."

I exchanged glances with Mo-bot and Sci.

"Tell me we're leaving," Justine said. "Jack? Tell me we're getting the first flight home tomorrow."

"They wanted me to kill someone," I replied. "This wasn't random. They were using you to coerce me and they chose us for a reason."

"You've told the cops, right?" she countered.

I nodded.

"Then we can go home," she said desperately. "We can leave this place and go somewhere we'll be safe."

"This was personal, Justine," I responded, sliding my arms around her. "I have to find out why and stop whatever they have planned."

She pushed me away. "No, you don't. You can leave it to the cops, and we can go and be safe. We don't have to chase danger, Jack. Danger finds us. Please don't go looking for it."

She looked to Mo-bot and Sci for backup, but they didn't give her any. They knew that if we didn't find answers this would remain an unresolved threat.

"There's no guarantee Roman and his people wouldn't come to Los Angeles," I told Justine. "This is personal. He wanted us dead on that mountain when he realized he couldn't coerce us anymore. There was hate in his eyes. We need to know why. It's the only way we'll ever truly be safe."

Justine hesitated and tears filled her eyes. I knew she was afraid, but she was also a professional and she recognized the truth of my words.

Finally, she nodded. "Okay. We find out why they came for us, and if we get the chance to hit them, we hit them hard."

CHAPTER 32

THE APARTMENT MO-BOT had rented on the Boulevard de Belgique was on the ninth floor of a block near the intersection with the Boulevard du Jardin Exotique, one of the main roads out of Monaco. We picked up essential supplies from a convenience store a couple blocks from the property and accessed the apartment using keys collected from the building concierge.

The five-bedroom penthouse was furnished like a contemporary hotel suite. The tan hide-covered furniture and light beech cabinets and tables were spotless. Huge windows opened onto large balconies and offered a view of the city and marina beyond.

"This must have cost a bundle," Sci remarked as we walked in and surveyed the place. "Last minute on Grand Prix week."

"The owner said they had a cancellation. It's the only reason we got it," Mo-bot replied. "But, yes, the nightly rental stings."

"It doesn't matter," I assured her. "We need to find out who these guys are and why they targeted us."

We put the bags of groceries on a counter in the large chef's kitchen, which opened onto the living room.

"I'll fix us something," I said. "It won't be gourmet, but we've got bread and cheese and cold cuts."

"I'll do it," Mo-bot responded. "You two should go and get yourselves cleaned up and relax a little. You've been through hell."

Justine smiled wanly.

"What about me?" Sci asked. "I got shot at doing that Morse code."

"You were well on your way back to the car before anyone got anywhere near you," Mo-bot told him. "But you go and have a cleansing bath if you like. Maybe with some scented candles and whale song playing?"

"That sounds lovely," Sci said with a grin. "Could you run it for me?"

Justine's smile broadened and I chuckled. It was good to be around friends who were acting normal.

"Shut up and help me," Mo-bot said, rifling through the bags.

Sci smiled and joined her, and Justine and I went exploring.

We walked along a corridor that connected the living room with the bedrooms and went into one at the front of the building. Like the rest of the apartment, it was decorated in neutral tan and white tones. Unobtrusive abstract prints lined the walls, and a king-size bed faced floor-to-ceiling windows. Beyond the balcony lay the twinkling lights of four city blocks and then came the marina with all the boats rising and falling on the gentle waves.

Justine put her arms around me and we kissed. We held each other in silence for a long while.

"I'm going to have a shower," she said at last. "Want to join me?"

She stepped away and took off her dirty T-shirt and, in that moment, I wanted nothing more than to join her.

But my phone rang, and when I saw it was Duval, I felt compelled to answer. He might have news on the investigation or could be trying to give us a warning.

"Philippe," I said.

He cut me off instantly.

"Jack, I'm scared. They're going to come for me and my wife and children. They will kill them if I call the police. I don't know what to do."

Justine realized something was wrong and eyed me with concern.

"Where are you?" I asked.

"At my office," he replied. "They know I was involved in the rescue . . ."

"Stay where you are," I told him. "I'm on my way."

CHAPTER 33

NO AMOUNT OF persuasion would convince Justine, Mo-bot and Sci to let me go to Duval's office alone. I'd pointed out the possibility that Justine's abductors were using him as bait to take one of us hostage, or that Roman was laying a trap to kill me and the others, but it didn't matter what I said, my friends insisted on facing the danger with me.

That's how the four of us ended up in a Renault traveling east to the Avenue des Citronniers. We sat in silence, each with our own thoughts. Justine and I were still in the clothes we'd worn during our escape from Roman, and we must have looked a motley bunch to our taxi driver, a middle-aged man I guessed was originally from Morocco because of the national flag air freshener that hung from the rear-view mirror. He was too polite, professional, or had simply seen too much, to comment on his disheveled passengers.

It took twenty minutes instead of the usual five because of diversions, restrictions and the sheer weight of traffic in advance of the Grand Prix, but we finally made it to the broad avenue where Duval had his office. The street was crowded with night-time window shoppers and people sitting outside cafes and restaurants. The city was really starting to fill up and the air of pre-race anticipation was palpable.

"Just here," I said to the driver, indicating a space in front of a cafe almost directly opposite Duval's building.

The driver nodded and pulled to a halt.

I paid the fare and tipped him five euros. Sci and Mo-bot had brought a couple of the gear backpacks we'd taken to the mountainside farm, and they retrieved them from the trunk of the Renault.

"I'm going in alone," I said, as the cab moved on.

Justine tried to say something, but I stopped her.

"If it's a trap, you can help me if you're out here. You're no use to anyone if you walk into something with me."

Sci and Mo-bot nodded sagely.

"I want eyes and ears on you," Mo-bot said, reaching into her backpack and producing a tiny camera disguised as a Stars and Stripes pin, which she fixed to my crumpled lapel. "Put this in."

She handed me a MARIE, a microphone and in-ear receiver, which I inserted into my left ear canal.

"Wait here," I said, indicating the cafe. "Have a drink. And if you see anything dangerous, let me know then call the cops."

Mo-bot paired a small flat-screen with her headphones and put them on.

"Say that again."

"Call the cops," I repeated, and she gave me a thumbs-up.

"Audio and video. You're good."

Justine took my hand and squeezed it. I kissed her before I crossed the street and headed for Duval's building.

I took the same route I'd taken the morning after her abduction, walking along the parade of stores, past the financial advisor's office, to the colonnaded entrance at the end of the terrace. I found the front door ajar and the reception area deserted. It was well outside office hours, and the absence of people was unremarkable, but the unlocked front door was disconcerting. I paid even more attention to every creak and rustle, alert to the slightest hint of danger.

I crept upstairs, listening to the sounds of an empty building settling after a hot day, and beyond its walls the hubbub of a city preparing for a huge party.

I headed for Duval's office and found his door half open. I pushed it wide and entered the lobby. The place was completely still. The only sound came from the street.

"I don't like it," Mo-bot said through my earpiece.

She'd be almost directly opposite the windows of Duval's office, and I had no doubt she, Sci and Justine would be clustered around the tiny video screen, watching what I was seeing.

"Where is he?" Mo-bot asked.

I didn't answer but instead crept toward Duval's private office. The door was closed, so I reached for the handle and twisted it slowly. I eased the door open, and as I did so, I heard an ugly, invasive sound rise above everything else outside.

The screech and scream of sirens. Close by and drawing closer still.

When I saw what was on the floor of Duval's office, I realized why they were coming.

Philippe Duval had been shot twice in the head, the visible powder burns suggesting a close-range execution. My new friend and prospective partner in Monaco had been murdered and I was the only person in the building. Was I being set up? Almost certainly.

Lying beside him was an FNX-45 tactical pistol with fitted suppressor. I had no doubt it was the murder weapon and would be free from prints.

I'd walked into a trap, but it was one that went completely beyond my expectations. Duval's phone call had made me fear for his life, not think I would be framed for his murder.

"Get out, Jack," Mo-bot said, as the sirens reached the Avenue des Citronniers, and the first tires screeched outside. "Run!"

CHAPTER 34

I HESITATED. NOT as a result of confusion or indecision, but because I noticed something in Duval's hand. I crouched to examine it and saw it was an old Nokia phone from the days before touchscreens and 5G. What was he doing with something like this, and why had he died clutching it?

I grabbed the phone as more sirens arrived with screeching tires, barked commands, and the sounds of commotion on the street below. I heard the tramp of heavy footsteps.

"Come on, Jack," Mo-bot said. "Get out of there!"

I ran from Duval's office, wondering why Roman wanted me to be framed for murder rather than luring me somewhere he could kill me. Why wouldn't he just try to abduct one or more of us again?

Maybe he was just getting me out of the picture while he

tried to take Justine or Mo-bot or Sci, I thought, and sudden panic sent adrenalin surging through my body.

"You guys need to leave now," I told Mo-bot. "I'll meet you at the apartment."

"But—" she tried. I interrupted her.

"No buts. I don't like this. We're all at risk. Go now."

"Okay," she conceded, and I heard her relay my instructions to Sci and Justine.

I crossed the lobby, but when I reached the door to Duval's suite, I was greeted by shadows rising up the stairwell wall and the sound of thundering boots. I knew the exit was blocked, so I retreated and shut the door.

I ran to a window behind the reception desk, grabbed the handle and pushed it open. A safety bar kept the gap to six inches. I picked up the receptionist's heavy chair and smashed it into the frame, breaking the restraint.

The window swung wide. I climbed onto the sill and looked around. There was a column rising to my right with climbable features, fleurs-de-lys, flowers and cherubs carved into the stone, that looked as though they could take my weight.

The door to Duval's suite burst open and a squad of police officers in black tactical gear raced inside. That was my cue to make a leap of faith and grab the cap of a floral motif. The stone held and I used it to haul myself off the window ledge.

Below me, dumpsters, pallets and recycling bins crowded the alleyway behind the building, but as I looked west, I saw police officers running from the street into the narrow cut-through, making a fall into one of the dumpsters a risky endeavor that would likely end in my capture.

I went up instead, climbing as fast as I could, ignoring the shouts and sounds of activity from inside the office below me. Within seconds, I was on the flat roof of the building, sprinting east.

I managed to get a fifty-foot head start on the first cop to follow me up. As we ran across the rooftop, with him yelling commands, he was joined by two of his colleagues.

With three police officers on my heels, I saw a fire escape on the adjacent building, but it was only as I closed in on it that I realized there was a fifteen-foot gap between the two structures. I couldn't risk getting arrested and thrown in jail where I'd be a sitting target, and I couldn't see an alternative to gambling.

I accelerated toward the edge of the roof, my legs pounding out an increasingly rapid beat, my heart thumping in my ears, and when I was a step away from falling, launched myself into a long jump, my arms flailing for purchase, my legs kicking out for something solid.

I flew across the gap, and when I slammed into the metal fire escape on the other side, tried to find a grip. My hands weren't quick enough and I dropped, plummeting a story down before I managed to catch hold of a railing and arrest my fall. I cried out as an arm was almost pulled from a shoulder socket, but I held fast for a moment before dropping the remaining fifteen feet to the ground.

I sprinted along the driveway onto Avenue des Citronniers and glanced both ways.

A crowd had gathered around the police vehicles outside the cafe where I'd left Justine, Mo-bot and Sci. There was no sign of them, but I did spy a man on a motorbike at the very edge of the gathering. He was straining to peer over the heads of the onlookers to see what was going on.

I sprinted into the street, jumped the flowerbeds and raced toward him. He was distracted by the lights and cops in tactical gear, holding his phone high above his head to capture the action. He didn't notice me until it was too late.

I pushed him off his bike, caught it before it fell, pressed the starter button, and as he came to his senses and realized what was happening, I raced away, leaving behind his cries of outrage, the flashing lights and angry cops as quickly as the little bike would carry me.

CHAPTER 35

I DITCHED THE bike in an alleyway off the Boulevard du Larvotto and covered the ground back to the apartment on foot, taking care to avoid busy streets, bright lights and crowds. I hurried along quiet residential roads and crossed to the other side whenever I encountered people.

After fifteen minutes I found the delivery entrance at the back of our building and pressed the buzzer for the apartment.

"Jack?" Justine said through the speaker moments later.

"Yes," I replied. "Buzz me in."

After a short pause, the door clicked, and I pulled it open and hurried up the back stairs to avoid the concierge. I had no idea whether I was now a wanted man, but I wasn't going to take any chances.

Justine was waiting for me in the stairwell. She threw her arms around my neck.

"I was so worried when I saw Duval," she said. She'd been watching the footage broadcast from my pin camera.

"I'm okay," I assured her.

"Come on," she said, taking me by the hand. "Mo-bot has found something."

I followed her out of the stairwell, along the corridor and into our apartment. I breathed more easily when Sci locked and bolted the door behind us.

He patted my shoulder. "Glad you made it, boss."

"Me too," I replied.

"Come on," Justine said, leading me into the large living room.

Mo-bot was at one of her spare laptops, which I assumed had been in one of the backpacks. On-screen was a photo of Roman. I recognized it as a mugshot, and the booking card read "Marc Barat" and identified the arrest as having been made by the Marseilles police.

"You okay?" Mo-bot asked. "Or do you need a breather?"

"I'm okay," I replied honestly.

Justine squeezed my hand and smiled at me. Tiredness would probably hit me soon, but right now I was too wired with adrenalin to feel the slightest fatigue.

"Earlier this afternoon, I sent stills of the drone footage we took at the farmhouse to Weaver and he identified this man, photo-matching a mugshot taken in Marseilles eight months ago," Mo-bot revealed. "I'm guessing the name is false, but it looks like he was busted during a drug deal."

"How'd he get out?" I asked.

Mo-bot shrugged. "It's not in the record."

I frowned. Why was a drug dealer targeting us? And who did he want me to kill?

"I want you and Sci to go to Marseilles," I said to Mo-bot. "See if you can talk to the arresting officer. Find out whatever you can about this guy."

Mo-bot and Sci nodded.

I turned to Justine. "Tomorrow we'll go back to the Automobile Club and find out what the biker who was chasing me was doing there."

"What if the cops put out a warrant for you?" Sci asked.

"I'll have to be nimble," I replied with a smile, before returning my attention to Mo-bot. "Can you keep an eye out? See if I'm flagged as wanted?"

Mo-bot nodded. I could feel exhaustion creeping in but my day wasn't yet done.

I took out my phone and called Eli Carver's private number. It rang through.

"Hello?" a voice said.

"Secretary Carver, please," I replied.

"Who's calling?"

"Jack Morgan."

"Mr. Morgan, I've heard a lot about you. My name is Henry Wilson. I'm one of the secretary's aides. He's in a meeting right now. Can I give him a message?"

"Have him call me as soon as he can," I replied.

"Of course," Wilson replied. "I'll let him know the moment I see him."

He hung up and I slipped my phone in my pocket. "We still

bouncing these things?" I asked, referring to the relay technology Mo-bot used to make our phones hard to track.

She nodded.

"Good. I don't want to give Roman any easy wins."

"We won't," she assured me. "Nothing is foolproof, but this is darned close."

The phone call reminded me of the device I'd taken from Duval. I pulled it out of my pocket and gave it to her.

"Duval was holding this when he died."

"I know," she replied. "We were watching."

"Sorry. I'm starting to feel the day catching up with me," I said. "See what you can get out of it?"

Mo-bot nodded. "Will do. You need to get some rest."

"Come on," Justine said, taking me by the hand. "You're done."

I didn't resist as she led me toward the bedroom.

CHAPTER 36

MO-BOT WAS TIRED, but she'd never needed much sleep, which was how she kept going while others rested. When she was younger, people had assumed she used drugs, stimulants, vast amounts of coffee, but the truth was she could function perfectly well on three to four hours' sleep per night. She felt drained now though and needed to recharge her batteries, which was why Sci was driving.

After an early-hours visit to the hotel to grab the gear and clothes they needed for the rest of their stay, Mo-bot and Sci had returned to the apartment where she'd connected Duval's phone to analysis software she'd designed. It would circumvent the rudimentary security of the old Nokia and provide a detailed log of calls, messages, and any other activity the device had been used for. She had left it running while she and Sci followed up the lead in Marseilles.

They had taken a cab to Nice Airport and collected the hire car Mo-bot had reserved in a false name, using a fake driver's license and credit card she carried for just such emergencies. They'd been at the rental desk when it opened at 7:30 a.m. and were on the road in the Ford Kuga, heading for Marseilles by 8:00.

Sci kept the car at a steady cruise once they hit the A8, a six-lane highway that would take them west through the dry foothills and mountains of southern France for almost 200 kilometers.

The journey time was a little over two hours and Mo-bot made the most of it, drifting off within five minutes of them joining the highway. The smooth road, steady rhythm of the wheels and gentle rocking motion of the vehicle lulled her into a deep, dreamless sleep.

When she opened her eyes, Mo-bot saw one of the most deprived neighborhoods she'd ever encountered. She and Sci were on a two-lane road, heading west toward a huge port. Cranes and container yards were visible in the distance. To their right was a flyover and beneath it a tramline. On the other side was an east-bound two-lane road. This broad, multi-level, multi-vehicle thoroughfare was flanked by a strange mix of gray late-twentieth-century office blocks and apartment buildings constructed in a rustic French style, complete with rusting balconies and flaked, rotting slatted wooden shutters. There was graffiti everywhere, and hardly any greenery. Mo-bot could see a single tree sticking through the cracked concrete beside a distant parking space.

"You were out," Sci remarked. "I thought I should let you sleep."

"Did I miss anything?"

"Aliens," he said somberly. "On the road outside Marseilles. They waved us in to be assessed for abduction but rejected us as atypical human specimens."

"I want to laugh, but I can't without hearing a joke."

"That's just cruel," Sci said. "Besides, who's joking?"

"You're such an idiot," she responded with a smile.

"You don't know. There could be someone out there," he said, pointing at the sky.

Mo-bot frowned at him before shifting in her seat. "Where are we?"

"Port district. Police precinct is that orange-and-brown monstrosity up ahead."

Mo-bot looked at the unusual building. It wasn't as drab as some of the concrete structures surrounding it, but it wasn't far off. An oblong structure with an orange fascia covering the exterior of the ground floor, the remaining four stories were adorned with brown metal slats. It looked like a depressing place to work.

Fifteen minutes later, after parking in the adjacent side street and presenting themselves in reception, Sci and Mo-bot found themselves in the office of Stéphane Porcher, a senior inspector they'd been told could answer questions about the Marseilles drug bust. He had a computer, but everything else spoke to a mind from another era. Books and files and papers were stacked everywhere. There was an old hi-fi system and record player on the bureau in the corner, and a mini-basketball hoop was hooked over the top of a corkboard covered in photos and case notes.

Porcher was lean with stubble so rough it looked as though

it could slice through rhino hide. His eyes were shadowed by too many years on the job, but his smile was wry and impish as though he was a bolt short of being fully hinged.

"Sit down, Americans," he said, showing Mo-bot and Sci into his time-capsule office.

The looked around and saw there was only one seat other than Porcher's and it was covered in books.

"That's okay," Mo-bot replied. "We'll stand."

"As you wish," Porcher said with a gracious wave. He lowered himself into his own seat. "What can I do for you?"

"We won't take up much of your time," Mo-bot responded. "We want to ask you about this man."

She produced the mugshot of Roman taken after his arrest.

"Ah," Porcher said, studying the photograph carefully. "*Le trépas*. Death. The Grim Reaper. I never thought I would see him again."

"Why?" Sci asked.

"Because I didn't think he was human," Porcher replied. "And I thought he had gone back to hell, where he belongs."

He paused and seemed to drift off. Mo-bot and Sci exchanged bemused looks.

"Come," Porcher said suddenly. "Let me show you how Death works."

CHAPTER 37

I WOKE EARLY and watched Justine sleeping. She looked so peaceful and at ease it was hard to believe she'd been a prisoner less than twenty-four hours earlier. Every so often, her face would scrunch into a frown, her legs would twitch, and she would whimper. I would stroke her hair and wonder whether she was reliving her escape or having a random nightmare.

A little before 7 a.m. I heard Sci and Mo-bot leave for the airport, where they would collect a hire car for their drive to Marseilles.

I checked my phone and responded to a message from Mo-bot telling me they'd been to get our gear from the hotel with a simple *Thanks*. I replied to other texts from Dinara Orlova in Moscow and Matteo Ricci in Rome, who congratulated me and Justine on our escape.

I didn't feel I deserved any congratulations. Justine had freed herself. I'd happened to be in the right place around the right time. And now a good man was dead. Had Duval been killed in retaliation for the escape? Or was he simply a pawn sacrificed in an attempt to frame me for murder?

I used my phone to check the local news, which was leading with Duval's death. There were photos of him with his family, his wife so elegant and warm-looking and his children happy and contented. It pained me to imagine what state they'd be in now, with their father's murder the talk of the city. To lose a former minister and prominent citizen in such violent circumstances was a shock to the tiny principality. I hadn't pulled the trigger, but I had brought death to this innocent family's door, and my role in involving Duval made me more determined than ever to catch the people responsible and see them punished.

None of the news coverage mentioned me, but there were reports of an unidentified man fleeing the scene. So it looked as though I'd been spotted, but had avoided identification thanks to the darkness and the confusion of the chase.

Justine stirred. I put down my phone and pulled her close to me.

"Morning," I said. "How are you feeling?"

"Like I've run a marathon," she replied. "You?"

"I've been better."

She gave me a sympathetic look and kissed me.

"I know," she said. "What happened to Philippe Duval wasn't your fault. Or mine. The people who killed him are the ones who should be held accountable."

The rational part of me knew she was right, but guilt was often irrational.

"Coffee and breakfast always make the day seem brighter," she said, rolling out of bed.

She looked amazing in her tight shorts and vest, but I was dismayed to see the heavy bruising on her arms and legs, which had matured to shades of dark purple and blue overnight. She saw me looking and appraised herself.

"They'll heal," she said. "Come on. Let's find the people who made them and give them hell."

An hour later, after showers, pastries and coffee, we were in Miriam Lambert's office at the Automobile Club. The room was spacious and elegantly furnished, and like everywhere else in the building, a passion for motorsport shone through in the framed prints that lined the walls. There was a classic Formula One steering wheel displayed in a glass case on Miriam's gleaming antique desk.

She looked harried, which wasn't surprising. The city was buzzing with anticipation for the weekend's race, and even this early in the morning the cafes and bars were packed with fans from all over the world getting the party started.

"I'm so sorry to hear about Philippe," I said, deciding it was probably better not to ignore the murder, which was national news.

"It's a tragedy," Miriam replied. "His children are so young . . ." Her voice faltered as her eyes filled with tears. She took a deep breath. "What can I do for you, Mr. Morgan?"

"This is Ms. Smith," I said. "She was the victim of the recent kidnapping."

Miriam was surprised by the revelation. "I'm glad to see you're safe and well."

"Thank you," Justine said.

"We know one of the abductors secured employment here," I reminded her. "It's possible there were others."

"What?" Miriam asked. "Why would that be?"

I shrugged. "I don't know. That's what I'd like to find out."

"How?"

"When I escaped from the kidnap gang, I saw the faces of some of them," Justine replied.

"I'm sorry that you suffered such an ordeal," Miriam said stiffly. "But if you think I can just let you look through our personnel records, you are mistaken. There are laws protecting privacy."

Today Justine was looking elegant in a black floral dress, but bruises were visible on her delicate arms and she made a point of staring at them, drawing Miriam's gaze.

"These men are violent," Justine told her. "What if they have planned something that could sabotage the Grand Prix?"

I didn't give Miriam a chance to answer. "There's nothing to prevent the Automobile Club of Monaco from hiring a private investigator to conduct a security review after discovering a suspected criminal was working here."

"It just so happens we're offering a new client discount of one hundred percent," Justine added. "So, it won't cost you a cent, and it will save a great deal of potential embarrassment if we discover any other criminals among your ranks. People who might threaten the security and safety of the Grand Prix."

Miriam nodded slowly, suddenly realizing the wider implications of failing to act on the intelligence we were giving her.

"I will arrange for you to have access to the employment files of all non-executive staff and temporary personnel," she said.

CHAPTER 38

MIRIAM MADE GOOD. She granted us access to an edited set of personnel records on a Club laptop, excluding those of long-serving senior members of staff. As we passed through the building we heard the hustle and bustle of a human resource command unit responsible for mobilizing a much larger race day army. People who experienced the glamor of watching the Grand Prix in Monaco would have little idea that delivering such a prestigious experience involved hundreds of staff with a near-obsessive focus on the mundane and practical details.

People here were fine-tuning the arrangements for barrier positioning, crowd control, free flow of local traffic while stands were built, roads were resurfaced and temporary buildings took over the city, travel arrangements for dignitaries, high-profile guests and drivers plus teams and families, catering, security, and race-day stewarding.

We sat in a third-floor meeting room, surrounded by photographs of past Grand Prix winners, each image a shot of the victorious car crossing the finish line.

Justine flicked through the employment records, clicking an arrow to cycle from photograph to photograph. In addition to the picture, these abridged records featured a name, a start date and their position within the organization. There were over a thousand currently active records, but the volume of files didn't faze Justine. By midday she'd already been through more than 500 of them.

I remained silent, not wanting to distract her from the rhythm she'd established. Every so often I would walk to the window and look down at the street to the rear of the building, which was lined with rigging trucks, TV vans, media and Automobile Club staff members hurrying about their business. I recognized Marc Leroy, the club's operations director, barking commands at his crew of coordinators.

"This is one of them," Justine said, and I turned to see her pointing to the photo of a man with short black hair and matching stubble. He was smiling in the photograph but there was an air of unease about it, unfamiliar and forced.

I recognized him as one of the men who'd opened fire on me in the gully after I'd knocked out their leader, Roman.

"Michel Augarde," I said, reading the man's name.

"Almost certainly false," Justine remarked, and I nodded.

False or not, we now knew her kidnappers were somehow linked to the Monaco Grand Prix, and if I'd been forced to place a bet, I would have said they were trying to infiltrate the event. Maybe to stage a murder or possibly something on a larger scale.

Justine hurried from the room and I followed her along the busy corridor to Miriam's office.

The personnel director had instructed us to interrupt her the moment we found anything, and we did just that, walking in on a meeting she was having with three members of her team.

"Michel Augarde," Justine said. "According to the system, he was hired as a rigger two months ago."

Miriam got to her feet. "We need to find Marc," she said. "Get me a radio." She directed her final remark at one of her colleagues.

"No need," I responded. "He's out back with all the big trucks."

Miriam led us through the building and we skipped down the stairs, weaving around club members and staff. Miriam swiped a keycard through a reader and took us into a service corridor that was full of scurrying personnel.

Finally, we reached an exterior door that took us outside to a loading area, where we found Marc, checking his phone and simultaneously speaking into his radio.

"Marc," Miriam said, and he looked up. "We need to talk to you about Michel Augarde."

Marc seemed puzzled by Miriam's request. I noticed his eyes dart toward someone further along the street. I followed the direction of his gaze and saw the man calling himself Michel Augarde removing scaffolding from a large truck.

His eyes met mine. The moment he registered me, he dropped the metal struts, which clattered loudly as they hit the ground, and set off at a sprint.

CHAPTER 39

"CALL THE POLICE!" I yelled before I raced after him.

He had a decent head start but I heard Marc yell to his staff, telling them to stop Michel. He raced past the first few people, who reacted to Marc's instruction with bemusement, but once the surprise had passed, other riggers and marshals lunged for the running man and he had to dodge their tackles and attempts to grab him, which slowed him down.

The memory of him shooting at me on the mountainside propelled me on. I sucked in air like a turbo-charged engine and closed the gap as Michel climbed up the side ladder of a rigging truck and ran across the roof.

From there he leaped onto the metal canopy of a cafe, startling staff and customers below as he thumped across the swaying structure and bounded in through an open second-floor window.

I followed, clambering up the ladder, racing across the truck and sprinting over the canopy. I jumped through the window and my instincts saved me when I sensed movement to my right.

I ducked and rolled as Michel swung a metal floor lamp at me. The heavy base hit the window and shattered the glass. As I got to my feet, he tried to swing it the other way, but I tackled him and he dropped the lamp as we grappled with each other.

We traded blows and ended up on the floor. I blocked his efforts and hit him in the face a couple of times. He rolled away, dazed, and staggered to his feet. I pursued him as he rushed for the door. He flung it open and set off through an open-plan office full of people, who were surprised to see two men engaged in a chase through their previously peaceful workspace.

Michel was bleeding from a cut above his eye and his face looked a mess, adding to people's unease. They rose from their desks and backed away from him as he darted around the office furniture and headed for the exit.

There were cries and shouts, but no one tackled either of us. I followed the fugitive as he barreled through a green fire door and chased him into a concrete stairwell, bounding after him, as we both leaped down multiple steps at a time.

He reached the landing above the ground floor and I took a gamble, jumping directly from the flight above. My bet paid off when I landed on him, sending him crashing into a wall. He lashed out instinctively with a vicious elbow to my chin, and I saw stars.

Dizzy, I backed off and he punched me in the gut before bolting down the last flight.

I caught my breath and ran after him, racing through the open door, which led into a large reception area.

Michel sprinted past a security guard and yelled something at him in French. The hefty uniformed man closed in on me threateningly while Michel raced through the main doors and ran onto the street.

I didn't have time to deal with the misguided security guard, so I vaulted the barrier by the reception desk, swerved to avoid his clutches and hurried outside.

There was a sudden blast of sirens further along the street and I was pleased to see two police cars round the corner directly ahead of Michel, but he kept running while the cars drove on, passing him without slowing.

They screeched to a halt a few meters from me and a uniformed officer jumped out of the passenger seat of the leading vehicle. He yelled, "Jack Morgan, you are under arrest. Stop where you are!"

"Wrong guy," I replied dejectedly, but I slowed to a halt and raised my hands in surrender.

CHAPTER 40

MO-BOT, SCI AND Stéphane Porcher were in a computer room in Marseilles police department in front of three rows of machines set on terminals. There were no windows, and at the heart of the front row was a bank of a dozen screens stacked three high by four wide to create a single massive display. Porcher's colleague, a gray-skinned man with long black hair that shone with grease, was trying to get the composite display to show a set of video files. Porcher hadn't introduced them, but Mo-bot gathered the man's nickname was Tifs and he seemed to have a prickly relationship with the detective.

Stéphane Porcher didn't move quickly, and neither did his colleagues.

Someone had to physically chase down and apprehend bad guys, but Mo-bot doubted it was Porcher, who seemed cerebral and slightly disconnected from the world, like Hercule Poirot or

Columbo. He had an aura of curiosity, as though it was the web of mystery and not the adrenalin of the chase or any strong sense of justice that attracted him to law enforcement.

"What did this guy do?" Mo-bot asked, hoping to move things along.

Porcher held up one palm and nodded at the screen in front of them, indicating that she should be patient.

She rolled her eyes at Sci, who smiled.

Stéphane and Tifs had a sharp exchange of words when the technology refused to cooperate. Mo-bot offered to help but both men ignored her, so she sat back and watched Tifs struggle on while Porcher grew increasingly exasperated.

There were three other tech specialists in the room and Mo-bot caught them all grinning and sharing mocking glances.

Finally, after an excruciating delay, six of the screens came to life and showed footage from different cameras within the precinct. The footage shared the same timecode, so Mo-bot realized she was watching six different viewpoints of the same night.

She knew it was night because she could see streetlights shining through the windows on a couple of the screens. One of the cameras was directed at the main booking hall of police headquarters, which was almost empty apart from two uniformed officers who chatted absently while doing paperwork behind a high counter.

The other cameras showed mostly empty corridors and there were two others aimed on the cell block.

"Watch," Porcher said, leaning forward and pointing at the screen that displayed the booking hall.

There was a blinding flash that turned the screen white. When the flare died away, Mo-bot saw part of the exterior wall had collapsed and four masked men in body armor were clambering through the breach. They held sub machine guns and opened fire on the two uniformed officers behind the counter. One of the cops managed to hit an alarm before he succumbed to his wounds, and the other screens showed cops running from offices and break rooms into the corridors.

The four assailants moved into the cell block and shot another cop who'd been quick to respond to the alarm.

There was no hesitation about any of their movements and Mo-bot realized these men knew exactly which cell to hit. They primed the door with explosives.

Two cops ran into the corridor nearby and were shot instantly. Mo-bot thought one of them looked a lot like Porcher. She caught his eye and felt his trauma on reliving the moment.

He nodded slowly, as if answering a question. "If it hadn't been for my colleague, I would be dead."

On-screen, they saw another police officer dragging Porcher out of the cell block and into an adjacent corridor where cops set to work on a tourniquet to stem the blood streaming from a gunshot wound in his thigh.

In the cell block, the masked attackers stepped away from the door and shielded their faces as the explosive charges detonated. A flak jacket was produced from a holdall and thrown over Roman, who was bustled from the cell like a president under heavy close protection.

Three of the masked attackers formed an arrowhead around

him, while the fourth went on point, shooting indiscriminately to clear a path.

The gang ran from the cell block to the booking hall, shot two more officers who'd equipped themselves from the armory, and fled through the breach they'd created.

The jail break had taken less than three minutes from beginning to end.

"Five wounded, four dead," Porcher told them.

"I'm so sorry," Mo-bot responded gravely.

"That's rough," Sci remarked. "I'm sorry for your loss."

Porcher waved their words away, but his eyes filled and he couldn't speak for a moment. Mo-bot wondered whether his slightly detached air was a consequence of antidepressant medication. She couldn't imagine what it would be like to live with the impact of such trauma.

When Porcher finally found his voice, he said, "We had arrested fifteen men that day. The information about the drug deal they were engaged in came from your American FBI. It was a huge bust for us, and the cells were full. They came only for this one man and left all the others. Why?"

He eyed Mo-bot and she wondered whether he was genuinely expecting her to have the answer.

"It is a question that has bothered me for months," he went on. "And now you come here looking for him. This was no street dealer."

"Who were the others he was arrested with?" Sci asked.

"The Outlaws," Porcher replied. "They control much of the heroin coming into Marseilles."

"Where would we find them?" Mo-bot asked, and Porcher smiled sardonically.

She had seen that expression before on the faces of people who thought she was crazy.

"They are extremely dangerous," the detective said. "My advice would be to stay away."

"We can't do that," Sci said. "We need to know who this guy is and why he matters so much."

Porcher shrugged, disassociating himself from this plan. "Then go and see Baba Saidi. He was arrested that day. He used to lead the Outlaws. Maybe he still does. He was in the cell next to the man who escaped."

"Where would we find him?" Mo-bot asked.

"Les Baumettes," Porcher replied. "He's in prison for the next twelve years and would probably welcome a visit."

CHAPTER 41

THE POLICE HAD taken my phone, watch, wallet, keys, belt, shoes and laces, and put me in the interview room in my suit and shirt. The floor felt cold through my socks, but I was glad of the sensation. My mind was flying through several possible scenarios, the most perturbing of which was that Roman and his people had friends in the Monaco force who would be willing to stage a suicide or accidental death in custody.

Every time someone walked past the interview room, I tensed. I wouldn't be able to do much against an armed attacker, but I wouldn't go down without a fight.

So far, though, the door had remained closed. I'd been left to stew.

The other scenario troubling me was that I was about to be charged with the murder of Philippe Duval based on circumstantial evidence, which might not be enough to convict me, but could be sufficient to keep me locked up and out of the way until Roman and his people had achieved their objective. They would now need to kill the target they had wanted me to eliminate for them. It might also give them more time to reach me in custody.

I shifted on the metal chair, which was bolted to the floor like the matching table and chairs opposite. The walls were an uninspiring white and looked to be recently painted, so I didn't even have old graffiti to distract me.

Without my watch or phone, I had no idea how long I'd been held in custody, but it must have been well over an hour, so I was twitchy and frustrated when the door finally opened and Valerie Chevalier entered together with a woman I didn't recognize.

"Mr. Morgan, I'm sorry to have kept you waiting. I was attending to another matter," the inspector said, closing the door behind her.

"Mr. Morgan, my name is Hannan Benyamina," the other woman introduced herself.

She offered me her hand, and I stood up to shake it. She was about five feet ten and exuded confidence. She wore a black trouser suit and a pastel-pink blouse.

"I'm your attorney. One of your colleagues instructed me in this matter."

I guessed Justine had moved to engage someone to represent me as soon as I was arrested.

"I specialize in complex criminal cases," Hannan said. "Here are my credentials."

She reached into a satchel and produced her resume. I

glanced at it but took it on faith Justine would have done her homework.

"Thank you, Ms. Benyamina," I said, offering her the seat next to mine.

"There's no need to sit," Valerie Chevalier said. "This won't take long."

Hannan seemed almost as surprised as me.

"Philippe Duval had a concealed surveillance camera system installed in his office. It recorded his murder at the hands of four masked men," the inspector revealed. "And later, your entry and flight from the scene, Mr. Morgan. Why did you go there?"

"Philippe called me," I replied. "Said he was in danger and asked to see me."

"And why did you run?"

"Because I thought you'd suspect me of murder," I replied. "And if it hadn't been for the secret video footage . . ." I let the implication hang for a moment. "I'm guessing the perps tried to frame me."

Valerie nodded. "They called the police as they were leaving the office after killing Monsieur Duval. We've matched when one of them uses a phone on the video to the time of the anonymous emergency call."

"So, you have no grounds to hold my client?" Hannan said.

"He had previously agreed to cooperate and share information with us," Chevalier responded. "And he'd been warned he would need to make himself available to us to assist with our investigation." She looked me square in the eye. "We had a deal, Mr. Morgan."

"We do," I replied, but couldn't force conviction into my delivery.

Roman and his men had known we were coming for Justine. They'd been planning to move location when she'd escaped, and that suggested a leak in the Monaco or French police force. But I couldn't tell Valerie Chevalier what I thought in case she was the mole.

"Where is Monsieur Duval's phone?" she asked.

I grimaced.

"Yes. The one you are seen taking from him on the video."

She turned to Hannan. "If we get the phone within an hour of your client's release, we won't charge him with interfering with a police investigation."

Hannan looked at me searchingly, and I nodded sheepishly.

"I'll make sure it's here within sixty minutes."

"Then you can go," Chevalier said. "But our information-sharing agreement is at an end, Mr. Morgan. And I'd suggest you stay away from this case. Too many people close to you are getting hurt or killed."

Her last line stung me, but I knew better than to react.

She opened the door and I got to my feet, eager for freedom.

CHAPTER 42

BAUMETTES PRISON WAS a huge complex south of Marseilles. Six-story cell blocks rose from the ground like monuments to misery, some a dirty brown, aged by years of Mediterranean sun; others new, boxy and soulless, painted white and green—the colors doubtless chosen for their neutral, calming quality.

The old buildings came from an era of retribution, when criminal justice had been primarily motivated by the concept of punishment, and it was evident in their severe architecture. The new buildings were about rehabilitation, an effort that went beyond the colors chosen. There were more plants and green spaces around them, larger windows, sports courts, and a general air of comfort lacking from the older iterations.

There were just under 2,000 prisoners on site, according to Mo-bot's cursory research, and she wondered how many of them were truly capable of rehabilitation and how many simply deserved retribution.

Baba Saidi was facing a twelve-year sentence, so he'd get plenty of both. Mo-bot had checked him out while Sci had driven them to the sprawling prison. Baba had been head of the Outlaws, who controlled much of the flow of heroin into southern France from North Africa. He'd been arrested along with thirteen members of his gang and Roman, who according to Baba's testimony had been the instigator of a deal to purchase thirty kilos of heroin. Baba had pleaded innocent, claiming Roman had been working with French police to entrap him. Baba was just an entrepreneur. The judge hadn't believed him and had given him a higher sentence than the eight years he'd been offered as part of a pre-trial deal. Mo-bot didn't feel sorry for the guy because Marseilles now had one ruthless criminal fewer on its streets. But as she read snippets of his testimony via Google Translate, she couldn't help feeling this was an egotistical man who'd had no idea how hard and fast he was about to fall.

And he'd fallen a long way. Sci parked the Ford Kuga in the visitors' section of the huge complex, and he and Mo-bot cleared security in an orange brick building that looked like it had been glued onto one of the modern cell blocks as an afterthought.

They joined a dozen other visitors, following a prison officer to the visiting room, an open-plan space with two dozen round tables, each surrounded by six chairs. All the furniture was hard resin and bolted to the floor. It was also very uncomfortable, and Mo-bot was in the process of shifting her weight to find a tolerable position when she saw Baba Saidi shuffle into the room with a puzzled expression on his face.

He had aged markedly in the months since his mugshot Porcher had shown them had been taken, as though prison had sucked the life from him.

His puzzlement was plain when one of the prison officers directed him toward Mo-bot and Sci. According to his police record, he was forty-four, but his short Afro was completely gray. The black hair in his mugshot must have come from a bottle, which might explain some of his loss of youth, but Mo-bot sensed it was more than that. He was thinner, gaunt even, and there was a slight stoop to his frame, which made him seem humble and hesitant. Had prison broken him?

He sat down opposite them without saying a word.

"Mr. Saidi," Mo-bot said. "My name is Maureen and this is my colleague, Seymour. Do you speak English?"

Baba sat stony-faced and said nothing.

"We work for a detective agency called Private."

His stare hardened and he got to his feet.

"Mr. Saidi," Mo-bot went on, as he turned his back on them, "we'd like to ask you about Roman."

It was as though she'd slapped Baba. He froze and then turned back slowly, a look of disgust on his face.

"*Howa ibna sharmouta*," he said with a vicious scowl on his face.

"I don't know what that means," Sci remarked.

"He's a son of a bitch," Baba replied, retaking his seat. He directed his gaze at Mo-bot. "Go on." His accent was a mix of French and Somalian.

"You were arrested with Roman, but he escaped justice," she said.

"When I was tried, I thought this man was a police inform-ant, that his escape was staged," Baba said. "But now I have had time to ask friends to check him out, I have learned the truth."

He fell silent and drifted away in thought. Mo-bot got the sense he was deeply conflicted.

"What truth?" she asked.

"They say he is no police informant but the devil himself. The tip-off came from the American FBI, that's why the Mar-seilles police raided us," Baba replied. "It was just bad luck. But the devil makes the most of bad luck."

"How?" Mo-bot asked.

"He could have helped me escape that night, but he saw an opportunity," Baba replied. "His organization is too well resourced to allow him to face justice. They rescued him and used my incarceration to take over my business. I don't have powerful friends like he does."

"What organization does Roman work for?" Sci asked.

"The Dark Fates," Baba replied. "My sources tell me his real name is Roman Verde."

Mo-bot and Sci exchanged looks of disbelief. The Dark Fates was a motorcycle gang they'd encountered in Rome, and Jack had shot the group's leader, Milan Verde, who was currently serving life in a Roman prison for his involvement in the Vatican murders.

"Roman Verde must be related to Milan," Mo-bot said to Sci, suddenly registering the physical resemblance between the two men. "That's why they targeted Justine and Jack. This is personal."

CHAPTER 43

WHEN I WAS finally processed and released, I found Justine waiting for me in the lobby of police headquarters.

"Jack!" she said, throwing her arms around me.

I pulled her close. It felt good to hold her and smell the vanilla in her hair and her jasmine perfume.

"Thank you," she said to Hannan, who'd supervised my release and walked out with me.

"You're welcome, but I really didn't do anything," the lawyer replied. "They had footage of the murder all along. They knew Mr. Morgan wasn't responsible."

Justine stepped away, irritated on my behalf. "Then why hold you?"

"To make a point," I guessed. "We'd had a deal to share information, which is apparently over because I've been holding out."

Justine frowned while Hannan moved to go.

"Well, if that's all, I should get back to the office."

"Thank you," I said.

"You're welcome. Call me if you need anything else," she replied. "Thank you for trusting me, Ms. Smith."

Justine nodded and Hannan walked toward the main doors, leaving the two of us in the middle of the busy lobby, surrounded by cops and civilians going about their business.

"The deal to share information is over?" Justine asked.

"That's what Chevalier said," I replied.

"And what if I knew where one of the kidnappers was?"

I looked at Justine in disbelief.

"After you were arrested, the guy you were chasing—Michel—stopped running, so I followed him. On foot at first, and then in a cab."

I smiled and slowly shook my head at her. "You're amazing."

"I know," she said flatly. "He's staying in a small apartment building in a neighborhood called La Turbie. It's just across the border in France. I rented a car. We could take a drive and talk to him."

Much as I relished the prospect of having a private encounter with the man, there was clearly a broader conspiracy at work that might involve the Grand Prix and put many lives potentially at risk. We knew at least one person would be targeted by this group, but they might have other plans. A terror attack at the race would send shockwaves around the world.

"I think we should share the intel," I said to Justine, whose mouth curled at the corners.

"After what the cops have just done to you?" she asked, then thought better of it. "I thought you might."

My phone rang. When I took it from my pocket, I saw the incoming call was from Mo-bot.

"Mo," I answered.

"Jack, you'd better be sitting down for this. The guy who took Justine is Roman Verde, brother of Milan Verde, leader of the Dark Fates."

I shook my head in disbelief.

"This is personal for him. Revenge for what we did to his brother," Mo-bot said. "We're on our way back to Monaco."

"We'll see you at the apartment," I told her calmly, but inside I was reeling.

The Dark Fates was the formidable criminal gang I'd encountered while investigating the Vatican murders. I thought it had been broken up by Italian authorities after its leader Milan Verde was imprisoned.

"See you there," Mo-bot replied before hanging up.

Justine looked at me expectantly.

"The man who abducted you is Milan Verde's brother," I told her.

While she reacted to the revelation with shocked disbelief, I reached a decision. "This is no street organization. There's a bigger play at work here, which means we can't keep any useful intelligence to ourselves. There's a chance the French or Monaco police deliberately blew the operation to rescue you, but we can't tackle something on this scale without trusting someone. We need to inform Chevalier about the suspect in La Turbie and see how she wants to handle him."

CHAPTER 44

JUSTINE AND I drove to La Turbie, a pretty town north-west of Monaco. Even though it was only three kilometers away, the drive from Monaco Police Headquarters took twenty-five minutes thanks to the heavy traffic caused by diversions on the roads in preparation for the race.

Justine had followed the man calling himself Michel Augarde to an apartment building on Avenue du Général de Gaulle in the heart of the small town. I had thought about informing Chevalier of our intention while we were still at police headquarters, but prior experience had taught me the cops moved slowly when there was any question of cross-jurisdiction. I had an idea how to ensure a rapid response if we found Michel at the apartment, one that would ensure he was taken into custody swiftly.

There was a line of parking spaces opposite his building and I pulled into one beneath the shade of an Aleppo pine. I studied the four-story block, trying to figure out how we could tell if our target was inside. There was a convenience store in the bottom left corner, a realtor on the first floor, but the rest of the building looked to be residential with large windows overlooking the broad avenue running through the heart of town.

"Come on," I said to Justine. "Let's kill two birds with one stone."

She gave me a puzzled look but nodded. We left the car and headed for the opposite side of the street. I saw a pink-washed building, three stories set above a bakery, that would be perfect for our needs. I glanced back at Michel's building and could see the flicker of TVs in a couple windows and dancing shadows that signified movement in others.

I took Justine to a recessed doorway beside the pink building.

"Stand here," I said, leading her behind a column that concealed her from the street. "When your phone rings, I want you to scream for help as loud as you can. Stay hidden but keep hollering."

"Why?" Justine asked. "Where are you going?"

"Up," I replied, indicating the roof of the pink building.

I hurried over to the wooden entrance doors and forced them open with a powerful shoulder barge. The lock snapped. I hurried into a narrow hallway and ran up the black-and-white-tiled stairs to the very top of the building.

It was a utilitarian block that smelled of dry plaster and homecooked food. When I reached the top of the stairs, I pushed the bar on the fire door to gain access to the roof and went to the balustrade facing our target's building. I settled into a crouch behind the low perimeter wall, ensuring I had a clear view of the front windows. I took out my phone and placed a call to Justine.

A few seconds later, her piecing cries of "Help me!" echoed around the quiet street, and people came running out of shops and cafes while the windows of nearby buildings filled with occupants drawn by the noise.

I kept my eyes on the building opposite and saw Michel glance down at the street from his third-floor window before swiftly withdrawing.

I dialed 112 and was connected to an operator.

"Do you speak English?" I asked.

"Of course."

"I'd like to report a woman being assaulted in a third-floor, north-side apartment, number twelve Avenue du Général de Gaulle in La Turbie," I said. "You can hear her now."

I held the phone out to maximize the impact of Justine's screams. This had been my original plan to ensure a swift response from the cops, but it had also served to get our target to reveal his location.

"Please send police officers," I said before hanging up.

I called Justine and she answered after a single ring. "Now what?"

"Come up," I replied. "I'm on the roof. The cavalry is on its way. We might as well settle in and watch the show."

CHAPTER 45

JUSTINE JOINED ME at the edge of the roof a few minutes later. We peeked over the balustrade and watched the building opposite. People drifted away from their windows in the absence of further cries for help, but soon returned when the sound of sirens filled the air. Once again people peered out of their apartments looking for the source of the commotion.

Not Michel though. He never came back to his window, and the next time I saw him was in circumstances I could scarcely believe.

He emerged from a side entrance beside the convenience store and hurried across the sidewalk to the corner of Avenue du Général de Gaulle and Avenue de la Victoire as the first police car arrived. Unlike the others that were approaching, this one didn't have its blue lights on and its siren was silent.

Justine glanced at me in surprise because instead of running when he saw the cops, our target approached the vehicle, nodded at the uniformed driver and his partner, and jumped in the back.

As the car rolled along Avenue de la Victoire, Justine's puzzlement turned to disbelief, a feeling I shared.

"Did he just . . ." she said, her voice trailing off.

"Let's go," I responded, and we hurried away.

Less than a minute later, breathless and with hearts pounding, we were in the silver BMW 3-Series Justine had rented. I gunned the engine and followed the cop car along Avenue de la Victoire, racing to catch up with our target.

The main convoy of police vehicles screeched to a halt outside Michel's building as we sped away, a blaze of sirens, flashing lights and loud, purposeful officers who had no idea they'd been betrayed by a couple of colleagues. Or maybe they did know? I had no idea how far the corruption went.

"So, they have connections to the cops?" Justine remarked.

I nodded. "Looks like it. More than connections. Protection."

The BMW roared along the broad avenue. When we reached Place Detras, I took a gamble and went west along the Route de Nice, following signs for the bus station. I guessed the cops wouldn't want a potential suspect in their car for long and would take him to a public transport hub.

We raced past slow-moving traffic, weaving onto the opposite side of the road and swerving to avoid oncoming vehicles. I ignored the shocked reactions of pedestrians on the sidewalks and the shouted curses of drivers enraged by what I was doing. It paid off. About fifty meters ahead I saw the cop car make a right turn on to a narrow side street.

"There," I told Justine. "Get video."

The BMW's engine growled as I dropped into second gear and hit the gas. We shot forward, darting around an old Renault Clio, which pulled abruptly to a halt.

Justine used her phone to film through the windshield. As we turned into the narrow side street, I saw the man calling himself Michel Augarde glancing back at us through the police car's rear window. He turned to speak to the driver. Moments later the Peugeot's lights and sirens came on and it accelerated as it sped north. Civic-minded drivers cleared a path and pedestrians hurried across the street. None of them could have known they were giving way to two corrupt cops who were spiriting a wanted criminal away from arrest.

But the cleared path worked for us too. I pushed the BMW until we were on the cops' tail. I could see the driver glancing in the rear-view mirror as both vehicles bounced and swerved along the narrow, winding street. A hairpin bend took us back on ourselves, and soon we were heading south, back toward the Route de Nice. I accelerated, driving so close our bumpers were almost touching.

"Make sure you get Michel on camera," I said to Justine above the roar of the chase, and she directed her phone at the man, who looked back again before ducking behind the seat.

I caught the police driver's eyes as our cars shimmied around the street, moving at speed. I fixed him with a glare. Corruption was an insidious form of injustice. I would make sure he and his partner answered for what they were doing.

CHAPTER 46

THE 3-SERIES SURGED forward, and I touched the bumper of the cop car as we neared the intersection with the Route de Nice.

Ahead of us, traffic paused on both sides of the main road, and the cop car swung a hard left turn, heading east, back the way it had come, toward our target's apartment building. I followed, staying close to the renegade cops, and the BMW's engine roared as I demanded more from it.

When we straightened up on the Route de Nice, there was a sudden screech of tires and the cop car swerved left, slowing as the driver used the handbrake to put the vehicle into a controlled drift. I stepped on the brakes and matched the maneuver, but as I turned, the tail of the cop car caught the front of ours and sent both vehicles into a spin.

We collided again and the BMW was flung into the fruit and vegetable display of a mini-mart. Produce scattered everywhere and we came to a crashing halt in the doorway of the store.

"Are you okay?" I asked Justine, who nodded.

I waved apologetically at the shocked man behind the checkout counter and reversed the BMW out of the entrance. We backed across the sidewalk and when we bounced off the curb and straightened up, I saw Michel jump out the cop car, which had collided with a streetlamp up ahead.

"He's making a run for it!"

I accelerated and the car devoured the distance between us. When we were thirty meters away and our target was just a blur running through the street market that sprawled across an entire block to our right, I stamped on the brakes so hard that Justine had to slap her hands against the dash to keep herself upright.

"I'm going after him," I told her. "Those cops will want your phone. Get out of here and I'll meet you at the apartment."

"Okay," she replied, taking my hand. "Be careful."

"You too," I said, squeezing her fingers.

I jumped out of the car and sprinted across the road, running at a diagonal, on a course to intercept Michel at the intersection with a side street leading to a church.

I heard the BMW engine roar and glanced over my shoulder to see Justine in the driver's seat, steering the car into an aggressive U-turn.

As I'd suspected, the cops mirrored the move and gave chase. Even though Justine had taken advanced evasion training and I had no doubt about her abilities as a driver, the part of me that loved and cherished her couldn't help but be worried.

I pushed these concerns from my mind and focused on the man who could unlock our investigation. I could see him now, running across the busy market square, and sprinted in pursuit of him.

CHAPTER 47

JUSTINE THOUGHT BACK to the hostile driving and evasion course she'd taken and recalled her instructor's advice: "Stay calm, be aware of your surroundings and use them to your advantage."

She glanced in the rear-view mirror to see the police car gaining on her. Ahead, the street was clear, the traffic pulled up haphazardly to either side in deference to the sirens and flashing lights.

Pedestrians clustered on the sidewalks, phones out, filming the chase. Justine hoped no one would capture more of her face than a blur as she sped by.

The BMW roared along the Route de Nice, west toward the edge of town where rustic buildings thinned out, giving way to the highway that connected La Turbie with the city of Nice.

Justine knew the open road wouldn't be her friend and made

a sharp left turn onto a narrow alleyway that cut through a quarter of old buildings.

She heard more sirens in the distance and felt the pressure. Without the suspicious presence of Michel in their car, the cops hot on her trail would appear to be in honest pursuit of a suspect, and she had no doubt they'd summoned backup.

As she raced south, Justine saw a break in the buildings ahead of her and in the distance, the shimmering blue of the sea. She followed the alleyway between low apartment buildings and villas with brightly painted wooden shutters until it joined a wider road where she raced east, tracking the sweep of a long bend so the sea was to her right.

Justine saw another police car further up the hill directly ahead of her, so she took the next right fork, down toward the seafront. She dodged around a blue-and-white bus that had pulled over in response to the sirens, and caught the expressions of amazement on the faces of the passengers, their noses pressed against the windows as she roared by.

Moments after passing the large vehicle, Justine saw a potential escape route. She floored the accelerator and the BMW growled as it found more torque, pushing her back in her seat. She glanced in the mirror as a parking lot flashed by on her right, and saw the crooked cops behind her swerve around the bus.

Justine swung a left into a tiny alleyway marked with a dead-end sign. The street was just wide enough for a car to drive down it. The sides of the BMW ground against the high drystone wall on her left and the yellow house on her right. She opened the sunroof, and when she drew near a bend in the alley, slammed on the brakes, unbuckled her seatbelt before the car had drawn to a complete halt, and pulled herself up through the sunroof.

The police car screeched to a halt behind her and the cops tried to jump out, but they couldn't open their doors in the narrow alleyway and the vehicle had no sunroof.

Justine jumped onto the hood of the BMW then skipped down onto the road ahead and ran toward a flight of steep steps with white-painted iron handrails to help pedestrians climb them. There was the roar of an engine behind her, and she glanced over her shoulder to see the cop car reversing back along the alleyway at speed. The driver wasn't calm or mindful enough of his surroundings and collided with a second police car that had just turned into the narrow route.

Justine left the corrupt cops to inspect the mangled wreckage and ran up the steps that took her to a courtyard behind a charming Mediterranean church. She slowed to a walk as she entered the quiet building. A sign told her it was the church of St Michel de La Turbie, which she thought was ironic given the name of the man they were hunting. She gave silent thanks to the saint and all the angels who'd watched over her as she made her way through a small crowd of tourists who were admiring the polychrome marble, devotional paintings, high organ and ornate Baroque ornamentation.

Justine walked through the building and emerged on Rue Capouane, a broad street lined with tall evergreens. A warren of alleyways ran off the square in front of the church. She picked one that would take her east to safety.

CHAPTER 48

THE MAN CALLING himself Michel Augarde cleared the market and set off along Avenue du Cap-d'Ail, a claustrophobic street lined with old buildings set close to the single-lane road. I hurried past the last of the bountiful market stalls and trailed him. The passing cars and motorcycles were so close I could have reached out and touched them. Ahead of me, Michel ran on, slowing slightly, legs starting to fail as fatigue hit him. He glanced back and saw me thirty feet behind him.

The sighting spurred him on. When he passed a terrace to his right, he dashed in front of a car, crossed the street and sprinted into an open-air restaurant, darting around tables and chairs shaded by parasols that bore the logo and name of Le Sol. He collided with a waiter who was carrying a tray of drinks, sending the man tumbling in a spray of beverages.

The waiter cried out as the cups and glasses shattered against the stone flags and some of the patrons got to their feet, muttering, but no one tried to stop Michel who ran into the covered part of the restaurant.

My heels reverberated against the cobblestones like bullets, pounding out a rattling beat. I sidestepped waiters, chairs and tables and dashed into the building.

Peripheral vision saved me as Michel swung a punch at me from his hiding place beside the entrance. I dodged the blow and barged into him, driving my shoulder into his gut and forcing him back until he collided with the far wall. I felt the air rush from his lungs, but he desperately tried to compensate by throwing another wild punch. I stepped clear and his fist found nothing but empty space. He lost balance and almost toppled forward. I seized the opportunity to drive a fist into his nose, knocking him back and setting it bleeding.

Dazed and covered in fresh blood, he flailed at me wildly. As I dodged his chaotic punches, I knew I had the advantage.

A heel kick to his shin deadened his left leg and he buckled; an uppercut to his chin caught him hard enough to make his eyes roll back. A couple of jabs followed by a right hook, and he crumpled like a dead weight.

I heard sirens approaching and knew I didn't have long before the place filled with cops. I needed some time alone with this man before he was taken into custody. There was no telling the true extent of Roman Verde's influence within the local police department, and no guarantee conventional methods of interrogation would yield any useful information.

I grabbed the man's arms and dragged him toward the place where I knew I could make him talk.

CHAPTER 49

"EVERYBODY OUT!" I yelled as I dragged the unconscious Michel into the small commercial kitchen at the back of the restaurant.

The head chef, her assistant and a waitress didn't need to be told twice. They hurried away through the fire exit. The door had been propped open by a food-waste container and I could see the place opened onto a narrow alleyway that ran behind the neighboring buildings.

I dropped Michel on the floor and shut the door to the restaurant, ignoring the inquiring looks from a man who was brave enough to peer down the service corridor. I locked the interior door but knew it wouldn't hold long against the police.

The distant sirens grew louder as I ran across the kitchen, dragged the bin away from the fire door and allowed it to swing shut.

I didn't have long and started with a physical search. I took the man's phone, tossing his wallet away because it contained nothing but cash and an Automobile Club swipe card.

I searched his pockets and rolled up the sleeves of his lightweight jacket to check for any distinctive markings. When I uncovered his left upper arm, I saw something that stopped me dead.

After a beat, I grabbed my phone and took photos of a tattoo of a fleur-de-lys inside a Jerusalem Cross. I'd seen this marking before in Rome; it signaled the man's membership of Propaganda Tre, the secret society linked to the Dark Fates that I thought I'd eliminated in the Eternal City.

The sirens were close now, their shrill notes rising above the bubbling sounds from pots on the stove.

I had to be quick. I slapped the man, who stirred.

"Who are you targeting?" I asked.

His eyes rolled so I slapped him again and he came to, suddenly snapping awake with a start.

"Who are you targeting?"

He focused on me and smiled. "You shouldn't have meddled in Rome," he said, his heavy French accent drawing out the word "meddled." "Everything that's happened during your time here was planned."

So, there was now no doubt we had been targeted because of our involvement in solving the Vatican murders.

"Who do you work for?" I shook him while I glanced around the kitchen for something to threaten him with.

I didn't believe in torture, but intimidation might get me the answers I needed.

"Is Roman Verde calling the shots?" I asked. "Is this revenge for his brother? Or does he answer to someone else?"

My eyes settled on a meat cleaver, resting on a butcher's block on the neighboring counter. I stood up to grab it, but Michel surprised me by kicking me in the chest and jack-knifing to his feet.

I was knocked into the counter and grabbed the cleaver as he pulled a knife from a nearby sink.

The sirens were almost on us as we faced each other.

"Are you going to take me, Jack Morgan? Can you do it before the police arrive? And if they take you instead, will you be safe in jail? Where do you think is beyond our reach?"

I heard cars pulling up outside and reached a decision.

I dashed across the kitchen. Michel gave chase. I slammed into the fire door, flung it open, and swung it shut behind me.

There was a dumpster beside it, which I shoved over just far enough to block the door. Michel cursed when he found his exit route blocked.

Satisfied I wasn't in immediate danger, I set off along the alleyway that ran behind the terrace of buildings. I didn't stop running until I was certain I was safe.

CHAPTER 50

A LOW AFTERNOON sun bathed the room, tinting our faces rose-gold so we looked a little like gilded statues as we sat trying to absorb the day's revelations.

Mo-bot and Sci had reached the apartment by the time Justine and I regrouped there, and they'd told us about their interview with Baba Saidi and how the French–Somalian gangster had confirmed Roman Verde's identity. Armed with the man's real name, Mo-bot had been able to pull his official records from the Italian Ministry of the Interior. He was a former special forces soldier turned criminal and had served time for gun and drugs smuggling.

We shared our account of the discovery of the man calling himself Michel Augarde at the Automobile Club, my arrest, and the intervention of the corrupt cops.

"So, we're up against an organization with resources and connections?" Mo-bot remarked.

Sci nodded. "Not just any organization. The Dark Fates."

"And Propaganda Tre," I added.

I told them about Michel's tattoo, which signified his membership of the influential secret society.

"Flip sides of the same coin," I explained. "The Dark Fates handle the street-level stuff while Propaganda Tre operates in the corridors of power."

"And they want someone or some people dead," Justine responded. "They involved us because they want revenge for what we did to Roman's brother Milan, but we're not the primary targets."

I nodded and decided to voice a thought that had been nagging at me since my encounter with Michel. "Did you pull anything from Duval's phone? Michel Augarde said every aspect of my trip here was planned."

Mo-bot rose from her perch on the end of the couch and went to her workstation.

"Nothing on the main files," she said, shaking her mouse to bring her monitor to life. "But he installed Signal." She was referring to the secure electronic messaging app that was supposed to be impervious to most hackers. "I left a combination-cracker running while we were in Marseilles."

She opened a file that showed an exchange of messages from the secure Signal app and scrolled through them.

"Friends, family, nothing unusual," she noted. "But let's see if there's an echo, the remnants of deleted messages."

She typed some commands. A shimmering icon appeared by a phone number that materialized at the top of the message list.

"Messages from this number were set to automatically delete after they were read, so I can't see what was said, but why would he instantly trash messages from just one number he hasn't even stored in his contacts?"

"Affair?" Sci suggested.

"Maybe," Mo-bot replied. "Or perhaps they implicate him in something?"

"The original attack took place outside his building," I remarked. "And I was suspicious of Duval until our background checks cleared him, but what if Propaganda Tre reaches as far as the government of Monaco? What if he was just very good at covering his tracks?"

"It's possible," Mo-bot conceded. "He knew where you'd be and when."

"And he knew we'd discovered Justine's location in the Utelle Valley," Sci remarked. "He might have been the one who warned Roman we were on to them."

I nodded and thought about all the phone calls Duval had made while we were preparing for the expedition. Even when we were on the mountain, he'd stepped away under the guise of calling Chevalier, but maybe he'd been warning Roman.

"So, what now?" Justine asked.

"I think we need to pay him a visit," I replied.

CHAPTER 51

SET IN THE foothills behind the Avenue Pasteur, the Princess Grace is Monaco's only public hospital and occupies a couple of city blocks. The main building is a tiered eight-story structure facing the bay. A huge, newly constructed extension to the east gave a sense of the gleaming curvilinear buildings that would proliferate in Monaco's future. Mo-bot's research told us the mortuary, which also served as the city's police morgue from time to time, was located in the old building.

In the warm evening Justine and I walked from our apartment holding hands, moving purposefully but not rushing. Duval was not going anywhere, and any secrets he might reveal would be there whether we arrived five or fifteen minutes from now. It was more important for us to reconnect, to find some equilibrium in the storm the world had unleashed on us.

"That could have been us," Justine said, nodding toward the

coast where dozens of parties were underway on yachts in the marina, and people had gathered in the bars and cafes that lined the streets around the seafront.

I nodded. It should have been us. We'd come to Monaco on vacation, and I had hoped to take Justine to the Grand Prix at the weekend. The race was the cause of all the revelry around us: motorsport fans staging pre-race parties, corporate sponsors hosting lavish entertainments . . . the whole city was lit up and alive with excitement.

"I'm sorry," I responded, squeezing her hand.

"You don't have anything to apologize for. You haven't done anything wrong."

"I could have taken us home. I could have let the police do their job," I said. "I could have chosen a different life."

"A lion can't be anything other than a lion," she replied. "You can't choose to be anyone other than yourself. The man I love."

I smiled and together we walked toward the hospital as the sounds of revelry drifted up the hillside from the coast.

The old building was elegant, but the new extension, two sixteen-story state-of-the-art towers, made it look insignificant by comparison.

We went through the main entrance into a quiet lobby, avoided the desk and two receptionists, who were too busy chatting to a third colleague to notice us, and followed signs for "*Pathologie*," where Mo-bot had assured us we'd find the morgue.

She and Sci had stayed in our apartment to study everything they'd been able to find on Roman Verde and put together some revised analysis of the Dark Fates and Propaganda Tre, given that we now knew that neither group had been wiped out by our recent operation in Rome.

The hospital, like most others, was a place of held breath, prayers for good news, and lives desperate to be lived. The clean, clinical corridors, devoid of soft furnishings or fabric, created a sense of space, reinforced by the echo of every footstep. Whether it was recovery from an operation, broken limbs, or treatment for heart disease, these were places that put normal life on pause. The sense of space, the echoes and amplification, reminded us there was so much more to be had from the world than what went on inside these bare walls.

We hurried ahead, following signs, avoiding drawing attention to ourselves, smiling at any healthcare workers we passed, trying to give the impression we belonged.

When we finally reached the pathology department located in a semi-basement at the very rear of the building, we found it was closed. Justine opened her bag and tried a universal key-card Mo-bot had given her.

A light on the reader beside the double doors flashed green on the second attempt and we moved inside quickly and quietly. We found the morgue down a flight of stairs. Even with the strip lights on, the white-tiled room was unnerving. I tried not to think about the procedures that had been conducted on the two stainless-steel tables that dominated the space.

The bank of refrigerators dominating one wall contained the earthly remains of the dead. No amount of learning or familiarity with death could shake the discomfort I experienced on finding myself near a corpse. I wondered how it affected people who worked with them daily.

"Philippe Duval," Justine said, reading the placard on one of the fridges.

She opened the metal latch and I helped her pull out the drawer that held Duval. His body was inside a mortuary bag.

Justine looked as unsettled as I felt.

"Okay?" I asked.

She nodded. "Whatever it takes."

I pulled down the zip and tried to ignore Duval's face and the ugly bullet wounds in his head, where blood was congealed and crusted. I reached for his left arm and fought the urge to recoil at the cold, meaty feel of his skin. I lifted his arm from the bag and studied it. Other than the grayish tinge, it was unremarkable, so I replaced it and did the same with his right arm.

I saw what I'd been looking for instantly. There, tattooed on the underside of his upper arm, was the fleur-de-lys inside the Jerusalem Cross, the insignia of Propaganda Tre.

Michel's words now made complete sense. Everything about our visit to Monaco had indeed been planned, including the invitation to discuss a potential business partnership with Philippe Duval. He was a member of the group we'd faced in Rome and had obviously been instrumental in helping them exact their revenge on me.

"I can't believe it," Justine said, staring at the tattoo. "If he's one of them, why is he dead?"

It was a very good question. One of many we had yet to answer, the most pressing of which was, who had they tried to blackmail me into killing?

CHAPTER 52

"WHERE'S SCI?" I asked when Justine and I returned to the apartment.

There was no sign of him anywhere and the whole place was very still. Mo-bot hardly moved when she was at her computer, and casual observers might have been forgiven for thinking her a sculpture: the white-hat hacker at work.

"He went for food," she said, glancing round. "You two look as though you could use a drink."

I nodded, and she rose and crossed the living room to the kitchen. Sci had bought a couple bottles of liquor when we'd stocked up at the grocery store, and Mo-bot settled on a spiced rum. Justine and I went to the terrace while Mo-bot took three glasses from one of the cabinets and followed us outside with the bottle.

Music filled the night. Thudding from bars, blaring from

apartments, disco lights flashing here and there, the noise of crowds from the seafront and the hum of late-night traffic combined to give a sense of a vibrant, lively city. Everywhere was heaving, from apartments in the buildings around us to incoming sports fans in the streets. The hotels and bars closer to the sea were all packed. Our grim investigation seemed at odds with the city's party atmosphere.

Justine and I sat on one of the couches beside the glass barrier that marked the edge of the terrace. Mo-bot took the couch opposite and placed the glasses on the table between us. She proceeded to pour three generous measures of rum.

"No frills," she said, handing us our glasses.

"None needed," Justine replied.

"Thanks," I added.

"Hey!" Sci called out.

I glanced over to see him step into the living room carrying a stack of pizza boxes.

"Where's mine?"

"Grab a glass," Mo-bot told him.

He hurried to the terrace and deposited four boxes on the table. As the rich smell of sauce and melted cheese filled the air, I realized I was starving.

Sci went inside, grabbed a glass, returned to take a seat next to Mo-bot, and watched expectantly as she poured him a drink.

"Cheers," he said, and the four of us raised our glasses in salute.

I took a swig. As the warm rum hit my empty stomach, I needed food more than ever.

"Pepperoni for Mo and Jack," Sci said, distributing the boxes. "Napoli for Justine and four cheeses for me."

We said thanks as we took the pizzas.

"What did you find?" Mo-bot asked.

I sighed. "Duval was a member of Propaganda Tre. I can't believe I was played by him."

"Me neither," Mo-bot remarked. "His background check was clean. It takes real skill not to leave a trail I can find."

We were silent for a moment. Sci opened his pizza box, picked up a slice and took a bite.

"We're only human," he remarked. "Eat. Everything will seem better then."

I nodded and started on mine. He was right, I felt better after the first mouthful.

"There's no way Carver is part of this, is there?" Mo-bot asked.

I shook my head. "I don't see it, but if you'd asked me if Duval was clean, I'd have given you the same answer up until earlier today."

"You can't feel bad for trusting him," Justine said. "I'm trained to spot liars, and he got the better of me too."

"These groups are designed to be invisible," Sci added.

"Why did they kill him?" Justine asked.

I shrugged. "Maybe they knew we were getting close? Or maybe he'd betrayed them somehow? I can't imagine being in a group like that, engaged in such evil, unable to really trust anyone because everyone around you is crooked."

"I've been looking at what Rome police uncovered during the prosecutor's investigation of Milan Verde," Mo-bot said between mouthfuls. "Like us, they believe the Dark Fates are the street arm of Propaganda Tre. Thugs and enforcers used for dirty work."

"But they believed they'd smashed both groups," Sci remarked.

"So did I," I replied. "But they wouldn't be able to smash parts of the organization that stayed hidden. Particularly those outside Italy."

"Do you think Duval joined recently?" Justine asked. "Or was he a member when he was in government?"

"It's a good question," I replied. "And I think there's only one way we'll find out the answer."

CHAPTER 53

I'D PARKED THE Ford Kuga on a quiet road that curved around the hillside. Justine, Mo-bot, Sci and I stood next to it in a turnout overlooking the city, now almost at peace. It was a little after 3 a.m. and only the hardcore parties were still going on in the distance, but even they had a dwindling vibe about them.

We stood beside a concrete barrier. Immediately below it was a high rockface that loomed over a small estate of six villas set in well-maintained gardens. The estate was demarcated by a high perimeter wall and a gatehouse by the main road to the south, where two security guards kept constant watch on comings and goings.

Philippe Duval's villa was directly below us, the property's garden ending at the rough, high rock wall that led up to the turnout barrier. The house itself was a modern Mediterranean-style home with a lot of stone and glass. It couldn't have been more than five years old.

"Just coming up to the vent," Sci said, and my attention was drawn to the remote control slung at his chest. A night-vision image of the side of Duval's house filled the screen as Sci piloted the tiny drone toward one of the air-conditioning units that serviced the property.

Moments later the drone was inside, flying through the vent, along a duct and through a grille to enter the interior of the house.

The place was spacious and tastefully decorated, with stripped wood floors, large pieces of abstract art, lush houseplants and striking sculptures. It seemed to be deserted.

"Check the bedrooms," I suggested, and Sci piloted the tiny aircraft up the stairs and into each of the rooms.

"Guard is doing another foot patrol," Justine said, gesturing toward the gatehouse.

This was the second patrol since we'd arrived.

Mo-bot checked her watch. "Looks like they're every thirty minutes."

"There's no one home," Sci remarked, pointing at the screen, which showed an empty bed in the last bedroom.

"His wife must have taken the kids to family," Justine suggested.

I nodded. "Makes sense. Must be a terrible time for them."

"Looks like we're good to go," Sci confirmed.

"Then I want us ready to move the moment the guard finishes his patrol," I replied.

CHAPTER 54

ONCE THE GUARD had returned to the gatehouse, a line attached to the tow-loop of the Ford and a simple waist- and thigh-belay was all we needed to descend the rockface into Duval's garden. Mo-bot was the one who found rappelling the hardest, but even she managed it with only minor complaint.

Soon, Sci was at the back door, working the locks with his pick. Moments later, we were inside a modern kitchen that contained a large family breakfast table.

Mo-bot hurried toward an alarm panel that had started beeping the moment we entered. She connected a handheld code-cracker to one of the terminal posts and forced the system to reveal its secrets. She input the code displayed on her device, and the alarm system fell silent.

We were in.

"We'll check his office," Mo-bot said, nodding to Sci.

"We'll search the rest of the place," I replied, and we split into two pairs.

Mo-bot and Sci went upstairs to Duval's home office, where the drone had revealed a computer and filing cabinets, and Justine and I began searching downstairs. We started with the kitchen cabinets.

"You think his wife knew?" Justine asked, as we moved quickly and methodically through the room.

"About him being part of Propaganda Tre?" I asked.

Justine nodded.

"I doubt it," I replied. "It would have put her in danger."

"Unless she was also a member," Justine noted. "Women can be in secret societies, you know?"

"Can they?" I asked. "I'm not sure they can. Most of these corrupt organizations are just for men. Maybe we're more easily led?"

"Maybe," Justine scoffed. "Men-children playing at being spies and gangsters, trying to dominate the world rather than make it better."

"Sounds about right," I conceded.

"Imagine living a lie like this though," she continued. "A normal family home, but beneath the veneer of respectability you're part of a criminal conspiracy. The deception must eventually take its toll."

I nodded. "I never want to find out what that's like."

"You couldn't keep something like this from me." She smiled. "You're too honest. I can read your thoughts on your face."

"I can lie when I need to," I replied.

"It's really not something to boast about," she said. "Come on. There's nothing in here. Let's check the rest of the house."

We moved into the hallway. A few streetlamps dotted the estate and their light fell through the windows at the front of the property, giving us just enough to see by.

I opened the door to the understairs closet and immediately sensed something was off. The dimensions didn't feel right. It didn't seem as long or deep as it should have been given the size of the staircase, and the space was devoid of any sign of family life. There were no coats or shoes or shopping bags, just bare white plasterboard.

I felt around the space and found a switch concealed above the inner door frame. I pressed it and a panel slid open in the wall in front of me, revealing an alphanumeric keypad.

"Mo!" I yelled.

Justine peered over my shoulder to see what I'd discovered.

"Mo, get down here," I shouted past her. "I've found something."

CHAPTER 55

SCI, JUSTINE AND I waited in the hallway while Mo-bot worked on the keypad under the stairs.

"Just . . . another . . . second," she said, spacing out the words carefully, so the loud clunk came the instant she finished saying "second."

"Would you look at this?" she remarked, and I peered through the door to see her stooping to enter a room concealed behind a hatch to the rear of the closet.

I followed her in, beyond a four-inch-thick metal vault door that had been covered in plasterboard so as to blend seamlessly with the understairs wall. The room the door concealed was about the size of a prison cell. There were four bunks and shelves full of supplies.

"Panic room," Mo-bot suggested, as Sci and Justine joined us in the cramped space.

I nodded. "You think you can open that?"

I gestured to a large floor safe tucked in the corner of the room at the end of one of the bunks.

Mo-bot crouched to check it out.

"Keypad," she observed. "So, it's probably between a four- and an eight-digit code. I should be able to do something."

She got to work, prizing open the panel.

Sci sat on the bottom bed of the bunk opposite. "Imagine living the kind of life where you need a place like this to keep your family safe," Justine remarked, looking around what was effectively a small survival bunker. "He probably told them it was because he'd been a government minister."

"Looks like it's a basic four-digit code," Mo-bot said. She'd connected her cracker to the safe and was interrogating the keypad. "Here we go."

She input the code displayed on her cracker, and the safe-locking mechanism shifted open with a clang and a click.

My heart thumped almost to bursting the moment Mo-bot pulled the door open, because a loud alarm sounded and rang throughout the house.

"Shit," she said. "There must be a kill switch somewhere."

I didn't waste any time trying to find it because we'd already given away our presence. Instead, I looked inside the safe to see four phones, passports, cash and half a dozen USB drives.

"Grab that and let's get out of here," I yelled above the deafening ringing.

Mo-bot swept everything into her gear bag, and the four of

us made a swift exit through the understairs closet and kitchen, before hurrying out of the house and into the garden.

"You go first," I told Mo-bot.

She handed me her gear bag as we approached, immediately starting to climb the rough rockface, which thankfully had plenty of chunky hand- and footholds.

When Mo-bot was halfway, Sci started up, and then Justine, and I went alongside her, conscious of the twin torch beams of the gate security guards heading toward the Duval home.

When I was two-thirds of the way up, I heard sirens approaching, but we crested the top of the rock wall, climbed over the turnout barrier and were in the car and moving at speed before the cops arrived.

CHAPTER 56

WE WERE BACK at the apartment less than fifteen minutes later.

Mo-bot went straight to her workstation and ferreted in her gear bag for the phones and USB drives she'd taken from the safe.

"I'll get to work on these," she said, settling into her seat.

"Coffee?" Sci asked, heading for the kitchen.

"You ever known me to say no?" she countered with a smile.

"I don't suppose there's any point me suggesting you get some rest?" I asked.

"Ha!" she scoffed. "Jack Morgan playing dad. You know me better than most. You think I'm going to let these little treasures keep hold of their secrets while I sleep?"

Mo-bot was one of the few people I knew who was capable of making me look like a slacker. She was tireless and relentless in her pursuit of the truth.

"Don't let me stop you though," she said. "This will take more than a minute, so you should get some rest while you can. Boost your reserves for whatever lies ahead."

Justine nodded. "The workaholic is right—"

"Hey!" Mo-bot interrupted, feigning hurt.

"We should try to get some rest," Justine went on. "It's been a tough few days."

Sci looked over from the coffee machine, a home version of something a barista might use, where he was making a couple of brews.

"I'm going to run the bank notes and see if we can identify where they were issued. They look fresh," he said, referring to the crisp euros Mo-bot had found in Duval's safe.

"Let me know if you find anything," I said, taking Justine's hand. "Come on."

I led her through the apartment to our bedroom and she pulled me into a tight embrace the moment the door was shut.

"Just hold me, Jack," she said. "Tell me everything is going to be okay."

"You know it will be," I replied.

I took in the scents of vanilla and jasmine that infused her hair, my favorite smells in the world.

"I need to hear it," she countered softly.

"Everything is going to be okay," I whispered in her ear, before kissing her.

She smiled and sat on the bed to take off her shoes. She looked beat, but then I probably did too.

"I'm going to grab a shower," I told her, and she nodded absently.

When I stepped out of the steamy en suite bathroom ten minutes later, Justine was curled up under the covers, deep asleep.

I slid into bed beside her and held her. I watched the glittering city and the port lights of the yachts in the distant marina until my eyelids felt too heavy to stay open, and when I finally fell asleep, I dreamed of happier times together.

CHAPTER 57

"HEY," MO-BOT SAID.

I woke to see her standing in the doorway. Justine lay against me beneath the covers, still wearing the clothes she'd fallen asleep in. We hadn't even had the energy to close the drapes. Morning sunshine now painted the city with bright color.

"You need to see what we found," Mo-bot told me.

"Give me a minute," I replied, and she nodded and shut the door.

"Can't we sleep a little longer?" Justine asked as I got out of bed and started to dress.

She yawned and stretched, while I put on a fresh dark blue linen suit and white shirt.

"I need a shower," she said, looking down at what she was wearing.

"Take your time, honey," I replied, leaning down to kiss her.

I left her to do her thing and joined Mo-bot in the living room. She was at her workstation, holding a large cup of coffee. Sci was nowhere to be seen.

"He crashed about an hour ago," said Mo-bot. "Sometimes I forget you're all only human."

"Very funny," I said, taking the chair beside her. "What have you got?"

Mo-bot suddenly became somber. "It's not good, Jack. Duval has been at this for years."

She opened a folder on her workstation showing an email archive.

"This was on one of the USB drives," she said. "They're messages from an anonymous account Duval ran, all sent to another anonymous account. The messages contain intelligence he acquired as Monaco's Minister of the Interior. There's even stuff in here on Eli Carver—conversations they'd had, likely US policy and attitudes on contentious geopolitical issues. They might call it a secret society, but Propaganda Tre made a spy out of this man."

I sighed and shook my head. I'd sworn an oath as a Marine to defend America against all enemies, foreign and domestic, and had never felt any inclination to join the Freemasons or other secret societies that I knew operated within the US, precisely because of my oath. I never wanted to be part of any group whose objectives might set me at odds with the vow I'd made to my country. Too often people joined political or social groups not realizing the split allegiance or inherent conflict implied by such a membership. Duval should have been an honorable pillar of his community. Instead, his membership of Propaganda Tre had turned him into a criminal and a traitor.

"We also found this tucked inside one of the passports," Mo-bot said, producing a black debit card. "He had a secret bank account, which according to the latest statement on this USB drive has a balance of over five million euros."

I whistled. "So, they made sure he got rich from his treachery?"

"Looks that way," Mo-bot said. "Sci was able to track the notes to a bank here in Monaco. And when I checked Duval's statements, he only ever used this card to withdraw money from a single cash machine located in the Chalmont Casino."

The Chalmont was one of the oldest and grandest casinos in Monte Carlo and was located on the waterfront near the Yacht Club.

"Why there?" I wondered. "Why that one machine?"

Mo-bot shrugged. "It's definitely not convenience. There are at least a dozen machines between his home and five between his office and that one. Maybe it's a front? Somehow connected with Propaganda Tre?"

"Maybe," I agreed. "See what you can find on the place." I got to my feet. "I'm going to make us all breakfast."

CHAPTER 58

"THE CHALMONT IS owned by Raymond Chalmont," Mo-bot said as she took a seat at the breakfast table on the terrace.

Sci and Justine joined us, he in his customary jeans and heavy metal T-shirt and Justine in a lightweight tea dress. Sci poured us all coffee as I served the pancakes I'd made.

Mo-bot used a tablet computer to show us all a photo of Raymond Chalmont. Chiseled good looks, thick blond hair, and even in the paparazzi shots he had an air of calm superiority.

"His family are old money," Mo-bot said. "Roots back to French and Belgian aristocracy. Been in Monaco more than a hundred years."

"Exactly the sort of man Propaganda Tre would try to recruit," I remarked.

"These are pretty good." Sci gestured at his partially eaten pancake, which he'd covered in syrup.

"Thanks," I replied.

"Yeah, he fits the profile." Mo-bot took a sip of coffee. "But so do a lot of people."

I nodded. "True. But how many of them own a casino used by a crooked government minister to withdraw cash from a secret bank account?"

I looked at Justine, whose hair was still a little damp from her shower.

"You got any lunch plans?"

She replied with a puzzled look.

"Because I hear the house salad at the Chalmont Casino is to die for."

CHAPTER 59

THE CARNIVAL THAT followed Formula One around the world was in full swing in the heart of Monaco. The city hummed with activity and excitement, which wasn't surprising considering the population was estimated to swell by a factor of five for the race weekend, from a little under 40,000 to more than 200,000. Every restaurant, bar and store was overflowing, and there were crowds of people everywhere.

Justine and I had walked to the seafront from our apartment and experienced the wild party atmosphere for ourselves. The Grand Prix course ran through the heart of the city, which meant massive traffic diversions were in place during the qualifying heat and the actual race, but the organizers did a remarkable job of keeping most routes open in the run-up to the event. Still, the swollen population, crowd control and closure of some streets meant there was slow-moving traffic everywhere. Supercars idled behind taxis and delivery vans in long lines, powerful engines rattling nearby windows, drivers looking around non-chalantly, obviously hoping motorsport fans would notice their state-of-the-art vehicles.

People in silly oversized hats spilled from bars, clearly drunk despite the early hour, and on hotel terraces more sedate corporate events took place behind discreet barriers.

The Chalmont was located in a grand four-story, hundred-year-old building with large arched windows overlooking Port Hercules. A sweeping U-shaped drive joined the casino to the Boulevard Albert 1er. It was currently packed bumper to bumper with millions of dollars' worth of supercars. Tourists and race fans stopped to take photos of the sleek machines, making the casino something of a draw for the crowds that had already gathered on the seafront.

A small group of paparazzi hovered near the casino entrance, eying passersby hungrily, eager for their next high-value celebrity sighting.

Justine had changed into a long green halterneck dress, and I was in a black suit, white shirt and blue tie. She led me along the drive to the stone steps leading to the grand entrance, where a doorman smiled and greeted us as we entered the vaulted reception area.

Three women in black suits sat behind an obsidian counter. Two were already dealing with guests, so we went to the third.

"*Bonjour, M'sieur, Madame,*" she said with a warm smile.

"Hello," I replied. "We tried to make a reservation for lunch, but the restaurant told us we should come and see if there were any cancellations."

I was telling the truth. The Jardin Restaurant at the Chalmont was world-famous and was booked weeks in advance at the best of times, never mind in the run-up to the Grand Prix.

"Of course, sir, madam, please go through," the receptionist said, waving us toward the inner doors, which were flanked by a pair of security guards in dark gray suits.

One of them held open a door and spoke words of welcome as we entered.

The Chalmont was even more impressive on the inside. A narrow corridor lined with obsidian walls was lit by inset LEDs that formed gently pulsing patterns as we walked.

At the end of the corridor was the large vaulted space of the main casino floor. About the size of a football pitch, the room had been created by merging the first two stories of the building. Black girders and wires made up for the loss of structural supports, giving the otherwise elegant structure an industrial feel. Inside there were roulette, baccarat, poker and blackjack tables, where the monied rich were already trying to beat the house, despite its only being just past noon. Servers moved around the place carrying drinks and snacks to the tables.

"Hey," Justine said, pointing toward a discreet black-and-gold sign. "ATMs."

The sign guided us to some nearby steps. We went down them and found ourselves in a small basement chamber that might once have been a wine cellar or fuel store, but which was now painted black and gold and home to four cash machines, including one belonging to Frontières Banque, the entity that was home to Philippe Duval's secret account.

Justine and I looked around the unremarkable space and I shrugged. There was no obvious reason to explain why Duval would have come to this specific machine.

We walked back upstairs, but as we reached the top and stepped onto the main casino floor, she grabbed my arm and pointed to someone sitting at one of the poker tables. He had light brown hair and a face that looked as though it had been battered by years of fighting. He wore a sky-blue shirt, dark blue trousers, and had a matching suit jacket slung over the back of his chair.

"He", Justine said, "is one of the men who kidnapped me."

CHAPTER 60

THE MAN IN blue spotted Justine and we locked eyes for a split second before he moved like a startled animal, jolting out of his chair and heading full tilt across the casino floor.

"Call Inspector Chevalier," I said to Justine as I set off in pursuit.

His pace kicked up a gear when he saw me in pursuit and we both dodged and weaved our way around tables, servers with trays, and gamblers staggering around stunned by a big loss or too much drink.

Soon we were running full pelt across the huge vaulted hall, and when he crashed through a pair of red leather-upholstered doors on the far side of the room, I followed and found myself in a wide carpeted corridor lined with oversized framed photographs of historic Monaco.

The corridor was empty. When the doors swung to behind me, the sound from the main floor faded to a muted hum.

I couldn't see any sign of my target so I hurried on, passing function rooms with names such as the Corniche Suite. As I ran past a door leading to the Princess Grace Suite, I heard movement behind me and turned to see the man I was chasing come barreling through, shoulder down, ready to tackle me.

I sidestepped just in time, grabbed his shirt and gave him an extra shove to propel him into a print of Stirling Moss winning the 1961 Grand Prix.

He cried out as the glass shattered on impact, but swiveled, already swinging, and caught me with a lucky right hook, which knocked me back a couple of steps and dazed me.

He didn't press his advantage, but instead took the opportunity to run.

I came to my senses and set off after him, sprinting to the end of the corridor and following him up a flight of stairs to the left.

He barreled through some glazed double doors and I chased him into a reception area, where a blonde woman and a dark-haired man sat behind a long counter. They both gasped when the man I was chasing passed them and sprinted down a corridor to their right. I followed, hot on his heels.

He reached a door at the end and burst through it. Moments later, I did the same and found myself in a large, opulently furnished executive office.

Seated on two long couches were Raymond Chalmont,

Roman Verde and two very large, heavyset men I recognized from Justine's escape from the farm.

The man I'd been chasing turned to me, a smile on his face. "You never stopped to consider whether you were the hunter or the prey," he said in a heavy Spanish accent.

The two large men stood and grabbed me. I tried to shake them off, but Roman Verde joined them and punched me in the face, stunning me.

Chalmont got to his feet looking agitated. "Your business should never intrude on my domain," he protested. "That was our deal. Whoever this man is, whatever you do to him, it happens elsewhere."

Roman nodded, and the two thugs who had hold of my arms whisked me off my feet and dragged me from Chalmont's office.

CHAPTER 61

JUSTINE CALLED MONACO police as she hurried across the casino floor. Jack's pursuit of the gang member had caused a stir, and people were busy craning their necks to see if they could catch any more of the action. There was muttered conversation, sounds of shock and disapproval all around, but no one had paired her with Jack so she moved on undisturbed.

She didn't bother trying to talk to Chevalier but instead spoke to the emergency operator, who eagerly took down details of the violent brawl at the Chalmont Casino. Justine figured they'd get a swifter response from an emergency call than from a harried detective who might well be off-site or not even on duty.

With assurances the police were on their way, Justine slipped her phone into her bag and went through the red double doors on the far side of the giant room.

She immediately noticed broken glass from a smashed

picture frame about halfway along a corridor. She hurried on, and as she neared the end of it, heard movement to her left. Shuffling footsteps and voices.

She peeked round the corner to see five sets of shoes coming down a flight of stairs. She recognized Jack's in between two unfamiliar pairs. There were another two behind them.

Justine withdrew before any faces came into view.

"Take him out the back way." She recognized Roman Verde's voice. "We'll deal with him at the safehouse."

Justine's mind was racing. What was Roman Verde doing in one of the most prestigious establishments in Monaco? How had they captured Jack? And how could she get him back?

Direct confrontation was not an option but Justine had a flash of inspiration and ran back the way she'd come.

She burst through the double doors, praying she'd be quick enough, and raced across the casino floor. The entrance corridor and lobby went by in a blur, and she ignored protests from the security guards. As the first rays of sunlight touched her skin and she felt the sea breeze on her face, she heard the familiar sound of approaching sirens.

She ran over to the huddle of paparazzi, who gave her a cursory once-over as she approached.

"You'll never guess who's been playing in one of the private rooms," she exclaimed breathlessly. "Timothée Chalamet."

The paparazzi were suddenly alert, like wolves catching the scent of prey on the wind.

"They brought him in through the back and they're trying to sneak him out the same way right now," Justine revealed. The nine freelance photojournalists moved with a sense of unity and purpose she'd rarely seen outside law enforcement or the military.

She followed the pack as it raced around the side of the building, along an alleyway to a service road at the rear.

They arrived just as a van was pulling up and Jack was man-handled out of the building.

"Timothée! Tim!" the paparazzi yelled, not really registering who was in the huddle ahead of them.

Roman Verde and his associates were startled and shielded their faces, which only added to the photographers' curiosity.

Justine didn't waste a moment. She stepped forward and grabbed Jack's hand.

"Come on, honey," she said, pulling him away from the men who'd abducted her, men who were now shying away from the cameras in an attempt to protect their identities.

It was beginning to dawn on the photographers that there was no celebrity, certainly not Timothée Chalamet. As Roman and his men retreated inside the building, the paparazzi started grumbling at Justine, but she didn't hang around to listen to their complaints. Instead she led Jack toward the approaching police cars.

CHAPTER 62

WE BYPASSED THE cops who'd just pulled up in a pair of liv-eried vehicles and headed along the Avenue du Port toward our apartment.

"You're amazing," I told Justine.

I glanced behind us to make sure we weren't being followed and saw four cops hurry from their cars toward the casino entrance. Their arrival had caused more of the seafront crowd to gravitate to the grand old building, creating a strange carnival atmosphere around my brush with danger.

"You'd have done the same," she replied, taking my hand.

She checked around us before pulling me into a kiss.

"I probably would have been more direct. Not as imaginative."

"Well, I'm not going to take on four guys," she replied as we resumed our journey. "That wouldn't end well."

I grinned. "What you did was perfect."

She smiled back.

We took a circuitous route to the apartment. We reversed, went through a couple cafes, making use of their service entrances to seek out new roads. I kept my eye on the sky for any sign of drones, and we both looked for tails—the same faces showing up, eyes that lingered just a little too long—but we saw nothing. When we were finally certain we were clear of danger, we hurried up the hill, inland, through the buzzing city, to safety.

It was a little before 2 p.m. when Justine and I stepped into the living room to find Sci and Mo-bot where we'd left them, analyzing files and photos on their computers.

"Well?" she asked without looking up.

"We had a run-in with Roman Verde," I revealed, and they both looked round with expressions of concern on their faces.

"What?" Sci exclaimed. "At the casino?"

"At the casino," Justine confirmed.

"Why would a street criminal be at a place like the Chalmont?" Mo-bot wondered.

"I was hoping you could tell us," I said, taking a seat on one of the couches. "See if there are any intelligence advisories on the place."

The NSA and other intelligence agencies used sophisticated artificial-intelligence network analysis to examine the relationships between known terrorists, organized criminals, and other notable individuals connected to suspicious entities around the world. It was possible the Chalmont had been flagged as a risk by one such agency.

"If it's a good front, they will have been careful to avoid being flagged by law enforcement or any basic analysis," Mo-bot said. "It's not a run-of-the-mill laundry. We might need access to the NSA. You think we can trouble Weaver?"

I shrugged. "Carver said whatever we need, but I'll call him to be sure. I need to tell him what we've learned about Duval anyway. Depending on how close they were, Carver's friendship with him might represent a security risk."

"Drink?" Justine asked.

I nodded as I took out my phone. "Water, thanks."

I dialed Carver's personal number. After a moment's silence, the call was answered.

"Yes?"

"Secretary Carver, please."

"One moment, Mr. Morgan."

The line briefly went dead then I heard a familiar voice.

"Hello, Mr. Morgan, this is Henry Wilson, Secretary Carver's aide. I'll just get the phone to him."

"Thank you."

I heard people, lots more voices, vehicles, cheers, music somewhere in the distance. It sounded as though Carver was at a festival.

"Jack," he said when he came on the line. "I was going to call you once I'd settled in. I'm here."

"Here?" I asked.

"In Monaco," he replied. "Assuming you're still here. I wasn't sure the summit would end early enough, so it wasn't a definite, but we got the negotiations done in time for me to make qualifying. It's such a relief to have got the treaty signed, but more importantly I get to watch the race."

He chuckled, but my mind was suddenly whirring.

The US Secretary of Defense here in Monaco. Someone I had unique and direct access to. Carver couldn't be the target, could he?

How would the Dark Fates and Propaganda Tre have even known his schedule, let alone something as tenuous as a contingency plan for a personal jaunt if the summit finished early?

"I'd like to invite you and Justine to be my guests at the race. And qualifying of course," Carver went on. "I've got great seats. Perk of the job."

"Thank you, Mr. Sec— I mean, Eli," I replied. "But we're too hot right now. I was calling to see if it was still okay to access the asset you made available to us."

"Of course."

I hesitated.

"And?" he asked.

"And I wanted to let you know we found evidence Philippe Duval was a member of Propaganda Tre, the criminal group we encountered in Rome."

Carver was completely silent and the line filled with the background sounds of Monaco.

"I'm sorry, Eli," I said. "I think he might have passed on sensitive information about you."

"Shit," Carver replied. "Can you send me what you've got?"

"I can, sir," I assured him.

"I appreciate it, Jack. I've got to go, but I'm at the Fairmont if the heat cools for you," he said, referring to the hotel near to where Justine had been taken. "I'll keep a couple race passes aside for you both, just in case. I've got a bunch of seats overlooking the Louis Chiron chicane. It should be an experience like no other, so I hope you can make it."

"Mr. Secretary, sir—"

He cut me off. "Just in case—send me the information, Jack. We'll talk soon."

And with that he was gone.

I turned to Mo-bot, unable to shake off a growing feeling of unease.

"Send everything we have on Duval to Eli Carver," I said. "And he's okayed us conferring with Weaver again."

"What's up?" Justine asked, handing me a glass of cold water.

"Carver's here," I replied.

"In Monaco?" Sci remarked, and I nodded.

"He's a petrol-head," Justine said.

"I keep asking myself a question," I revealed. "What if they knew he'd be here? What if he's the target? What if this wasn't just about revenge? What if they chose us because they knew I could get close to the Secretary of Defense?"

CHAPTER 63

I COULDN'T SHAKE that feeling of unease while we went over the evidence in the apartment.

Mo-bot messaged Weaver, but it was too early for an East Coast analyst to have started his day, so we were forced to wait.

In the meantime, Mo-bot and Sci checked their European sources for anything that would link the Chalmont Casino to Roman Verde and the groups he was a member of.

"I'm guessing money laundering," Sci said. "Dirty cash in for a few hours, play some small hands. Take clean cash out and claim you won it at the casino. It's an old trick."

Mo-bot scoffed. "You think people still launder cash in the age of crypto?"

"People like me," Sci responded.

"Dinosaurs," Mo-bot quipped.

"Even with crypto, you still need a way to distribute dollar or euro assets to your organization," I remarked. "Crypto back end, casino front end could be a powerful combination."

Mo-bot nodded. "Sure."

"He suggests it and you take it seriously," Sci said, playing hurt.

"He's the boss," Mo-bot countered.

"Can we see where the five million came from?" I asked. "The money in Duval's account."

Mo-bot shook her head. "I can't access the account, and none of the statements Duval stored on his drive show the incoming transfers. That's something Weaver might be able to help with."

It was 4 p.m. when Weaver replied to Mo-bot's message asking for more details on the casino. She sent everything we had on Duval, Raymond Chalmont, his casino, and Roman Verde and the Dark Fates. She also provided a rundown of our experiences with Propaganda Tre.

Weaver replied almost immediately, telling her he'd need a while to dig deep.

I paced the living room restlessly.

"Jack, what's up?" Justine asked. "You've been on edge ever since the call with Carver."

Part of being an effective investigator is learning to trust your intuition. I'd learned to listen to mine, and even though I didn't always understand it, I knew I had to follow where it led me. I believe our brains absorb far more information than our conscious minds can process. Somehow the analysis of all this data is fed back to us as intuition, so while it might appear to be magical or lack an obvious grounding in evidence, it is in fact built on rational analysis.

"I don't like being in the dark," I replied. "And I don't like Carver being here. It's too much of a coincidence."

"I don't like it either," Mo-bot said. "Coincidences are for daytime soaps and fairy tales."

I came to a decision.

"You want to take a walk?"

"Now?" Justine asked. "What about Roman and his people?"

"We'll be careful," I assured her. "They don't control the city."

"You hope," Sci scoffed unhelpfully.

"You want to see Carver?" Mo-bot asked.

I nodded. "I want to tell him what we know and check his security arrangements. Find out if there was any way Propaganda Tre would have been able to find out he would be coming to Monaco."

CHAPTER 64

IT WAS LATE afternoon by the time Justine and I neared the Fairmont Hotel. We avoided the Avenue des Citronniers and approached the iconic property from the seafront.

"You okay?" I asked her as we neared the spot where she'd been taken.

She nodded but was silent, and I could see she felt uncomfortable about the reminder of her abduction. I knew what it was to feel powerless and out of control. I'd most recently experienced it at the casino, when Roman Verde and his men had seized me, but I'd suffered many instances of having someone else's will imposed on me, and understood the panic it could induce.

I took Justine's hand and squeezed it gently. "We're together and we're safe."

She smiled at me and nodded again, this time more emphatically and at ease.

The Fairmont was one of the most desirable hotels in Monte Carlo, and it was easy to understand why. It was conveniently located in the heart of the action, on the racetrack itself, and many of the rooms had views of the notorious hairpin turn, with, on the far side of the property, glimpses of the seafront and marina.

The city was heaving, and the streets were packed with people in various stages of excitement and inebriation. The foot traffic grew heavy as we approached the hotel and were funneled into pedestrian channels beside the newly resurfaced road.

Qualifying started tomorrow, and the course was now closed to traffic as the final preparations were made to ensure it was safe for the powerful Formula One race cars.

The keen anticipation felt by so many race fans charged the air with the kind of energy normally reserved for Halloween or New Year's Eve.

We navigated the specially constructed walkways and finally made it to the hotel grounds, abuzz with some sort of large function. There were a lot of people crowded around the entrance, and a security team was holding most of them at bay and only allowing a select few to enter.

Justine and I pushed our way through the crowd until we encountered a man in a dark gray suit who blocked our path. He eyed us up and down. Justine had changed into a long black dress, and I was wearing my black suit, but had changed into a matching shirt, which was open at the neck.

"Hotel or party guests only," the man said. His Boston accent and the way he carried himself told me he was probably Secret Service.

"Jack Morgan and Justine Smith," I replied. "We're guests of Secretary Carver."

I took a chance that Carver's invitation to the race also extended to pre-event parties.

The man in gray checked a list on a tablet computer and nodded.

"ID," he said.

Justine and I produced our passports.

"Okay," he said. "Security is to your right as you enter."

He stood aside and signaled to a metal detector staffed by other men in suits who looked as though they'd attended the same school of intimidating deportment. The way they moved made them seem as though they were confident they could handle anything and was intended to discourage potential trouble-makers. I was familiar with the theory of force projection from my time in the Marines, the idea it was better to use displays of power to prevent violence than deal with its consequences.

We went through the metal detector and I was given a wand and fingertip search while Justine was waved on. I joined her in a large lobby. The floor was covered in cream marble tiles, and there were white leather couches and benches dotted between thick tan-colored pillars that supported a soft white ceiling inset with gentle spotlights. A wall of glass overlooked the terrace where a busy party was taking place.

We were about to go to the crowded reception desk and ask for Carver's room number when I saw him on the terrace near the exterior bar. He was at the very heart of the party, surrounded by people, including several Secret Service personnel whose eyes were everywhere.

"Come on," I said to Justine, who had also spotted him.

We were stopped by another man at the entrance to the lobby bar. He was clearly part of Carver's close protection detail and wore a Stars and Stripes pin.

"Names and ID," he said, not bothering with any niceties.

Justine and I presented our passports again, and when he'd checked us against his digital list, we were allowed through.

I'm not one for keeping up with the celebrity pages of the tabloids, but even I recognized some of the faces around me as we moved through the party. Musicians, actors, politicians, social media influencers, all talked and laughed in animated groups, while a DJ near the interior bar filled the room with mellow house music.

We stepped onto the terrace and pushed our way through the crowd. Carver saw us when we were a few feet away from his group, and broke away to greet us.

"Jack, Justine," he said enthusiastically. "So good to see you."

He shook our hands and pulled us toward the people he'd been standing with.

"This is my aide, Henry Wilson." He introduced us to a blond man who looked as though he'd stepped out of the pages of a Tommy Hilfiger catalogue, complete with sweater tied over his shoulders. "And Princess Elizabeth of Saxony," indicating a middle-aged pencil-thin woman in a striking red halterneck dress. She nodded at us. "Here's Chloe Waveley,

TikTok superstar." A woman in a short black dress with blue hair and a body covered in tattoos smiled at us. "And Clive Russell. He's a boxer."

Clive looked the part, his muscles barely contained by a suit that was just a little too small.

Justine and I greeted them all, and I wondered where else in the world one would find such an eclectic group. But we weren't here to make small talk.

"Mr. Secretary . . . Eli," I said, "we were hoping to get a couple minutes in private."

"Do you ever stop working, Jack?" he asked with a teasing smile.

I didn't indulge his attempt at humor with a response but left my request hanging.

"Okay," he said at last. "Henry, you'd better come. I think this is going to be official."

Henry was chatting to Chloe and looked disappointed to be dragged away from the attractive social media influencer, but he joined us as we followed Carver to the edge of the terrace. His Secret Service detail reconfigured around us.

"Well?" Carver asked.

"The men who abducted Justine were trying to blackmail me into killing someone," I said. "They never revealed the target."

Carver looked at Henry, both of them blank-faced.

"You think it was me?" Carver asked suddenly.

It sounded vaguely ridiculous hearing it said out loud like that.

"Why?" he went on. "Do you have any evidence?"

"No, sir," I replied. "Just a hunch that they chose me so as to exploit our relationship."

"No one knew I'd be in Monaco," Carver said. "My plans were entirely contingent on the summit and nobody outside my Secret Service detail and private office had any inkling. Hotel reservations, race tickers, travel were all booked by an agency the State Department uses whenever it wants to do things anonymously. There's no way anyone would have had enough advance knowledge to put something like this together."

"I know, sir," I replied. "I just—"

"I appreciate the concern, Jack," Carver said, interrupting me. "But sometimes shadows are just shadows and there aren't any monsters lurking in them. Look around you. Does anything about my security feel deficient?"

I glanced at the Secret Service agents positioned around us and the others dotted around the terrace and interior of the hotel.

"No, sir," I conceded.

"The Secretary is safe, Mr. Morgan, Ms. Smith," Henry assured us. "We take his safety extremely seriously."

Carver patted my shoulder and gave me a sympathetic smile. "I'm sorry you got caught up in something like this, Jack," he said. "And I hope you can resolve it quickly, because it would be good for you to be able to enjoy life. Even I'm not on all the time. Speaking of which, if you'll excuse me, I need to get back to having fun. It's been a stressful couple weeks and I need to unwind."

He moved back to the party, and, after giving us a pitying smile, Henry joined him. The Secret Service detail shifted to a new formation around their principal, leaving Justine and me behind.

CHAPTER 65

MO-BOT LEANED BACK in her chair and stretched. They were still waiting for a response from Weaver, but she knew complex network analysis could take some time, so she wasn't quite reaching the levels of frustration Jack had experienced hours ago.

She looked at the panorama visible through the picture windows. Jack and Justine were out there somewhere in the last rays of the afternoon sun, braving a city that seemed to have lost its mind over a motor race.

Mo-bot couldn't blame Jack for being twitchy and impatient or for wanting to check Carver's security. His feelings were those of a man dedicated to making the world a better, safer place.

Like Jack, she didn't believe in coincidence, and Carver's arrival in a city where Jack had faced attempted blackmail engineered to make him commit murder, combined with the corruption of Duval, a former government minister and friend of Carver, were an uncomfortable combination.

Sci was beside her, yet again going through the physical evidence they'd taken from Duval's safe. Double- and triple-checking was Sci's way of combating his impatience. Even though he seemed lost in concentration, revisiting each and every item from the safe, she knew he was desperate for progress. They all were. The waiting game was the worst part of being a detective.

"Well, this is a thing," he said, turning to face her.

He was holding one of the passports they'd found in Duval's safe, a fake Italian issue that contained Duval's photograph but was made out in the name of Filippo Massimo.

"What?" Mo-bot asked.

"The biometric chip in this passport isn't actually a bio chip." He held out the relevant page for Mo-bot to see. "And look, the laminate comes away so you can access it."

Sci demonstrated, raising the plastic page cover and taking the tiny silicon wafer from beneath it.

"I think it's a phone SIM," he said, studying it closely. "I can't believe I missed it before."

"It looks like a biometric," Mo-bot replied. "We see what we expect to see. Let me take a look."

He handed her the tiny wafer, which she inserted into a SIM reader connected to her workstation.

She opened a reader program and input some commands.

Moments later the SIM's data files appeared, showing two numbers that had been called using the card.

"Isn't that Jack's?" Sci asked.

Mo-bot nodded. "I bet if we check with him, the number of this card will match the one Duval used to call him and make the arrangements for his visit to Monaco."

"What's the other number?"

It was an American cell number and looked like a Chicago area code. Mo-bot ran the number through public directories and soon got a hit.

"Kendrick Stamp," she said.

She pulled the public records for all the Kendrick Stamps in the Chicago area and only recorded a single hit.

"Looks like he was FBI, now retired," Mo-bot remarked. "And Marine Corps before that."

"Why would Duval call a former FBI agent?" Sci wondered.

Mo-bot switched windows to Amadeus GDS, one of the most widely used hotel reservation systems in the world. She accessed the database via a backdoor she'd created a few years ago to enable her to run queries. The NSA and other intelligence agencies had been able to interrogate hotel and airline reservation systems for decades, so she knew how useful such access could be. She did a search of hotel bookings in the name of Kendrick Stamp in the past three months and wasn't surprised when she got a hit.

"He's here," Mo-bot revealed. "Or at least someone called Kendrick Stamp is staying at the Metropole."

"You think he might be the other shooter Roman Verde was talking about? The backup plan?" Sci asked.

Jack had told them about Roman's remark that a good general never relies on one plan.

Mo-bot shrugged. "The Metropole is ten minutes from here. You want to put on your walking boots?"

CHAPTER 66

MO-BOT PHONED JACK as they were leaving the apartment building, but the call went to voicemail so she left a message.

"Seymour and I are going to check out a lead. Kendrick Stamp at the Metropole. Details are on my computer."

"Would you look at all this?" Sci remarked, when she hung up.

He gestured at the street around them, which was thronged with people and clogged by near-stationary traffic. Monaco had surrendered itself to festivities and was full of noise and energy that intensified with each passing minute. Maybe it was just perception, or their direction of travel, which took them toward the heart of the city, but the music seemed to grow louder, the laughter wilder, and the chatter more frenetic with each step they took.

"It's too much for me," Mo-bot confessed.

"I prefer two wheels to four," Sci said, referring to his love of big motorcycles. "But these cars are some of the most sophisticated pieces of engineering on the planet. What we're witnessing is really a celebration of math and science."

A group of men further along the street cheered loudly. One of them was wearing a jester's hat with Formula One cars hanging from the points in place of the usual bells.

"A celebration of math and science?" Mo-bot said dryly. "Okay."

It took less than ten minutes to reach the Metropole, a colonial mansion-style hotel that stood six stories high. Arched windows, imperial columns, Roman statues and manicured gardens all spoke to the grandeur of the city's ancient past, but the hotel, located just off the Avenue de Grande Bretagne, somehow managed to feel modern and fresh.

Mo-bot and Sci crossed a cobblestone courtyard, passed a decorative fountain and went inside. They moved through the grand lobby, which featured a magnificent atrium and giant skylight, to reach the elevators.

Mo-bot's search of the reservation system told them Kendrick Stamp was in room 408, so they took one of the cars to the fourth floor and stepped into a quiet corridor, which reminded Mo-bot of a first-class train carriage. Chandeliers hung from the ceiling at regular intervals, and bench seats set in alcoves lined the walls. A vase of fragrant lilies had been placed in between each pair of doors on both sides of the corridor, filling the air with their heavy scent. The thick carpet felt so soft and luxurious, Mo-bot had the urge to take off her shoes and walk it barefoot.

They found room 408 a short distance from the elevator, and could hear a TV playing CNN through the door.

Sci knocked. The TV was switched off almost immediately.

"Yeah?" a man asked through the closed door.

"Kendrick Stamp?" Mo-bot replied. "We'd like to talk to you, please."

The spyhole darkened for a few seconds before the door opened a short way, restrained from going any further by the chain.

The man who peered through the gap looked haunted. He had dark shadows around his eyes, days of grown-in stubble, and the dry lips of someone who had spent too long inside an air-conditioned room. He wore a white vest and jeans and was barefoot.

"Who are you?" Stamp asked.

"Maureen Roth and Seymour Kloppenberg. We work for Private—"

"The detective agency?" Stamp interrupted. "I've heard of you. I was at the Bureau until a few months ago. Medical retirement."

"I'm sorry to hear that," Sci said.

"It is what it is."

"Why are you in Monaco, Mr. Stamp?" Mo-bot asked, and he stiffened slightly.

"Vacation," he replied.

"Alone?" she pressed.

Stamp didn't respond.

"A colleague of ours was abducted," Mo-bot said. "The people who took her attempted to blackmail another colleague, trying to force him to do something to ensure her safe return."

Stamp remained impassive.

"I think I saw something about a kidnapping on the news," he replied at last.

"So, you're not traveling with anyone?" Sci asked, and for a split second Stamp's strained smile wavered.

"No," he said. "I'm alone."

"Your wife is called Angela, right?" Mo-bot remarked. They'd found details of the couple on Angela's social media feeds. "Goes by Angie."

Stamp tried not to glare at Mo-bot, but he looked wounded.

"She not with you?" Mo-bot asked.

Stamp shook his head. "I told you, I'm alone."

"Because if anything has happened to her, we can help," Mo-bot told him. "If she's being used to coerce you, we can support you. Don't trust these people if they're—"

"I said I'm alone," Stamp interrupted. "I hope they find your friend who was kidnapped."

"Oh, we found her and she's safe," Mo-bot replied, registering her words hit home with him. "That's what we're saying. We can do things to help you. Real, practical things, like recovering people who've been taken. But we can only do those things if you tell us what kind of help you need."

Stamp hesitated.

"None," he said finally. "I don't need any help."

He signaled Mo-bot to draw near, and she leaned forward.

"You should go," he whispered. "They're watching me. It's not safe for you here."

CHAPTER 67

STAMP TOOK A step back.

"I don't need any help," he said loudly for the benefit of an unseen audience. "Good luck with whatever you're involved in."

He shut the door and Mo-bot looked at Sci.

"What did he say?" he asked.

"That he's being watched," she replied.

An elevator chime sounded. Mo-bot looked at Sci nervously.

"Let's take the stairs just in case," he said.

They started toward a door marked "*Escaliers*," a few feet away and had only taken a few steps when a trio of men in dark urban wear emerged from the elevator lobby.

"Hey!" one of them yelled, producing a pistol from inside his jacket.

"Run!" Mo-bot pushed Sci forward and he burst through the stairwell door as the man started shooting.

Bullets zinged through the air behind Mo-bot as she joined Sci, and the two of them barreled down the stairs as fast as their legs would carry them.

People would sometimes tease Mo-bot for hardly moving from her computer, but this was why. The digital world offered her control. If bad things happened, they generally didn't involve gunfire and the threat of death.

The gunman was first through the door, but he couldn't get a clear shot and he and his two accomplices raced down the stairs in pursuit of Sci and Mo-bot, who bounced off the walls, taking the descent at a hazardous pace.

Mo-bot stumbled at the top of the final flight, but Sci caught and steadied her and together they raced toward the exit.

They burst into a corridor that led to the lobby and saw another pair of hostile eyes on them. They belonged to a man Mo-bot had noticed on the way in. Unshaven and wearing casual sportswear, he'd been unremarkable at first but now was clearly identifiable as an enemy.

He made straight for them through the crowded, opulent lobby. Mo-bot and Sci turned and ran the other way.

They raced along a short corridor to a busy bar and restaurant and flashed past a startled hostess standing beside a menu station. Mo-bot glanced behind them to see the trio led by the gunman burst through the stairwell door. The three angry, hostile men joined their accomplice in pursuit of Sci and Mo-bot.

They danced around tables, servers and ornate floral displays, running toward the kitchen doors.

They hurtled through one marked "*Entrée*" and found themselves in a huge, frantically busy catering kitchen, where staff were sweating their way through the afternoon service and prepping for dinner on the busiest week of the year.

Mo-bot spotted an open door on the other side of the kitchen, which appeared to lead to a service corridor.

"Come on!" she told Sci, and they ran toward the opening, ignoring yells from angry chefs whose fury intensified when the band of pursuers burst into the kitchen.

Mo-bot heard the buzz of alarmed chatter from the dining room as the door swung back and forth, and she had no doubt hotel security and police would already be on their way.

A gunshot rang out and a bullet ricocheted off a pan rack. The cries of anger from the kitchen staff turned to exclamations of fear. The chefs and their assistants hurried to escape the danger and fled into the dining room.

Another shot, this one close by, but Mo-bot and Sci were near the doorway now and she could only focus on the light shining through. They had to make it! They were almost there . . .

"Move!" Mo-bot shouted, as she and Sci bundled through the open doorway to the safety of the corridor beyond.

CHAPTER 68

MO-BOT AND SCI stumbled into a service area. Above their heads, a large duct ran the length of the corridor. As they dashed on, breathless and exhausted, they saw doorways to their right. They sprinted past a series of offices before reaching an intersection with another corridor. They turned as their pursuers entered the corridor behind them, and the gunman took a few potshots. The bullets hit the wall behind them as Sci led them down a branching corridor, which opened out into a wider space.

To their left was an office, to their right a huge industrial laundry full of large washing machines and steaming presses. Ahead of them was a loading bay, and beyond the vehicle area was a raised roller shutter that opened onto the street.

"Come on!" Mo-bot told Sci, pushing him toward the loading bay.

She glanced back to see the four gangsters enter the corridor. She and Sci ran through an archway into the vehicle area. She pushed him to the right and followed him, out of the path of the gunfire that whined through the air around them.

"Jeez!" Sci exclaimed, jumping down from the loading platform into one of the vehicle bays.

Mo-bot followed, and the two of them sprinted across the bay toward the roller shutter and the street beyond. They were inches away from escape. Mo-bot could see the Avenue de Grande Bretagne at the end of the alleyway that accessed the loading bay. They were going to come out very close to the cab rank that served the hotel.

"Nearly there," Mo-bot told Sci breathlessly, and he nodded.

There was another shot, but this time there was no ricochet or rush of whipped air as the bullet failed to find its mark. Instead, there was a quiet grunt from Sci and a misstep that sent him lurching forward as they cleared the shutter.

He stumbled and fell into the alleyway. Mo-bot realized he'd been shot in the back, near his right shoulder. The bloodstain was already spreading across his T-shirt.

"Don't you stop on me!" she yelled, grabbing him. "Get up, Seymour!"

She slipped her arm under his and was grateful when he pulled himself up. She couldn't have carried him.

He smiled thinly, his face as pale as a cloud-covered winter sky.

"I'm still here," he said, and together they staggered to the end of the alleyway.

Mo-bot guided Sci toward the cab rank a short distance away, supporting him as they stumbled to the first vehicle.

"We need to get my friend to hospital," she told the driver, who looked startled and afraid.

Mo-bot followed his gaze, glancing over her shoulder to see the gunman emerge from the loading bay. She didn't wait for the driver to respond, opened the rear door and shoved Sci inside.

"Just get us to a hospital," she yelled, stepping into the vehicle.

She heard two shots and immediately registered two stabs of searing pain in her back around her left kidney.

She slumped forward onto Sci and heard the roar of an engine. She was vaguely aware of the cab moving off at speed but she was on her own journey, one that tuned out life, color and light and sent her into inescapable darkness.

CHAPTER 69

JUSTINE AND I left the Fairmont Hotel. As we started west toward the apartment, I checked my phone and saw I'd missed a call from Mo-bot while we'd been in the loud party with Carver. I listened to her message as we picked our way along the crowded street, following the pedestrian walkway around the racetrack toward the seafront.

"Mo and Sci have gone to follow up a lead," I told Justine. "Some guy called Kendrick Stamp."

"Any idea why?" she asked.

I shook my head. "Mo-bot didn't say."

We hurried through the city. The sun was falling rapidly and I was sure the coming of darkness would take the festivities to a new pitch. I wondered if locals liked the race or whether it was viewed as an economic boon to be endured. Did they leave the city, make a bundle renting out their homes, and return when the kerfuffle had moved on to the next country on the Formula One tour? I imagined the race brought in tens of millions of dollars at a minimum, so expected there was general good feeling toward the event.

The race fans thronging the city were already excited and I wished I could be one of them, carelessly partying the night away. But I'd chosen a different path through life, one that took me into harm's way far too often. One that regularly meant my choices weren't my own.

I looked at Justine, so beautiful, so intelligent, her face tight with stress. She deserved better than this, surely? Even if I didn't feel I did. She should have a life of comfort and ease with someone who could make her the center of his world. Someone whose mission in life wouldn't put her in danger.

She caught me looking at her and smiled. The darkness in my heart faded a little, and I smiled back. My logical mind might believe I should surrender her to a better life, but my heart couldn't let her go. She was my world and I loved her.

Twenty minutes later, we were back in the apartment. There was no sign of Mo-bot or Sci. I checked Mo-bot's workstation and found some information about a man called Kendrick Stamp. He was a former FBI agent, who'd served as a scout sniper in the Marine Corps before joining the Bureau, but there was no indication of why Sci and Mo-bot were interested in this man. There was a hotel reservation in his name at the Metropole, which would explain the lead they were following up.

I tried Mo-bot's phone but there was no answer. Sci's also rang through to voicemail.

By 6:30 p.m. Justine and I were starting to get worried.

"I don't like this," I said, fidgeting restlessly by the dining table.

Justine was flicking through the local channels, looking for news. "They'll be okay," she assured me, but I could see the concern writ large on her face.

"I think we should check the hospital," I said. "And go to the hotel. Ask around. See if anyone has seen them. Talk to this Kendrick Stamp."

"Jack," Justine said, pointing at the TV.

She put the volume up on a news report in French. I couldn't understand the detail, but it was clearly giving details of a shooting outside the Hotel Metropole in Monaco earlier in the day. I caught the gist of a police appeal for witnesses and the fact the victims were two American tourists, but that the attack was targeted and there was no evidence there was a danger to anyone else.

"You don't think . . ." Justine began.

I didn't get the chance to reply. My phone rang and I answered immediately.

"Mr. Morgan, this is Valerie Chevalier. Your colleagues Maureen Roth and Seymour Kloppenberg have been shot. They are in the Princess Grace Hospital receiving treatment. Their conditions are grave."

"I'm on my way," I said, before hanging up.

Justine looked at me expectantly, but it took me a moment to break the news because a pit had opened inside me and sucked all the sense and joy from life.

Their conditions are grave.

I understood the significance of those words and could hardly cope with the horror of them being applied to my friends.

Finally, I looked at Justine, my eyes wet.

"Mo and Sci have been shot."

CHAPTER 70

WE ALMOST RAN to the hospital. The exertion was a welcome antidote to the numbness I'd felt in the apartment.

I'd lost friends and comrades before, but familiarity didn't make the trauma of death any easier. Mo-bot and Sci hadn't gone, but the Grim Reaper had one hand on them. Police officers and government officials didn't use the word "grave" unless there was a serious risk of death, and my mind reeled at the prospect I could lose my friends. I'd been feeling guilty about Justine's abduction and my role in placing her in harm's way, but if I lost Mo-bot and Sci because of their association with me, I didn't know how I'd cope. For now, I channeled the guilt, fear and frustration into a bottomless pit of anger at the men who'd done this to us, and most of all Roman Verde whom I was eager to confront.

Our journey through the city, full of anxiety, anger and dismay, was at odds with Monaco's mood, which was one of delirious excitement. As we headed toward whatever nightmare awaited us, parties were gathering momentum all around.

Chevalier was waiting for us in the hospital and I was glad because it was an obvious place for Roman Verde to target, knowing we'd be very likely to visit our colleagues. I had to assume his people were behind the shooting and that he knew from the news reports that Sci and Mo-bot had survived. As Monaco's only public hospital, the Princess Grace would be a safe bet for their admission.

"I'm so sorry," the inspector said as we rushed through the main doors. "This way."

She led us across the lobby, where three uniformed officers were posted.

"You think there's an ongoing threat?" Justine asked.

"Possibly," Chevalier replied. "To you as well as them. The police presence will discourage opportunist attacks."

She took us to one of the private wards on the fifth floor. There was another cop by the elevator, and a fifth standing guard on the ward itself.

Chevalier nodded a greeting as we approached, and the officer stood to attention.

"Mr. Kloppenberg is in there," she said, gesturing to a room on our right. "He's had emergency surgery."

Justine gasped and I felt hollow deep inside, my legs barely supporting me.

I peered through the observation window and saw Sci, unconscious, connected to a plethora of monitors and IV drips. He looked in a bad way.

"Oh, Sci," Justine said, taking my hand. In that moment, it took every ounce of self-control to prevent myself from breaking down.

These were our friends.

"Miss Roth is in here," Valerie said, signaling to the room directly opposite.

Justine and I moved across the corridor. When we looked through the observation window, I was surprised and relieved to see Mo-bot was conscious. She had her head turned toward the exterior window, which gave her a view of the city and the starry night sky. She must have sensed movement because she turned to us, smiled faintly, and beckoned us in.

"The doctors say she cannot be disturbed for long," Chevalier informed us. "That's why I haven't taken her statement yet."

"We'll be quick," I assured her, and she followed us inside.

I'd never seen Mo-bot look so frail and vulnerable. Her skin was paper white and her movements were shaky.

"Excuse the mess," she said, gesturing at the various machines and drips surrounding her.

"Mo," Justine responded, moving swiftly to her side. She took our friend's hand, the one without the canula. "I'm so sorry."

"I'll be alright, kiddo," Mo-bot said.

Her voice was thin and small. I could already feel her creeping fatigue.

"What happened?" I asked, leaning in.

"We went to follow up a lead," Mo-bot said. "It turned out to be nothing, but some of Roman Verde's men spotted us in the street and they shot us."

I got the sense she wasn't telling the whole truth and she didn't mention Kendrick Stamp at all. I guessed there were things she didn't trust Valerie with. Mo-bot's attention drifted for a moment, and I couldn't tell whether it was from exhaustion or getting lost in the memory of trauma.

"Is Sci okay?" she asked at last.

"You don't need to worry about him," I told her. "He's in good hands. Just focus on yourself."

She smiled. "Okay, Dad."

"What was the lead?" Chevalier asked.

"Oh, it was a ridiculous hunch I had about some of Roman's men using the hotel as a meeting place," Mo-bot replied, and I knew for sure she was trying to keep something from the inspector.

"Maybe not so ridiculous," Chevalier remarked. "What made you think they might be there?"

"I'm tired, Jack," Mo-bot replied. "So tired."

"We should leave," I said.

The inspector hesitated and then nodded reluctantly.

"Feel better," Justine told Mo-bot before steering Valerie toward the door.

"I will send a Photofit artist when you are well enough," Valerie told Mo-bot.

She and Justine left the room.

"Mo, I want you to—" I began, but she cut me off, suddenly more alert.

"If you tell me to focus on myself," she interrupted, "or to concentrate on getting better, I'll kick your butt into the next room."

There was fire in her eyes.

"My body will do what it needs to do to heal. I want you to get the men who did this to us," Mo-bot said. "I guess we're still not fully trusting the cops after the obvious corruption and security breaches?"

I nodded.

"That's why I didn't mention Kendrick Stamp. He's at the Metropole. Room four-oh-eight. I think he's the second assassin Roman talked about. In fact, I'm pretty certain of it. He told me he was being watched before we were attacked. His number and yours were the only ones on a SIM Philippe Duval had hidden in his safe. Stamp is married and got really cagey when we asked about his wife. I think Roman and his men have her."

I took her hand and squeezed it gently.

"You did good work," I said.

"Don't praise me, Jack. That's not what I need," she replied, her eyes filling in a rare display of vulnerability. "Find the men who did this. Find them and make sure they answer for what they've done. Promise me."

I nodded. "I promise."

CHAPTER 71

I SAW CHEVALIER and Justine watching us through the observation window, and their eyes stayed on me as I left Mo-bot's room.

"What did she say?" the inspector asked, after I'd shut the door.

"She wanted me to pass on some messages to her team," I replied. "And family."

Chevalier frowned.

"Do you know why they went to the Metropole?" she asked.

I shook my head. I was going to leave it at that, but I was angry at what had happened to my friends and the way we'd been treated since arriving in the city. I stepped closer to Chevalier.

"We found evidence Philippe Duval was working with the men who shot Mo and Sci," I said. "My government is looking at it right now."

I caught Justine's startled expression, and the side-eye from the uniformed cop posted guard.

"What . . . Philippe?" Chevalier exclaimed in what seemed like genuine disbelief. "What evidence have you?"

"We can't share it with you just yet," I told her. "If your Interior Minister was compromised—"

"Former Interior Minister," she said.

"This was going on while he was in government," I revealed.

Her mouth opened and closed a few times before she finally said, "So, you don't think you can trust us."

"No," I replied. "Nor the French police. Two cops helped the Automobile Club suspect escape arrest. Justine has the footage."

Chevalier looked at Justine who nodded.

"Can you send it to me?" she asked.

I nodded, and Justine said, "Yes. I'll message you a download link."

"If what you say is true, then these people have infiltrated institutions we should be able to trust," the inspector remarked.

"Exactly," I agreed. "If an Interior Minister can be compromised and officers induced to break the law, then you'll understand why we're wary of the authorities."

"My people are—" she began, but I interrupted her.

"Honest? Trustworthy? Can you really vouch for everyone who works for you?" I asked. "We'll share the evidence when we know it's safe. In the meantime, you need to reassess the people you trust."

Valerie Chevalier looked punch drunk but there was nothing

more to say. Justine and I left her dealing with the implications of our revelations while we walked to the elevator.

Minutes later, we were outside the hospital amid the sights, sounds and smells of a city heading for new heights of revelry.

"What now?" Justine asked, when we were well clear of the building.

"We go to the Hotel Metropole. Mo-bot thinks Kendrick Stamp is the second assassin. Former Marine scout sniper and FBI special agent," I said. "So, he has the skills."

"What if Roman's people are still there?" Justine asked.

"I hope we run into them," I replied grimly.

Twenty minutes later, after navigating the crowded streets, we stepped into the grand lobby of the Metropole, which showed no signs of any shooting. The large atrium was packed with new arrivals waiting to check in. Others had spilled out of the bar and were holding drinks, talking and laughing animatedly.

We went directly to the elevators and took one to the fourth floor. We found room 408 and I knocked on the door. I could hear the TV playing inside, but there was no other sound. After a couple beats, I knocked again.

Justine wandered idly along the corridor until something stopped her in her tracks.

"Jack, come and look at this." She beckoned me over, and as I approached, I realized she was pointing at a bullet hole in the plush wallpaper on the far side of the stairwell door. "Do you think the cops even know about it?"

I shook my head. There would be a slug in that wall, but knowing what I knew about the Dark Fates and Propaganda

Tre, I was almost certain it wouldn't lead to a traceable gun. Still, the police should at least analyze all the available evidence and try to piece together a trail.

"Tell Chevalier about it when you send the footage you took in La Turbie," I said, and Justine nodded.

I returned to room 408 and knocked for a third time. After another couple beats, I glanced along the corridor and, seeing it was clear, barged the door open with my shoulder.

There was a loud crack as it split from the frame, and another bang as it swung wide and slammed against the stopper.

Justine and I hurried into the room to find the TV on, but the room empty. The closets were devoid of clothes and there was no sign of habitation anywhere.

A twenty-euro bill on the pillow spoke to a decent character, but also suggested Kendrick Stamp had checked out.

I picked up the housephone and made a call.

"Reception," a man said.

"This is Marc from housekeeping," I replied. "I just want to confirm Mr. Stamp from room four-oh-eight checked out early."

There was a brief pause.

"Yes. He settled his bill a couple of hours ago. It's marked on the turndown rota."

"I see it now. Thank you." I hung up and turned to Justine. "He's skipped. They must have moved him after the shooting."

CHAPTER 72

I WAS SEETHING by the time we returned to the apartment, and I suspected Justine shared my mood, because she said nothing on the journey back. Our friends were lying somewhere between life and death while the men who'd put them there roamed free, able to inflict further evil on the world.

The apartment seemed lifeless without Mo-bot and Sci. Everywhere I looked I saw reminders of them. Sci's spare boots, Mo-bot's reading glasses. I felt angry at the men who'd hurt them, but also furious at myself for having failed to protect them.

"You want something to eat?" Justine asked.

I shook my head. "I'm not hungry."

I sat down at Mo-bot's workstation and used the emergency password she'd given me in case anything ever happened to her. The screens came to life and I saw she'd received a message from Weaver. He'd provided a full breakdown of who was behind the

Chalmont Casino, and his network analysis concluded the business wasn't entirely legitimate.

I printed off two copies of the analysis and handed one to Justine. She sat next to me as we went through the document. We also reviewed the information Mo-bot and Sci had pulled on Kendrick Stamp.

We spent hours poring over everything, occasionally rising to make each other coffee and grab chips and snacks as the rage-fueled adrenalin wore off and was replaced by hunger.

"Listen to this," Justine said, as I returned with a fresh cup of steaming java. "Kendrick Stamp received a Bureau commendation for international cooperation. Intelligence he provided was used by French police to bust a drugs gang. The bust resulted in multiple arrests."

"Where was this?" I asked. "You don't think it was the Marseilles bust involving Roman?"

I sat down at Mo-bot's machine and messaged Weaver to ask if he could provide details of the investigation that had led to Kendrick's commendation.

"That would give the Dark Fates a personal grudge against him," Justine remarked. "Like they have against us."

I nodded and continued reviewing the Chalmont network analysis while I waited for a reply from Weaver. As I looked at the document, I realized I'd missed something that had been staring me in the face since the intelligence analyst had emailed across the information.

"There's a small shareholder in Chalmont called Entreprises du Soleil," I said, showing Justine the corporate records.

"So?" she asked.

"Look at the address for Entreprises du Soleil," I suggested.

I used Mo-bot's computer to search the address and it displayed a mountainside in southern France.

The Utelle Valley.

The pin dropped on the high farmhouse, the one where Justine had been held hostage.

She looked at me in disbelief.

"So, we've got proof Raymond Chalmont is tied to these people."

An alert sounded, notifying us of a new message from Weaver.

"Easy question," he wrote. "Kendrick Stamp was on a joint DEA–FBI taskforce that picked up intelligence of a major heroin deal going down in Marseilles. He advised the Marseilles Police who arrested a gangland kingpin called Baba Saidi. Stamp received a commendation for his work. It was his last big investigation before he was signed off sick."

"We know the Dark Fates have connections in the French police," I said to Justine. "Which means Roman could probably have identified the source of the intelligence that led to his arrest and the disruption of the deal, giving him a personal motive for revenge."

"Putting Stamp in the firing line," Justine remarked.

I nodded. "You got the energy for a drive?" I asked. "I want to check something out."

CHAPTER 73

WE DIDN'T SPEAK as I followed the road up the Utelle Valley. The Ford Kuga's engine strained against the steep inclines and its tires churned up gravel from the surface. The clatter of loose stones against the chassis and the growl of the engine were the only sounds as we climbed higher up the mountainside.

The headlamps sliced a wedge of light into the nothingness of night. I stuck to the center of the road, avoiding the sheer drops and hairpin turns, the deep ravines spanned by narrow bridges.

I remembered how close we'd come to death on this mountain, and how narrowly we'd escaped the bullets sent our way by the men who'd made Sci and Mo-bot targets. Seeing them in hospital had shaken me and reminded me just how vulnerable we all were. Skill and luck had been my allies then, but what would happen if they deserted me?

"What if there's someone there now?" Justine asked, bringing me out of my maudlin self-reflection.

"Then we'll turn back," I replied.

Chevalier had told us the place was deserted by the time the police had arrived.

"I won't let anything happen to us," I assured Justine.

She smiled at me. "I don't need you to protect me, Jack. You know that. I just wanted us to have a plan."

"I . . ." I hesitated. I wasn't sure what she was getting at.

"You don't have to carry the responsibility for saving me," she explained. "I'm my own person. I can assess risk for myself and if I make a mistake, it's on me to fix it."

"Is this a rage against the patriarchy?" I asked. "Because I'm not your white knight. I don't view it as me saving you. I see it as us saving each other. We look out for each other because we both care. Equality."

She looked a little contrite. "I guess. I just wanted to be clear, I don't want you carrying me as well as everything and everyone else."

"If you're carrying me and I'm carrying you, no one's carrying a burden," I said.

"Confucius?"

"Jack Morgan," I replied with a smile.

I got what she was saying, but there was no way I was going to stop protecting her. It was ingrained in me to look after others, but I wasn't going to press the issue. She looked after me too, so did Sci, and Mo-bot. I'd lost count of the number of times my life had been saved by others. It wasn't an admission of weakness; it was a recognition of the hazards we faced in our line of work.

We were almost at the farm, so I pulled over at the next turnout and killed the engine.

"We go on foot from here."

I'd changed into jeans, a T-shirt and a lightweight racer jacket, which I fastened against the cool wind blowing up the valley. Justine was in black trousers and a matching rollneck. We set out through the trees toward the farmhouse.

I stayed alert for any signs of patrols or sentries, but there was nothing except the unpredictable sounds of nature. An owl, something scurrying in the undergrowth, branches creaking, leaves rustling.

We moved quickly toward the cobblestone courtyard, and I saw Justine eye the building where she'd been held hostage. The door was open, but neither of us moved toward it. Instead, we headed for the main house, its roof partially burned by the incendiary drones Sci had rigged and dropped during Justine's escape. There were no signs of life, no vehicles in the yard and no lights or indications of activity in the building. The front door stood open.

I went first, using a small torch to light our way. It pushed back the shadows to reveal a largely empty property.

There was no art or decoration of any kind. Just plain painted walls and functional furniture. The main living room was full of bunks, which were all unmade, and a couple mattresses had been tossed on the floor.

The kitchen contained a large farmhouse table surrounded

by more than a dozen chairs, and I pictured Justine's abductors in here together, eating, laughing and joking, or perhaps grimly plotting murder, while she was trapped in the small store outside. What pushed men like them to normalize such evil?

We continued through the house, moving upstairs to find more bunks and finally the master bedroom with one king-size bed. I guessed this was where Roman Verde slept, a perk of leadership.

The bed was unmade and the closets were bare, but when we checked the bathroom, we found evidence of a fire that was nothing to do with the burned roof because the ceiling above was still intact.

A small metal trash can stood in the center of the room, its sides blackened. I looked in the can and found the charred remains of papers. Most had burned to ash but a few might be recoverable.

Carefully, I gathered as many fragments as I could, and held them gently in a stack.

"I think this is it," I said. "The cops must have taken everything else for analysis, or there wasn't anything here when they were looking. I don't think we're going to find anything else."

Justine nodded.

"We should go."

"Happy to," I replied.

She'd masked it well, but I could tell the return to the place where she'd been held prisoner had been hard on her.

"You're safe," I assured her, as we left the room.

"I know," she said, but I didn't feel the tension leave her until we were in the car, heading down the mountain.

CHAPTER 74

BY THE TIME we returned to the apartment, Monaco was finally asleep. The streets were empty and devoid of crowds. I got a more complete sense of just how much the race altered the city. The diversions, signs, barriers, specially constructed walkways, elevated tunnels, hoardings, stands and temporary buildings stood out as transient additions to the small Mediterranean principality.

Justine took care of the charred documents while I drove us back. When we entered the apartment, we laid them out on the table. I went to Sci's gear bag and took out one of his traveling crime-scene kits. I found a processing pan and prepared a solution of two parts water, five parts alcohol and three parts glycerin, which I added to the pan. The chemical cocktail was designed to strip away the charring to reveal anything written or printed on the burned paper we'd recovered. The process involved the destruction of the documents, but in the absence of a full lab, it was the best way to retrieve whatever information Roman or his associates might have been trying to destroy.

Justine and I worked methodically, placing each fragment of paper in the solution. We watched them absorb the liquid, sink and then disintegrate, and after each iteration, I would drain the pan, clean it and prepare a new bath for the next document. The first five pieces of paper gave us nothing. They were either blank or contained generic words or numbers that had no special significance, but the sixth and final piece gave up something useful.

First came a logo, Port Hercules Fuel Depot, followed by details of a transaction: 500 liters of marine diesel, invoiced to a boat that had been fueled the previous week. I used my phone to take a photograph of the information.

"They have a boat," Justine remarked.

"Kendrick Stamp was a scout sniper," I replied. "They gave me an undetectable pistol for a close kill. It makes sense to have a long-range shooter as backup. Different method in case I was compromised."

"You think he'd be able to take a shot from a boat?" Justine asked.

"Why not? Why else would they need one? And why try to destroy this invoice if it wasn't important?"

I watched the fragment of paper sink to the bottom of the pan and begin to disintegrate.

"What now?"

I shrugged. "I don't know. Do we trust the cops with this? Or if we tell them, do we run the risk of the information leaking, forcing the assassin to switch to a different method?"

"It would be easier if we knew the target," Justine remarked.

"Until we know otherwise, I'm going to assume it's Eli Carver," I told her, aware I had nothing but the fact I was close to the man and Duval's sharing of intel to support my hunch. "If we can get to the fuel depot, we can use the invoice number to identify the vessel."

I searched my phone for the details of the filling station at Port Hercules, and discovered it opened at 7 a.m.

"I'm going to make sure I'm there first thing," I said.

"We should get some rest in the meantime," Justine suggested. "You look beat."

I shook my head. "I'm fine. I'm going to stay up a while and review everything. I can't help feeling there's something we missed."

Justine pulled up a chair next to me.

"Don't," I said.

"Hey. What's good for the gander is good for the goose," she said with a smile. "Mo and Sci are family to me too and I want to do whatever I can to catch the men responsible."

I took her hand and squeezed it. We kissed tenderly before getting back to work.

CHAPTER 75

I WOKE WITH a start, suddenly aware of noise rising from the street. In the distance I could hear powerful engines roaring like wild animals. I was lying with my head on the dining table and must have fallen asleep where I'd been working. I sat up and checked my watch, dismayed at my failure to stay awake.

It was 8:30 a.m. The fuel depot had been open for ninety minutes.

I looked around and saw Justine asleep on one of the couches.

"Jus," I said, moving toward her.

She stirred as I leaned down to kiss her.

"Justine, come on," I said. "We fell asleep."

"Oh my God," she exclaimed with a start. "Oh, no. What time is it?"

"Eight-thirty," I replied. "We need to get moving. It sounds like they're warming up for qualifying."

Nothing can prepare a person for the sound of a Formula One car, and the noise of the state-of-the-art machines dominated the city.

Justine nodded and stretched as she stood up.

"I'm sorry," she said. "I just had to sleep."

"Turns out I did too."

"You find anything?" she asked, gesturing to the mass of paper spread across the table.

"I don't even know," I replied. "It all became a blur."

I returned to the table and looked at the evidence we'd amassed from our investigation into Duval. I picked up the messages we'd pulled off the four phones we'd found in his safe. One device had contained a peculiar set of messages sent by him over the course of a year: a series of numeric codes. I don't know whether it was the benefit of sleep, or a little distance from the intense focus I'd applied to them, but I finally saw a pattern in them. The first eleven numbers were repeated in each message.

"What is it?" Justine asked, joining me.

"These texts," I replied. "I think I can crack the code."

I grabbed a blank piece of paper and wrote out the first eleven numbers.

21716131316

I assumed it was an alphanumeric and that the larger numbers referred to letters further into the alphabet. Through a process of trial and error, I broke the sequence into:

2-17-16-13-13-16

and then tried to fit letters to each one. After a few minutes I realized it was a simple plus one code that read:

APOLLO

"What's Eli Carver's Secret Service code name?" I asked, and Justine grabbed her phone to search the internet.

"According to a *Rolling Stone* profile, Secretary Carver has mixed feelings about his code name," Justine read from the article, "'because he isn't quite as fleet of foot as the Greek god Apollo.'"

"I bet this is information Duval was supplying on him," I said. "Can you send these messages to Weaver, while I call Carver?"

Justine nodded and sat at Mo-bot's workstation.

I dialed the Secretary's personal line.

"Yes?" a woman said.

"Secretary Carver, please."

"One moment."

The line went silent, then I heard heavy breathing and the sound of sheets rustling.

"Mr. Morgan, this is Henry Wilson. How can I help you?"

"I need to speak to the Secretary."

"Secretary Carver has given strict DND orders," he replied.

"DND?"

"Do not disturb. He'll surface just before qualifying, I imagine. You're very welcome to join us."

"I have reason to believe the Secretary is a target. We discovered—"

He cut me off. "Mr. Morgan, we've discussed this."

"We found text messages on a conspirator's phone that mention the name Apollo. I haven't been able to decipher the rest of the coded messages, but that's the Secretary's code name, isn't it?"

There was a moment's hesitation.

"Mr. Morgan, do you have any idea how many threats the Secret Service addresses every single day? Do you know how sophisticated our threat matrix is?"

"I don't give a damn," I replied, allowing my frustration to get the better of me. I wished I'd controlled my emotions more effectively because I must have sounded a little unhinged. "I'm telling you, this is a real and present threat."

"Thank you for your concern, Mr. Morgan. I'll inform the head of the Secretary's detail. I do hope we'll see you later."

And with that he hung up on me.

"That son of a . . ." I said.

"I've sent the messages to Weaver," Justine responded. "But he probably won't see them for hours. It's the middle of the night on the East Coast. What do we do now?"

"We're going to have to split up," I replied. "I want you to find Carver. Make him listen to you. He'll be at the grandstand overlooking the Louis Chiron. It's one of the most famous features of the course."

"What are you going to do?"

"I'm going to the port to find the boat Roman is using," I said. "If you can't get Carver and his people to listen, we're going to need to stop this ourselves."

CHAPTER 76

JUSTINE WALKED WITH Jack as far as the corner of Avenue du Port and Boulevard Albert 1er. The city was packed with race fans being channeled along the temporary walkways and tunnel bridges. The noise of the crowd and race cars being prepped and tuned was deafening. The atmosphere before qualifying already rivaled the excitement of any event Justine had experienced, so she struggled to picture what the energy of the city would be like for the race the next day. But she couldn't get caught up in the anticipation and enthusiasm: she had other things on her mind.

"Be careful," Jack said before giving her a kiss.

"You too," she replied.

He headed south, climbing steps to a tunnel bridge that would take him to the grand port and marina, full to bursting with luxury yachts.

Justine went east toward the race command center and the

Louis Chiron, the infamous chicane located nearby, directly opposite the port. The first roaring Formula One car racing along the city streets told Justine qualifying was underway. In between the sound of gear changes came the cheers of crowds in the grandstands and gathered around the city.

She headed for the Monte Carlo Casino stand, which was located opposite the Louis Chiron. Carver had told Jack that's where he'd be, and as Justine worked her way through the crowded walkways and neared the location, she could see why the Defense Secretary had chosen this stand to watch the race from. It was in a magnificent setting on a tight bend that forced the powerful cars to slow in front of the spectators, before rocketing onto the next straight. The stand was set tight against the bend, so the people in the front row might believe they could reach out and touch the cars, putting them in the action, rather than consigning them to merely spectating.

Justine surveyed the stand at a distance, but couldn't make out Carver, so she approached an entry gate and joined a small group of people looking to get into this section of the race. She was soon at the front, facing an admissions marshal.

"Pass?" he said.

"I don't have one," Justine replied. "I just need to talk to someone in the Casino stand."

"You can't enter without a pass," the marshal said.

Justine suddenly remembered Carver had invited them to be his guests.

"I have a pass, but it's with my friend," she responded. "He invited me."

"If your friend has arranged a pass," the marshal said, "it will be available for collection at a ticket kiosk."

He gestured toward a row of white huts on the other side of the pedestrian walkway.

"Simply present your passport or identification card."

"Thank you," she said, before joining a line for one of the booths.

Ten minutes later, after making it to the front of the line and presenting her passport, she was given her pass. She went back to the gate and this time was allowed in.

As she crossed a footbridge to take her to the grandstand, Justine's senses were assailed by the roar of a race car passing beneath her, the smell of high-grade fuel, and the cries of the crowd.

She hurried on, eager to reach Carver before it was too late.

CHAPTER 77

I FELT UNCOMFORTABLE leaving Justine, but our team was short of people and I wanted to make sure Eli Carver was fully informed of the threat.

The route to the marina was crowded and took in more loops and turns than would have been normal so as to avoid the race-track, the temporary media center, and stands around the edge of the port. I could hear a car tearing around the track, engine screeching at the upper end of the revs, the vibration so forceful I felt it touch my bones. It was something no television or home speaker could convey, the sheer body-trembling power of the vehicle was awesome, and sufficiently loud to drown out the cheering of the crowds it passed.

I pressed my way through the crush of slow-moving pedes-trians and finally managed to turn off the main walkway serving the marina berths and toward the fuel depot. There wasn't a single empty mooring, and shoals of tenders skimmed across the water carrying people from vessels anchored in the bay to the shore, and vice versa. The yachts closest to the promenade were full of spectators on their highest decks, trying to get a good view of qualifying.

When I glanced over my shoulder, I could see the Monte Carlo Casino stand in the distance, but I wasn't able to pick out Eli Carver or Justine on any of the balconies.

I hurried along the main jetty toward the branching pontoon that was home to the fueling station. There were two attendants dressed in smart navy-blue overalls. One was filling the fuel tank of a Beneteau motor yacht while the other stood by a small office and watched.

"*Oui?*" the unoccupied man said to me.

"Do you speak English?" I asked, and the man nodded.

"I need to know about a boat that refueled here last week," I said. "Invoice number one-six-one-nine."

"Why?" he asked.

"I'm a detective," I replied. "They owe a client of mine some money."

The man frowned.

"I'm willing to pay for the information," I told him, producing my wallet.

"I'm a friend of justice," he replied with open arms.

"Invoice number one-six-one-nine," I repeated.

He sauntered into the office and picked up a ledger. He removed his sunglasses and flipped the pages until finally settling on one.

"Oh, yes," he said. "I can believe they owe money. They didn't give a gratuity."

I took five twenty-euro notes from my wallet and handed them to him.

"The yacht is called the *Sunset Prince*," he revealed. "It left port a few days ago. Probably moved along the coast."

I frowned. That was not what I expected.

"Are you certain?"

He nodded. "I saw it leave."

"Thank you," I said, before turning to go. I wondered what to do now.

"That's not true," his colleague said, looking up from the fuel tank he was filling. "They left, but they took a mooring in the bay. I saw them on my way in this morning."

He nodded toward a RIB with a single 150 horsepower Yamaha outboard engine.

"Where?" I asked.

"South-east, maybe half a kilometer offshore," he replied.

Well within sniper range for a good marksman.

He stopped filling the tank and stepped away from the motor-boat, leading me to the edge of the pontoon.

"Over there, you can just see the black-and-white navigation unit," he said, pointing into the distance.

As I peered through the forest of masts, I could make out the satellite array he was talking about. It belonged to a large motor yacht.

"How much to charter your RIB?" I asked, and the two fuel attendants exchanged a look that told me we were about to start negotiating.

CHAPTER 78

JUSTINE HURRIED ALONG the walkway toward the Monte Carlo Casino stand, but was stopped by a man in a dark gray suit. His large build, aviator sunglasses, buzzcut, Stars and Stripes pin and MARIE transceiver in his left ear all screamed Secret Service.

"Ma'am, this stand is off-limits," he yelled above the thunderous roar of an approaching race car. His Texan accent was another giveaway.

"I'm a guest of Secretary Carver," Justine said. She craned to peer around the man, but couldn't get a view of the stand, just the steps that led to the seating area.

"Name, please," he responded automatically, producing a tablet computer.

"Justine Smith."

He checked the device and frowned.

"I'm afraid your invitation to be in the Secretary's party has been rescinded, ma'am," he revealed. "I'm sorry. You'll need to make your way to another part of the course."

Justine stood in stunned disbelief for a moment.

"Ma'am, you'll need to move along."

She couldn't understand why Carver would retract her invitation.

"What about Jack Morgan? Is he still on the list?" she asked.

"Ma'am, I can't share any details about other people in the Secretary's party," he replied. "I have to ask you to move along, please."

Justine found herself eyeing the stand. She couldn't have been more than forty feet from the steps and thought about pushing past the huge guy and making a run for it, but there were two more agents by the grandstand, and she had no doubt the men were armed and would shoot her if they deemed her a threat.

"Could you check with Secretary Carver," she said. "I think there's been some mistake."

The thunder of the engines, clamor of the crowd and wild atmosphere made the conversation even more difficult and fraught.

"I can't do that, ma'am," the agent replied loudly. "The list doesn't make mistakes."

"I saw the Secretary yesterday," Justine said. "He reiterated his invitation. Why would he have done that?"

The Secret Service agent shrugged. "I can't answer for the Secretary, ma'am."

"Could you please, please, please check for me?" she asked again. "I really do think there's been a mistake."

He set his jaw and his tone turned darker. "You need to move along, ma'am."

Justine glanced around desperately and saw a familiar face coming along the walkway. Henry Wilson, Carver's aide, was talking on his phone. His jovial expression fell away momentarily when he saw Justine, but he recovered with a quick, false smile. She wondered why she was suddenly unwelcome. Was it because she and Jack had warned of danger? Were they regarded as obsessive alarmists?

"Ms. Smith," Henry said, a little too sweetly. "I'm surprised to see you here. I thought you had your hands full."

"I need to talk to the Secretary," she told him. "But this gentleman says my invitation has been rescinded."

"We reviewed the Secretary's security protocols on your recommendation and pared the guest list down to the absolute minimum," Henry replied.

"Does he know?" Justine said.

The aide didn't respond.

"Does he know? Or did you do this?"

Henry drew close. "Ms. Smith, please don't cause a scene. The Secretary doesn't need the scandal associated with your abduction and alarmist talk of conspiracy with the Dark Fates, Propaganda Tre and Roman Verde."

Justine stepped back and studied him.

"Who told you about Roman Verde?" she asked.

"The Secretary. It was in the intel you sent him," Henry replied, but he seemed flustered.

"His schedule had to have been leaked by someone close to him," Justine remarked.

"Oh, come now," he scoffed. "You don't seriously think . . . Please don't draw me into your web of insanity."

"Show me your arm," Justine said, and lunged for him. "Show it to me!"

He stepped back. "I don't know what's got into you, Ms. Smith, but this is precisely why you were removed from the list."

He turned to the Secret Service agent.

"Get her out of here. Eject her from the course and take her pass. Now."

The huge guy grabbed Justine, who screamed and fought against him as he marched her toward the exit. Her cries were lost beneath the cacophony of the race and hardly anyone noticed her being taken away.

CHAPTER 79

THE YAMAHA 150 outboard growled as I piloted the RIB through the port. The yacht berths were jam-packed port to starboard and bow to stern. The bay beyond was smooth as a boating lake.

The popularity of the race was advantageous to me because all the vessels gave me useful cover as I took a circuitous route to the *Sunset Prince*.

I steered the RIB on a wide, sweeping arc west, keeping as many boats as possible between me and the large motor yacht that was now my target. My aim was to approach the vessel from its port side because I figured if there was a shooter on board, all eyes would be on the race and the open-water side would be less likely to be watched.

I could hear the roar of engines in the distance, the rising and falling cheers of the crowds, and from the decks nearby came the excited shouts of people watching qualifying from their boats. I hoped Justine had reached Carver but couldn't count on him or his people to take the threat seriously.

I turned north toward the *Sunset Prince*, a blue-and-white Beneteau 46 powerboat with four decks. I couldn't see any obvious signs of a shooter, but I was coming at the vessel from the wrong side of the action.

When I was fifty feet away, I cut the RIB's outboard engine and ran silent, allowing momentum to carry me toward the stern of the *Sunset Prince*.

Despite being within the confines of the bay, the large yacht bobbed on the waves, which would make any shot a challenge, even for an accomplished marksman. If he was on the other side of this vessel, Kendrick Stamp must have been utterly desperate to agree to do this. Roman Verde must have some powerful hold over him, and given the man's MO in our case, Mo-bot was probably right to think they had Stamp's wife hostage.

Momentum and tide carried me into the swimming platform attached to the stern of the yacht. I jumped onto the wooden decking and secured the RIB's line to a cleat, before climbing a short ladder and boarding the vessel.

"Hey!" a man yelled as I climbed over the stanchions.

I turned to see a heavyset guy coming from below deck, up a gangway that led to the cabins.

I rushed him before he reached the top of the stairs and kicked his torso, sending him tumbling down into the galley below. He cracked his head against the wooden floor and his eyes rolled back before he passed out.

I hurried to the starboard side and peered around the bulkhead to see Kendrick Stamp on the high deck above the pilot's wheel. In front of him was a McMillan TAC-50 sniper rifle, a sophisticated long-range gun with telescopic sight. It was mounted on a platform with side panels that concealed it from casual observers, and the platform itself was constantly moving, powered by gyroscopic servos that compensated for the movement of the boat on the water. It was an expensive, state-of-the art gun and stabilizing system. With this equipment, I had no doubt a man like Stamp would be able to assassinate Eli Carver.

CHAPTER 80

JUSTINE STRUGGLED AGAINST the large Secret Service agent, but it was hopeless. He had hold of her left wrist and had twisted it behind her back into a position that inflicted immediate pain if she deviated even slightly from where he was directing her. Any further pressure and she feared her wrist might snap.

They were moving away from the grandstand toward the nearest exit across a raised walkway. The celebratory atmosphere, roaring cars and excited crowds meant no one paid them any attention.

Justine became increasingly desperate but fought a sense of panic, which she knew could only steer her down the wrong path. Even as she was led away from her objective, with no way back to warn Carver plus the nagging suspicion Henry Wilson was working for the enemy, she tried to find calm.

"What's your name?" she asked, raising her voice to be heard above the din.

Her captor remained silent.

Justine's mind whirred frantically, but she fought the tumult of fears and frustrations and reminded herself that the truth was the most powerful weapon. Good people recognized the truth when it was plainly spoken.

"You know my name is Justine Smith. I work for Private, the detective agency run by Jack Morgan."

She glanced over her shoulder and saw a glimmer of recognition in the man's eyes.

"You know that name. I bet everyone on the Secretary's detail knows that name because Jack saved your principal's life at Fallon Airbase in Nevada."

The agent's grip on her wrist loosened slightly.

"Jack is out there right now." Justine nodded toward the port. "He's looking for a shooter we believe is targeting the Secretary. And I think Henry Wilson is one of his co-conspirators."

The agent stopped moving and let go of Justine. She rubbed her arm as she turned to face him.

"Ma'am, do you have any idea how crazy this sounds?"

"I don't care how it sounds," she replied, having to yell to make herself heard over the noise of the race. "I care about Secretary Carver's life. You need to take me back so I can talk to him."

The agent's expression hardened.

"Or don't, but have his detail move him. Get him to a less exposed location and keep him away from Wilson."

Justine saw the conflict in the Secret Service agent. If she was an alarmist, he would face embarrassment and censure, but if what she was saying was true, the alternative would be catastrophic: the death of the man this agent was sworn to keep safe.

"This is a serious threat," she said. "Don't let the bad guys win."

"My name is Greg Campbell," he said at last. "And I think you'd better talk to the Secretary yourself."

CHAPTER 81

I STARTED UP the gangway toward Kendrick but was surprised by a man who thrust a pistol in my face. It was Michel, the man I'd chased from the Automobile Club. His face was twisted into a vicious snarl.

"Up," he said. "Slowly."

He stepped back and allowed me to climb the narrow steps that led to the pilot's deck. I moved at a deliberate, steady pace.

"Up," he said, gesturing at another short run of steps that would take me to Kendrick Stamp.

I did as Michel said. As I reached the upper deck, Stamp looked around. He seemed haunted and I could sense the conflict within him. He didn't want to be there, and his eyes blazed with hatred when Michel climbed the stairs to join us, his gun on me the whole time.

We had a clear line of sight to the Monte Carlo Casino

grandstand from up here, and I watched the crowd rise from their seats as a qualifying car sped round the Louis Chiron bend.

Michel approached me, brandishing his gun. "You've caused nothing but trouble."

"You don't have to do this, Kendrick," I said to Stamp. My attempted intervention earned me a smack from the gun, which made the world turn white with pain and set my ears ringing.

Once the pain had subsided, I stood tall and glared at Michel.

"Take the shot," he ordered Stamp. "Or your wife dies."

He produced a cell phone.

"One call from me and you'll never see her again," Michel said. "You want to live with the guilt of knowing you could have saved her?"

Kendrick looked at me and his eyes welled with tears. I could see the turmoil within him. Like me, this man had devoted his life to protecting and serving others. His record in the Marine Corps and FBI suggested someone with a strong sense of right and wrong. Being faced with this choice must have been tearing at his soul.

"Don't take the shot," I said. "We can find Angie and get her back."

Kendrick frowned at my use of his wife's name, and Michel hit me again. This time he opened up a nasty gash on my forehead and, as blood ran into my right eye, I felt the pull of unconsciousness. I fell to my knees and put out a hand to steady myself. The world swam and the pain was excruciating, but I rode the waves of agony until they settled.

Kendrick Stamp looked down at me. I saw nothing but

conflict in his eyes. This was a good man torn between doing what was right and what was necessary.

I locked eyes with him and shook my head slowly. Tears overflowed and wet his cheeks as he turned to face the shore. He wiped his face, before pressing his right eye to the scope.

"You can watch your friend, the Secretary of Defense, die," Michel said to me. "And then I'll send you to Hell to join him."

He pressed the muzzle of the pistol to my temple. He would kill me the moment Kendrick hit the target.

CHAPTER 82

SECRET SERVICE AGENT Greg Campbell made good on his word and led Justine back to the entrance to the stand.

"She's good," he said to the two agents posted by the stairs, and they nodded him and Justine through.

"Thank you for doing this," she said, as they started up the steps.

"You'd better be on the level," Greg replied.

"I am," Justine assured him.

They went up and over the rear of the stand, and when they reached the top of a run of steps on the other side, Justine got a proper view of the Louis Chiron chicane and the port beyond. It was a magnificent spot from which to watch the race, which was also broadcast on two big screens set a short distance away from either side of the stand.

"He's down at the front," Greg said. He took hold of Justine's arm, gently this time. "You'd better not be a nut."

"I'm not," she replied, and he released her and followed as she started down the steps.

She saw Eli Carver in the very first row, glancing around excitedly. The next car was approaching the bend and Justine felt the phenomenal vibration of its engine as it neared. There was a roar as the car changed gears, and a magnificent Formula One car entered the Louis Chiron chicane in front of the grandstand. For a moment, the rest of the world ceased to exist as the sound and presence of the supercar cast everything else into shadow and silence. Reality returned only when it growled by, shifting gears as it sped out of the turn.

Justine's eyes flicked from the fast-disappearing car to Eli Carver, but she caught someone else looking directly at her: Henry Wilson, sitting two seats away from his boss.

"What's she doing here?" he yelled. "Get her away from the Secretary."

The sound of the cheering crowd died away and Henry's voice seemed loud in the lull that followed.

"I said get her out of here!"

Carver turned and was initially puzzled to see Henry shouting at Justine. He looked from one to the other, bemused. "What's going on?"

"Mr. Secretary, this person is a threat to your—" Henry began, but Justine cut him off.

"Eli," she said, making a conscious decision to use familiarity to remind him of their friendship, "we have reason to believe there is an imminent threat on your life. Jack is—"

Justine didn't get the chance to complete her sentence.

There were two loud cracks as a pair of bullets struck the grandstand directly below where Carver was sitting. Justine only recognized them as gunshots because she was expecting violence, but most of the nearby spectators looked around in confusion, and people a few rows away from Carver didn't even register what had happened because of the general noise and commotion.

Carver's Secret Service detail knew exactly what had happened. The agent nearest the Defense Secretary leaped to protect him and yelled, "Shots fired! Shots fired!"

Another agent shouted, "We gotta get Apollo to the secondary location."

Justine felt Greg's hands on her arms. He steered her toward the guard that had suddenly formed around Carver. She felt herself being swept away, following the phalanx out of the stand through a side exit at the end of the front row.

Events had moved beyond her control, but at least Carver was safe for now. She hoped the same was true of Jack.

CHAPTER 83

"YOU MISSED," MICHEL said bitterly, and his face reddened with fury as he watched the commotion on the grandstand.

I couldn't make out the details, but I was pretty sure the press of bodies was Carver's close protection detail taking him to safety.

Kendrick Stamp unclipped the rifle from the gyroscopic platform and turned it on Michel.

"I missed that target," he agreed. "But I won't miss this one."

He pulled the trigger and shot Michel in the chest. The force of the high-caliber slug delivered at deafeningly close range drove Michel across the deck, and he collapsed against the other side, pawing weakly at the hole in his chest.

Stamp put the rifle down and helped me to my feet.

"Thank you," I said.

His eyes shimmered with tears. "I didn't do it for you. I did it for my wife."

"I appreciate it nonetheless," I told him.

"I missed on purpose. I couldn't do it. I couldn't shoot him. I swore an oath." He hesitated. "Help me find her. Please."

"Do you have any leads?"

He nodded. "They let me speak to her this morning. I was hooded, but she was there with me, in person, in a house or warehouse. It was definitely inside. I felt the breeze when they took me out afterwards."

"Any ideas on the locality?" I asked, wiping blood from my eye.

"After the shooting at the hotel, they came and took me. Put a hood on me and moved me somewhere about twenty minutes' drive away. They turned and doubled back so much, I can't tell you the direction of travel. I spoke to Angie inside and then they led me away and brought me here by boat. I was still hooded, but the boat was waiting right outside the location. There were steps down and sand, so wherever she is it has to be on the waterfront. Angie is somewhere over there."

I walked over to Michel, who was taking rapid shallow breaths. He groaned as I approached, and I ignored his pathetic attempts to fight me off as I reached into his pocket for the phone he'd threatened Stamp with earlier.

I stepped away and used it to call Justine. She answered almost immediately.

"Hello?"

"Jus, it's me."

"Jack, thank God! When Carver was shot at, I feared the worst."

"I'm okay," I assured her. "Where are you?"

"In some sort of equipment store with Secretary Carver and his people," she replied. "They're preparing to evacuate him."

"The threat here is over. I don't know if there are others, but Kendrick Stamp did the right thing and missed on purpose," I said, looking at Stamp, whose eyes shone with fear and uncertainty about his decision.

I knew exactly how he felt, having lost Justine to these men a few days earlier.

"I need you to ask Carver to run a trace on the last five numbers into and out of this phone. And I need it now. Angie Stamp is being held hostage somewhere in Monaco, and I've promised we'll find her, so I need the location of any device that's had contact with this phone."

"I'm on it," Justine said, before hanging up.

I turned to Stamp, who signaled to Michel. His eyes were glassy and his bloody chest was still. He was dead. I felt no pity for a person who'd been part of such evil.

"We need to be ready to move," I told Stamp as I crouched to pick up Michel's fallen pistol, a Dan Wesson DWX, which was an excellent close-range weapon.

Stamp grabbed the sniper rifle, and took an ammunition box from beneath the gyroscopic platform.

"I'm ready," he said.

"Good. Let's go," I replied, and we headed for the RIB.

CHAPTER 84

JUSTINE STOOD BESIDE Greg Campbell in a corrugated-steel equipment store built beneath the grandstand. She'd been bustled into the room by the big Secret Service agent who had followed his colleagues. They'd done a magnificent job of clustering to shield Carver and had got him to this secondary location in under a minute.

The atmosphere in the equipment store was tense. The ranking agent in charge coordinated with the extraction team via radio, urging them to make ready. Justine heard an announcement on the public address system in French and English, saying qualifying had stopped pending the resolution of certain technical issues. She wondered how many people who'd been sitting near Carver would know the true meaning of the phrase "technical issues" and whether news of the shooting would spread. Even if it did, members of the public who reported an unconfirmed assassination attempt on social media would likely be dismissed as conspiracy cranks. There would undoubtedly be race footage of Carver being hurried from the stand, but TV companies might not release it, and even if they did, the Secretary's media team could say the two events were unrelated. The public would only know about the assassination attempt if Carver or the US government wanted them to.

The sour note in the room was the presence of Henry Wilson, who stood in the opposite corner near the door. He didn't take his eyes off Justine and Greg, and prior to Jack's call, Justine had been wondering what to do about this man who probably wanted her dead.

She clasped her phone tightly and made for Carver, who seemed bewildered. He sat on a metal equipment chest and caught his breath. His detail bristled as she approached, and a couple of agents stepped toward her.

"Please stay back, ma'am," one of them said.

"She's okay," Greg told his colleagues, but his words didn't really register because Wilson yelled over him.

"Get this woman out of here! She poses a security risk."

"Henry?" Carver said.

"I think she's been working with the people behind all this," he replied. "The people who just tried to shoot you. She knew about the attack in advance. She caused a distraction when it happened."

"Me?" Justine said in disbelief. "Why would I warn you about an attack I was a part of?"

"That's something we'll have to find out," Wilson responded.

"*You're* the one who's behind this," Justine said. "You've been helping Roman Verde."

"I knew she'd do this," Wilson said with an exasperated sigh. "She's trying to make the people in this room distrust one another. Which is why she needs to be placed under arrest and taken away from here. She's the outsider. She doesn't belong. And she's dangerous. Get her out!"

Obviously tired of talking, he stepped forward and grabbed Justine's wrist, which was still sore from being manhandled by Greg. She wasn't about to allow herself to be assaulted by a man she suspected had betrayed his country and employer, and who had likely played a role in her own abduction and the attempted murder of her and her friends.

She slipped his grasp and slapped him hard.

He staggered back for a moment, but when his shock evaporated, he lunged for her, swinging his fists.

Justine ducked and dodged his wild punches, and Greg stepped in and responded to the attack with a right cross that caught the smaller man on the nose and knocked him on his backside.

"What the hell is happening?" Carver asked.

Henry Wilson wiped his bleeding nose gingerly and tried to stand, but Greg pushed him back down.

"Stay there," he said, before turning to Justine. "You wanted to look at his arm. Which one?"

"No!" Wilson protested. "You can't do this."

"Both," Justine replied.

He tried to resist as Greg came at him.

"Pete, can you get hold of this guy?" Greg asked, and one of his colleagues stepped forward, squatted and put Wilson into a chokehold.

"It'll be easier on you if you cooperate," Greg said. "But you don't have to be conscious for this."

Henry Wilson stopped struggling while Greg ripped open his shirt and pulled his jacket off to expose his bare upper arms.

There, tattooed on the inside of Henry's upper right arm, where the skin was at its softest and most sensitive, was the fleur-de-lys inside the Jerusalem Cross, the mark of Propaganda Tre.

CHAPTER 85

"IT'S JUST A tattoo," Wilson said.

"I know exactly what it is," Carver responded coldly.

His aide's indignation and anger melted away to be replaced by shame. He started shaking and seemed to shrink as he cowered on the floor of the store.

"Why, Henry?" Carver asked, gesturing at the tattoo. "What's going on?"

He didn't answer. Tears filled his eyes. He looked like a child caught out in a lie, and Justine's experience told her the shame he felt was for his exposure, not his wrongdoing. Criminals who repented rarely did so immediately, and this kind of reaction was grounded in self-pity and a sense of humiliation rather than genuine contrition.

"I can answer your questions, Mr. Secretary, but right now I need your help," she said. "Jack's trying to find someone, and he believes they were in communication with this number." She held out her phone and showed him details of the most recent call. "I need you to run a trace as fast as you can."

Carver nodded. "Do it," he said to the man called Pete, who'd had his arms around Wilson's neck.

Pete approached Justine and took a photograph of the number displayed on her phone screen.

"Thanks," she said. He remained impassive.

With the air of someone who rarely smiled, he stepped into the far corner of the room and typed a message into his phone.

Justine turned to Carver. "Jack suspected they were going to use him to target you because he could get close. They gave him a 3-D printed resin gun and bullets to circumvent security. The other shooter was meant to be a backup, but he became their primary after I escaped, didn't he?"

Her question was directed at Wilson, who didn't respond.

"But this was a contingent trip. It would only take place if the summit ended early. And it wasn't known outside your immediate circle, which is why we suspected someone was working against you, feeding information to Philip Duval, who was sending it on to Propaganda Tre. I never expected that person to be a member of the group too."

Carver looked as though he'd been punched. "Is this true, Henry?"

He couldn't even bring himself to look at the man he'd betrayed.

"I bet an investigation will find he has a secret phone he used to send coded messages giving information on your movements to another phone in Duval's possession."

Wilson's expression of shame seemed to intensify.

"Your friend and colleague set you up, Mr. Secretary," Justine said, noting Carver's pained expression. "The only thing I don't know is why."

"They didn't tell me," Wilson responded, finally breaking his silence. His eagerness to talk suggested to Justine he was lying. "I'm low down in the organization."

Carver's face hardened. It was one thing to hear Justine's explanation and speculation, quite another to hear a confession. The Secret Service detail closed around the disgraced aide and Justine could feel their anger. She guessed they weren't just enraged by the betrayal of their principal, but also by the fact the aide had put them in the line of fire.

"I don't think he's telling the truth," Justine said. "I think he's lying and that he knows why you were targeted, Eli."

Wilson scowled at her.

"I want him taken into custody," Carver said. "I want him on the next plane home, and I want him to be given special VIP treatment. And when he's told us everything he knows, I want him to stand trial."

Carver pushed his way through the gathered Secret Service agents and stood over Wilson.

"I'm going to make you regret you were ever born."

Pete looked up from his phone. "We have a hit, sir. The number Ms. Smith gave us was used to call a phone in Monaco. I'll have a location in a few seconds."

CHAPTER 86

WE WAITED IMPATIENTLY. I sat at the stern with the outboard motor idling, while Stamp was in the bow of the RIB, holding the line loosely looped around a cleat to keep it connected to the *Sunset Prince*.

I could feel the determination radiating off him, as though sheer force of will would bring him the location of his wife. I sympathized. That had been me a few days ago, when I'd been frantic and would have done anything to get Justine back. I doubted I could have sat as patiently as Stamp was doing now and could only admire the man's external stoicism in the face of what I knew was inner turmoil.

I regretted Michel's death and that of the other guy I'd kicked down the stairs into the galley. It turned out he wasn't unconscious; the fall had broken his neck, killing him instantly. This meant there was no chance of extracting Angie's location from either man, and instead of facing justice for their crimes, both had experienced quick and relatively painless deaths, which felt too much like an escape.

My phone rang and I saw Justine's number on screen.

"Jack, it's me. We've got a location. It's a villa on the coast in the Cap d'Ail and it belongs to Raymond Chalmont."

We must have disrupted their plans quite considerably for them to be using an address so clearly connected to one of their principals. Or perhaps it was simply arrogance on their part. Maybe Chalmont believed himself above the law in Monaco?

"I'm sending you a map pin," Justine said. "It will give you the exact location. Do you want me to notify the police?"

"Yes. Call Chevalier and ask her to bring a tactical unit and meet us there."

"Jack . . ." Justine began.

"I know," I said. "Be careful."

"No," she responded. "I was going to ask you to make sure these guys don't escape. I want them to get what they deserve. For me. For Sci. For Mo."

"You have my word," I told her.

"We're about to move to a more secure location," she said. "I've got to go. I love you."

"Love you too," I replied, before hanging up.

I checked my phone and saw Justine had sent me a map pin for a location a couple miles south-west of our current position.

"We've got it," I said to Stamp. "Let's go."

He pulled in the line and I backed us away from the yacht.

When we were clear, I twisted the throttle and the RIB

gathered speed. The bow rose and the boat bounced against the waves as we raced through wind and spray, engine humming, speeding toward the cruel, twisted men who held Angie Stamp.

CHAPTER 87

THE BOAT WAS fast. We crossed the bay in minutes and made it round the headland to the south-west, leaving the cacophony and turmoil of the race behind us. The waters beyond the headland were quiet, and high above us on the rock bluffs that rose from the sea stood magnificent villas and apartment buildings. A few had pontoons with little sailing dinghies and motorboats bobbing alongside them on the warm, crystal-clear water. It was a paradise on earth and I wondered why a man who had so much would gamble it all. Why would an establishment figure like Raymond Chalmont associate with men like Roman Verde and give his house over to them? Greed? Fear? Or belief? Based on what we knew of Propaganda Tre, I guessed belief, the organization's emphasis on far-right ideology and supposedly traditional values that were just a thin veneer for hate. But I wouldn't know for certain until I investigated the man.

Roman Verde was easier to understand. A hardened criminal once motivated by greed, now driven by revenge and whatever corrupting agenda Propaganda Tre had twisted him and his men to believe. I hadn't thought much about my own beliefs since leaving Rome, and in truth had been afraid to probe them. I'd met good and bad in the Vatican and had left the city resolved to continue with my own way of making the world a better place. It might not involve the dogma and observances of the Church, but I was on the frontline, waging a battle against evil every single day.

I was doing it now, facing down these men, taking Stamp to find and save his wife. He had stayed at the bow, spotting, while I piloted us toward the marker Justine had sent. The spray and fresh air felt good against my face. In any other circumstances, this would have been a beautiful trip, but instead it was darkened by the fact we were trying to outrun death and reach Angie before Roman executed her for Stamp's failure to complete his mission.

I checked my phone. We were close now. The run of pontoons ended and the hilltops turned wild for a while as we traveled westward. There were no obvious signs of habitation.

"Ahead," Stamp said, pointing to a lone pontoon that extended into the water like a solitary finger. "Slow down."

I did as he suggested and could see why. There were two men patrolling the pontoon, tiny figures in black combat trousers and T-shirts, each holding a sub machine gun.

With the engine cut, the RIB soon drifted to a complete stop. Stamp knelt and positioned the rifle against his shoulder. It would be a challenging shot.

"Wind is coming from the west. About fifteen knots," I told him.

He nodded his thanks and calibrated his sight. There was no gyroscope here, so he would have to compensate for the waves by moving his body and timing his shots perfectly.

The men seemed to be looking our way, but at this distance they couldn't possibly know who we were, and without field glasses or telescopic sights they wouldn't be able to see the rifle and scope. To them we were probably a couple of fishermen poaching their waters.

I willed Stamp to take the shot nonetheless, because there was a risk one of them would catch reflected glare off the scope or be sufficiently eagle-eyed to register his sniper stance.

He held his breath and squeezed the trigger.

The man to the right, closest to the beach, bucked, his head snapping back suddenly. He fell to the ground. His comrade to the left, further out to sea, registered the shot, looked at his dead companion and started running.

Stamp tracked him as he ran along the pontoon toward the shore and fired three shots in quick succession. The third struck him in his right leg and sent him tumbling into the water. As he thrashed, trying to make it to the short, sandy beach, Stamp shot him again, striking him in the back of the neck and killing him instantly.

"Good shooting," I said without emotion.

Stamp grunted, and I turned the throttle and steered us toward the pontoon.

My stomach tightened as I felt a rush of adrenalin flood my

body. I'd learned fear was an ally. It was not to be suppressed or fought; it was to be channeled. The most effective warriors used it to heighten their senses; they let it flow around them like electricity, giving them power, an edge over their enemies. Outwardly calm, they mastered their fear to their advantage, and I did so now.

When we reached the pontoon, Stamp jumped out and tied the line to a cleat. He left his rifle in the RIB and grabbed the sub machine gun and spare ammunition from the first man he'd shot.

I was content with Michel's pistol.

"Ready?" I asked.

Stamp nodded and we ran toward the beach.

CHAPTER 88

OUR FOOTSTEPS HAMMERED a rapid beat across the wooden planks and fell silent when we reached the soft sand. The beach was set in a small cove, with high cliffs enclosing the golden crescent on three sides. We hurried north toward a set of roughly hewn stone steps that curved round the cliffside and led up to the summit.

We moved in single file, me first and Stamp following a few paces behind with his sub machine gun raised and ready for action. We left the beach behind us and climbed the steps, creeping to minimize noise. The stairs became more finely crafted as we neared the top and were set with a decorative inlay. I peered over the last one and saw a path that wound through ornamental woodland. It led to a large lawn, beyond which lay a swimming pool, and behind that a large, beautiful Mediterranean villa. This was the kind of home most people could only dream of, and I wondered why it wasn't enough for Raymond Chalmont.

I caught movement to our right and saw one of Roman's men, dressed in black, smoking a vape and kicking the ground absently as he looked at the house. He was about twenty paces away and had his back to us.

I signaled Stamp to wait. He nodded and I climbed the final few steps and crept across the tufty grass at the top of the cliff. The man in black heard me moving toward him and turned. After a moment's shock he reached for a pistol tucked into his waistband, and I rushed him as he tried to pull it on me. He managed to get the gun out, but before he could bring it up, I hit him with my gun, catching him across the temple. The blow knocked him down and he fell still.

Stamp came up behind me and kicked the unconscious man in the ribs. I understood his anger, even if I didn't agree with his action.

We moved on through the trees. Sunshine danced between the gently rustling branches. This would have been a beautiful spot for a family picnic, but instead of using his resources for good, Chalmont had diverted them and made this a place of evil.

We reached the end of the wood and peered across the lawn to the house. There was a circular turret to one side of the building that gave the rooms that overlooked the sea almost 360-degree views.

"Lots of open ground," Stamp remarked, nodding at the rolling lawn.

"Yeah," I agreed. "I'll go first. You cover me."

He nodded, and I took a deep breath and started across the grass.

There was no point trying to be stealthy. I was exposed and vulnerable, in the full glare of the sun, and needed to change that as quickly as possible. My heart thundered as I sprinted across the lawn. Fear heightened my senses. I looked around, alert to danger. I was about halfway between the trees and the house when I saw another black-clad gunman rush through French doors at the back and use his sub machine gun to start spraying the garden around me with bullets. The air crackled as the turf ahead of my feet was churned and shredded by bullets. The gunman moved rapidly across the terrace toward the pool house, for some cover and to get a better angle of fire on me.

I shot at him and Stamp joined the effort, lighting up the area around the pool house with heavy fire, forcing the shooter to take cover behind the small structure.

I sprinted over the final stretch of grass, ran up a grand staircase, and crouched on the patio beside the pool, taking cover behind a stone balustrade, aiming my pistol so I was ready when the man broke cover.

Suddenly aware of movement behind me, I turned and fired instinctively, hitting another gunman who'd emerged from the bushes on the far side of the swimming pool.

Stamp signaled to me from the treeline, indicating he was going to make a run for it. I knew he was trying to lure the man behind the pool house out from his protected position. I nodded, and he ran across the lawn, legs hammering at full speed.

The gunman behind the pool house broke cover to target

Stamp. I trained my gun on the man and pulled the trigger twice. I shot him in the chest and he collapsed against the pool house wall and slid to the ground, his eyes glassy and lifeless.

Stamp joined me by the pool.

"You okay?" I asked.

He nodded and we set off around the swimming pool, toward the house.

CHAPTER 89

THERE WERE STEPS up to another terrace that was furnished with a large table, chairs, sofas, recliners and a wet bar. I imagined the parties that could have been held in such a place. Had Chalmont schmoozed Monégasque high society here? Had he used his power and influence to further the aims of his criminal accomplices? Despite the sun-kissed beauty of the place, I couldn't help but feel it was rotten to the core.

Beyond the broad terrace were some French doors. They stood wide open and led into a lavish kitchen.

As we headed there, the top of the exterior dining table beside us erupted, splintering as bullets hit it. Stamp and I took cover behind a patio sofa, and I peered round it to see a gunman in a second-floor window, inside the circular turret. He opened fire again, shredding the sofa near me, sending fabric and shards of wood everywhere. The noise was deafening and set my ears ringing, and I knew our flimsy cover wouldn't hold against such an assault for long.

"Second-floor turret window, third from the left," I yelled at Stamp. "You go right. I'll go left."

He nodded and I held up my fist to signal us to stay put while the storm of bullets continued to rain down.

The shooting stopped, I lowered my fist and we broke cover. I rolled out from behind the wall into a kneeling stance and aimed at the shooter. As the man targeted me in reply, Stamp opened fire from my right and a volley of bullets hit the marksman in the window, sending him bucking backwards into the shadows of the room.

I nodded my appreciation at Stamp, and he nodded back. Taking a life was rarely something to be celebrated, but sometimes it was necessary. I was always wary of those who reveled in killing. Stamp had the cold detachment of a professional soldier. I was glad to have him by my side.

We rose and ran across the terrace, and I went into the house first, barreling through the French doors, and rolling to my knees. I was glad I did, because a gunman appeared from behind a counter with a pistol in hand and shot the air where my head had been a split second earlier.

I responded with a single shot that hit his chest, and he fell back against a large silver double refrigerator, and slumped down, groaning.

"You have any idea where they were keeping Angie?" I whispered.

Stamp shook his head.

"Were you taken up or down any stairs?"

"No," he said quietly. "Not until we got outside. They led me down to the boat the way we've just come."

"Then she was on the first floor," I responded. "We search this place methodically until we find her."

We moved through the large kitchen, silently and carefully. I could hear the waves lapping against the sand in the bay below us, and the sounds of distant traffic, but the house was still. My heart pounded and my ears hummed, straining against the silence. The pistol felt heavy in my hand, and my eyes darted in one direction and then another as I searched for danger. I had no doubt it was close.

We stepped into a corridor that ran through the heart of the house. Elaborately framed paintings hung on the walls, and classical sculptures together with urns filled with flowers were displayed on marble plinths. The place screamed wealth, but it looked tasteless and overblown to me, particularly knowing the criminal enterprises of is owner.

Stamp stopped suddenly and I did likewise. He signaled to some double doors on the other side of the corridor and indicated he had heard a sound. I nodded, held my gun in the ready position, and the two of us moved toward the doors.

I reached for the brass handle and opened the door nearest me. I crept inside a huge drawing room, at least forty feet long and thirty wide. The space was furnished like the grand salon of a French château with chairs and couches in gilded frames, delicate Aubusson carpets over parquet flooring, and eighteenth-century paintings depicting scenes from Greek mythology.

Here, Zeus held a lightning bolt, ready to fling it against his enemies; there, Heracles fought the lion.

Standing in the middle of the room was Roman Verde.

He was holding Angie Stamp, with one of his hands over her mouth. The other clasped a pistol, which he pressed to her temple.

CHAPTER 90

"SECRETARY CARVER IS still alive," Roman said. "Which means your wife's life is forfeit."

"Don't," Stamp replied through gritted teeth.

I trained my pistol on Verde.

Angie couldn't talk, but her eyes told me everything. She was terrified, not just for herself but for her husband. Tears were visible when she looked at him.

"We're not here to have a movie standoff," Roman Verde said. He turned his gun on me and pulled the trigger.

The sound of the gunshot seemed too loud for the room. It cracked like thunder clouds colliding. My left shoulder immediately felt like it had caught on fire, and the flames instantly turned to agony as the bullet drilled straight through me.

It felt as though I'd been hit by a truck. I couldn't stop myself from tumbling back. As I crashed to the floor, I dropped my pistol and it clattered away, skidding toward one of the grand couches. I was suddenly painfully hot and broke into an instant sweat that cooled me far too fast, so that I swung between blazing heat and searing cold. The world swam, warping and bending into the most bizarre shapes.

Time must have slowed for me, because all of this happened the instant before Verde arced his gun around and shot Stamp in the right thigh. The former Marine and FBI agent crumpled instantly as the leg gave way beneath him. He cried out and dropped his gun so he could clutch at the wound.

"That's better," Verde said, his voice rising above the ringing in my ears, cutting through the pain that tormented me. "You people just don't get it. You wasted three lives today when you could have traded them for one. I'm going to kill you all. And then I'm going to kill your friends and loved ones. And when I'm done, I will make a new plan to deal with Eli Carver. You changed nothing except the date of his death and yours."

He took his hand away from Angie Stamp's mouth and she cried out, "Ken!"

I grimaced. I had to have answers and I wanted to play for time. "I know why you chose me. Revenge for your brother, but these two . . ." I indicated Kendrick and Angie Stamp.

"These two," Verde interrupted, "because he ruined a business deal and got me arrested. People who cross me pay the price."

"I don't even know you," Stamp protested, his voice strained from the pain he was in.

"That was your mistake," Verde said.

"What about Duval?" I asked.

"He failed us," Verde replied. "We don't tolerate failure. And knowing your reputation, I suspected you would tie him to us eventually. We are not a sentimental group, Mr. Morgan. Loyalty must be earned every single day."

It was the justification of a psychopath trying to excuse acting on their every whim.

"And why Carver?" I asked, casting my eyes around for a way out of this situation.

Verde sneered. I grew aware of faint sounds, which grew louder with each passing second.

Sirens.

Verde had clearly heard them too because he said, "We'd better get this over with before the police arrive. Which of you wants to see the other die?" he asked, addressing Angie and Kendrick Stamp. "Jack Morgan can watch you both, the last to taste a bullet, because I know how much he loves being a hero."

"Don't," Stamp managed to say, grimacing with pain.

I was in agony, but no amount of suffering could suppress the anger I felt toward this pitiless killer. I couldn't let us die here at his hands.

I steeled myself.

"If you can't make a choice, I'll choose for you," Verde said, and turned his gun on Angie. "You will watch your wife die."

"No," Stamp yelled as his wife broke into sobs.

Verde smiled and I saw his grip tighten on the gun. I rolled across the floor, ignored the explosion of pain that came with the movement, and grabbed my pistol. He reacted instinctively, pointing his gun toward me and opening fire, but his aim was off. I rolled onto my belly and shot him in the hip.

He staggered back, relinquishing his hold on Angie, and she ran clear, giving me an open target. Verde brought his gun up and round, but he wasn't fast enough. I already had him in my sights and pulled the trigger twice. A brace of bullets hit him in the chest. He fell back against a marble-and-gilt gueridon table before rolling onto the floor, where he lay moaning and gasping.

CHAPTER 91

I TOOK A deep breath and instantly regretted it. My shoulder was a fiery, bloody mass of pain, and I almost blacked out. I tried to hold on to the world, to fight the bleak pull of unconsciousness, but part of me wanted to surrender to the darkness.

Angie ran to her husband and the two of them embraced and kissed. Their loving display reminded me of Justine. I wanted to see her more than anything, and fought the black cloud fraying the edges of reality.

Pain cut through everything and shocked me to life. Like fear, I knew it could be channeled, so I tried to tame it. I wanted to escape it somehow and my body's autonomic processes knew unconsciousness was the best way, but I tried to convince myself I could outrun it and used it as a prompt to action, rising quickly and moving across the room once I'd got to my feet.

I heard sirens, close now, and knew I didn't have long. Twitchy with the searing pain, I staggered over to Stamp and Angie.

"You okay?" I asked, looking down at the wounded man.

He had removed his belt and was tying a tourniquet around his upper thigh to stem the flow of blood.

"I feel better than you look," he said. "You need a doctor."

I nodded and moved on. Standing still meant the pain would catch me. Movement helped me outrun it.

I lurched over to Roman Verde, who lay clutching the wounds in his chest. There was blood, but not the heavy, pulsing flow of a ruptured artery, so I thought I'd missed his heart. However, the bubbling, rasping sound he made with each gasping breath suggested I'd punctured a lung.

I loomed over him and kicked his pistol well clear of his grasp.

"Why?" I asked.

I bit my lip to keep myself from crying out in pain and resisted the urge to inflict my suffering on the man who'd done this to me. He was clearly in his own physical hell.

"Why?" I asked again.

He looked up from contemplating the holes in his chest and fixed me with hostile eyes. There was nothing but contempt radiating from the man, and he knew the feeling was mutual.

"Why Carver?" I pressed him.

He shook his head and for a moment I thought he wasn't going to answer.

"Peace," he gasped, his voice wet and rasping. "Peace is the enemy of all we stand for. He was supposed to die, then evidence would have been released implicating participants in the peace negotiation. The treaty would have collapsed, leading to permanent war in Europe."

"Why?" I asked. "What kind of people want never-ending war?"

He smiled. "If you have to ask that question, you wouldn't understand the answer."

"Who is behind Propaganda Tre?" I asked. "Who are you people?"

Verde smiled. It was insincere and full of hatred. "Keep looking over your shoulder, Jack Morgan."

The sirens were almost upon us. The first set of tires crunched over the gravel at the front of the house.

"Lying on your back, shot and bleeding out, and you threaten me? I can handle whatever you send my way. Can you say the same thing?" I growled. "All your people will meet the same end. Broken and ready to answer for what they've done."

Verde's smile fell away and his eyes narrowed.

We both looked in the direction of the front door, which cracked and splintered as it was smashed open. Then came the tramp of heavy boots over hardwood floors, and moments later Valerie Chevalier stormed into the room at the head of a squad of cops in tactical gear.

"Jack!" she yelled, and I followed her gaze to see that Verde had produced a second pistol from behind his back.

It was a snub nose .22 revolver, the kind of gun used in street muggings and gangland killings, and it was pointed directly at my head.

"Can you handle everything I send your way?" he rasped. "Goodbye, Mr. Morgan."

The sound of the shot turned my blood to ice. It took me a moment to realize it hadn't come from Roman's gun.

A volley of bullets tore through his left eye, creating a bloody crater and ripping a path deep into his skull. His other eye went glassy and rolled back as his body went limp. His hand fell to the floor and the gun clattered against the floor, but even in death he held it firm.

I looked round to see Kendrick Stamp holding his sub machine gun, the barrel still smoking.

"Thanks," I said.

"Don't mention it. We're even," he replied, pulling Angie close.

CHAPTER 92

I LOOKED DOWN at Roman Verde's body. He would never trouble anyone ever again, and while I regretted the fact that I wouldn't have the opportunity to question him further, I'd rather be alive without all the answers than dead and gone.

Police officers clustered around Angie and Kendrick Stamp, and one of them checked the tourniquet on Stamp's leg.

"Is it good?" Angie asked anxiously.

The police officer nodded at her and she smiled.

"You okay?" I asked, staggering over to her.

"Angie, this is Jack Morgan," Stamp introduced us. "He's the reason we're here."

Her smile broadened and her eyes filled to overflowing.

"Your husband is the reason we're here," I corrected him. "He could have taken the shot."

"And then they would have killed us both," Stamp responded.

"How did they get you out here?" I asked.

Stamp grimaced.

"I was retired from the Bureau on health grounds. Gunshot wound. They didn't think I still had what it takes. So, I was looking for jobs in law enforcement or adjacent fields."

He hesitated.

"And?" I asked.

"Philippe Duval got in touch and asked if I'd be interested in running the Private office he was setting up with you here in Monaco," Stamp revealed. "He invited me to interview and said I could bring Angie as his guest."

I shook my head and immediately regretted it.

"I didn't know," I said.

"I guessed that when you had no clue who I was," he replied.

"But I want you to come and see me in Los Angeles when you've recovered," I told him. "I can always use good people, and you've shown me exactly how good you are."

Stamp smiled and Angie hugged him again.

"Thanks," he said.

Chevalier had been coordinating with colleagues. She walked over to Verde, confirmed he was dead, and then joined us. The pain in my shoulder gradually retreated from a raging blaze to a smoldering fire with occasional flares and sparks of agony.

"There are ambulances on the way," she said. "Both of you need urgent attention."

"I'm okay," I replied.

She gave me a withering look.

"Okay, I'm not okay, but I will be," I said, and took a seat on one of the ornate Rococo chairs.

Chevalier came to stand beside me. "Secretary Carver is safe, thanks to you and your team. I'll need a full account for my report, but that can wait for now. I just wanted to thank you for what you've done. You saved his life, and you saved this city from scandal and terror."

I nodded almost imperceptibly. It hurt to move my head.

"And the owner of this house?" I asked. "Raymond Chalmont?"

"I don't yet understand how he is connected to what happened," Chevalier replied. "But we're looking for him."

A smart man would be on his way out of the country by now, if he hadn't already left. Nice Airport was a short drive away and could take a person west to the Americas, south to Africa or east to the farther reaches of Europe and Asia, but I didn't share these concerns with her.

"Jack!" Justine cried, straining to get past an officer in tactical gear who held her at the door.

"Let her in," Chevalier told her colleague, and he allowed Justine to pass.

She ran over and crouched down level with me, but hesitated when she saw my bullet wound.

"Oh my God," she said, her voice full of concern. "Jack."

"It's not as bad as it looks," I assured her, trying to conceal the pain I felt when talking. "It went straight through."

She winced and shook her head. "I'd hug you and kiss you if I knew it wouldn't make you pass out."

I replied in kind, forcing a smile through the pain. "Me too."

"And then I'd punch you for putting yourself in this kind of danger," she said, and my smile grew broader.

"I'd still hug and kiss you," I said.

"Me too. And I wouldn't really punch you," she responded tenderly. "You did a good thing. I'm just sorry to see you suffering. Both of you." She glanced round at Stamp before her eyes drifted to Verde's body. "And it makes me angry to see such meaningless violence because of the arrogance of evil men."

"I know," I told her. "What happened to Carver?"

"They took him back to his hotel," she revealed. "I get the impression it's become a fortress."

"And the race?" I asked.

"Qualifying restarted. They told everyone it was a technical difficulty."

"Carver can watch it from the hotel. The Fairmont Hairpin is a pretty spectacular section, and he'll have a suite with a view."

Four paramedics hurried into the room and split into two teams. The first pair went to Kendrick Stamp and the second came to me.

"He speaks English," the inspector told them.

"That's not his fault," the lead paramedic said. She was a thin, cheerful woman in her twenties with long blonde hair. "I'll speak slowly so he understands."

I smiled and so did her colleague, a man in his thirties with brown hair and a golden tan.

The lead paramedic lifted my shirt collar and I winced as the fabric pulled away from my wound.

"We'll patch you up in the ambulance," she said. "But you'll almost certainly need surgery at the hospital."

I nodded.

"Can you walk?" she asked.

"Yes," I replied. "I think so."

"Then let's go."

She and her colleague tried to help me to my feet.

"Please don't touch me," I said, rising gingerly.

Kendrick's paramedics had left the room to retrieve a gurney. He nodded at me.

"See you in Los Angeles, Mr. Morgan."

"Call me Jack," I replied through gritted teeth.

"We can get the wheelchair or a trolley," the lead paramedic said.

I had nothing against wheelchairs, but I felt it was important to leave this place under my own steam, to show the universe and myself that these men hadn't been able to drag me down.

The paramedics walked either side of me, and Justine followed us out.

The sunshine felt good against my face. As I shuffled toward the waiting ambulance, I was glad to have put our ordeal behind us.

CHAPTER 93

I WAS TAKEN to Princess Grace Hospital and scanned before undergoing surgery on my shoulder. My surgeon, Christos Argyropoulos, assured me it was a routine patch job. The scan showed the bullet had gone straight through with minimal tissue and bone damage. I went into theater, but the work was done under local anesthetic, so I got to listen to the Greek doctor cracking wise with his team while he worked. I wasn't squeamish, but there were times I had to look away as Christos and his American resident, Anthony Leonardi, sutured me inside and out. Thankfully the surgical team had music playing, which helped distract me, as did the back and forth of good-hearted banter between the doctors who constantly ribbed each other.

"Explain the role of T-cell differentiation in immunosenescence," Christos said.

Anthony scoffed, "I'm not a med student anymore."

"So, you don't know?" the senior surgeon countered.

"Of course I know, but I'm not educating you unless you agree to kale sandwiches for lunch."

"Urgh. Don't threaten me with that foul weed," Christos responded, his face scrunching in disgust. His expression changed and he was suddenly thoughtful. "We should get chili." He patted me on my good shoulder. "You're all done."

"Thank you," I replied. "For fixing me and for the laughs."

Their humor wasn't an indication of carelessness, it was a common trait in the Marine Corps and at Private. It was the mark of professionals who had confidence in their abilities and were trying take the heat out of what might have otherwise been a stressful experience for everyone involved, especially me. They'd given me exactly what I needed, and spending some time with people who took joy in everyday life was the perfect way to adjust back to normality. I was no longer facing immediate danger and needed to get myself out of the habit of viewing everyone as a potential threat.

I had my arm put into a sling and was wheeled out of surgery where I found Justine in the waiting area. Her expression was strained, but she smiled when she saw me looking so cheerful, and the tension melted out of her face.

"Jack," she said, hurrying over.

"I'm fine," I replied. "Much better."

I offered her my good hand, and she took it and squeezed it. We held each other as I was wheeled to my private room.

Justine stayed with me as I regained my strength, but we

passed much of the time in silence, simply enjoying one another's company and the joy of being alive.

At 8 p.m. Christos came to check my dressing.

"It looks good. Sutures are holding well," he said. "You can spend the night here or I can discharge you, provided you promise there'll be no exertion."

"It would be nice to go to the apartment," I replied. "Okay, no exertion."

"And if you notice any discharge or feel unwell in any way, you come straight back," he instructed.

I nodded.

"Okay. I'll write you a script for antibiotics and pain relief," he said. "You should be able to leave in twenty minutes."

The pain relief I'd had pre-surgery had reduced the agony in my shoulder to a dull ache and the sling restricted my movement to reduce the chance of my hurting myself. I felt confident I'd be comfortable out of hospital.

Half an hour later, once my discharge paperwork was complete and a nurse had given me a prescription, Justine and I left my room and took an elevator to the fifth floor.

We walked slowly, Justine giving me sidelong looks of concern as though I was made of glass and might shatter at any moment.

We rounded the corner and entered the private ward where I saw the police officer who was supposed to be protecting our friends was missing. My instinct for danger hadn't died in the operating theater and I felt a flush of adrenalin as I hurried to Sci's room and peered through the observation window.

His bed was empty and neatly made.

Had something happened to him? My heart sank. I couldn't take a loss like that.

Justine tapped my good arm and I turned to see her pointing at Mo-bot's room.

Sci sat on the side of her bed, playing cards with her. There was a mobile IV stand by his side, the bag hanging from it feeding a line into a canula in his left arm.

The cop was at the end of the bed, joining in the fun, clasping a run of cards tightly so no one could see them.

I smiled with relief and Justine and I went inside.

"Jack," Mo-bot said enthusiastically. "I see you've been making use of the facilities." She indicated my sling. "Come in. Sci has already lost his house to me. He's such a bad gambler."

"We're not gambling. This is just for fun," he replied.

"This is Officer Jean-Louis," Mo-bot said, and the young cop shifted uncomfortably.

"I need to return to my post," he said, shamefaced.

He sidled past us and shut the door on his way out.

"What happened?" Sci asked, gesturing to my injured arm.

"Roman Verde shot me," I replied. "He's not a problem anymore."

There was a moment of silent reflection, which Mo-bot finally broke with a single word.

"Good."

"I'm glad to see you up and around," Justine told Sci.

"Yeah, I don't do bed rest," he replied. "And you can imagine what this one is like stuck in here." He nodded at Mo-bot.

"Hey," she protested. "I can't help it if I feel fine and they want to drive me out of my mind with boredom by keeping me for another five days."

"They reckon it will be at least a week for me," Sci said. "Not quite the Riviera vacation I'd dreamed of."

"But you're alive," I said, "and that's better than any vacation."

"True," Sci replied.

"Do you need anything?" I asked.

"My computer," Mo-bot replied instantly. "Just the baby one so I can hack this place and bring my discharge forward."

I smiled and shook my head. "No chance. You're not doing any work until the docs sign you off as fully recovered."

"Killjoy," she countered.

"I think we're good," Sci said. "You should get some rest. You look pretty pale."

I nodded. "We'll check on you tomorrow. And we'll fill you in on exactly what happened with Carver and Roman Verde."

Justine and I headed for the door.

"Jack," Mo-bot said, and I paused. "Thanks for taking care of him."

I glanced back at her. "Wasn't going to end any other way," I said before leaving.

CHAPTER 94

I SLEPT THROUGH a long, dreamless night and woke at noon the following day when the sound of banging roused me. Justine stirred beside me. I groaned as I rolled out of bed, aware the painkillers had worn off. My shoulder felt raw and battered as though someone had hit it with a meat-tenderizing hammer a couple hundred times. But it was bearable. Just.

I fumbled with a pair of shorts and managed to pull them on one-handed as there was another knock at the door. Justine sighed and got up. She slipped into a T-shirt as I staggered out of the bedroom, aware the pitch of the pain in my shoulder was rising, throbbing a little more urgently. I needed a fresh dose of painkillers, but whoever was knocking at the door was doing so insistently now.

I opened it and was greeted by four faces. Eli Carver and three of his Secret Service agents, all somber, large men in dark suits. Wearing nothing but shorts, I suddenly felt very exposed.

"Mr. Secretary . . . I . . . well," I stammered. My head felt fuzzy, and I most definitely wasn't at my sharpest.

"I'm really sorry to walk in on you like this, Jack," Carver said, entering the apartment. His entitlement was strong, but I couldn't hold it against him. "I wanted to check you were okay. We heard about what happened at Raymond Chalmont's place."

"You'd better come in," I told his detail. They'd hovered on the threshold, waiting for instructions.

"Thanks," the lead agent said, and they entered and spread out around the living room.

"I also wanted to invite you and Justine . . ." Carver glanced at the corridor leading to the bedroom, where she had just appeared in her long T-shirt. "Morning," he said to her. "Sorry to intrude. I'd like to invite you both to be my guests at the race today. If you're up to it." He looked at my sling.

"Morning, Eli," Justine said. "How's your arm?" she asked me.

"I'll live. I just need some pills," I replied. I turned to Carver. "I guess you won't take no for an answer."

He smiled.

Two hours later, feeling more myself, fully dosed on painkillers, my hunger sated by a light sandwich lunch at the Fairmont, we joined Carver in the Monte Carlo Casino stand where we watched the race build up. I was glad Justine and I had accepted the invitation. As she sat next to me, holding my hand, I looked at her with adoring eyes, grateful the threat had passed and that we could be together without fear.

Carver sat on my right, and we talked to him about the great races and drivers of the past, the likes of Schumacher, Hill, Senna, Prost and Vettel. Carver was very knowledgeable and had nuggets of information about all of them.

It wasn't until almost an hour after arriving at the stand, minutes before the race was due to start, when the hush of expectation had swept over the crowd, that he turned the conversation to more serious matters.

"I owe you my life again, Jack," he said quietly.

"I did what was necessary, Mr. . . . . I mean, Eli," I replied.

He smiled at my use of his name. "You went above and beyond, and I might not be here now if you hadn't done so. I'm in your debt again."

"What happened to Henry Wilson?" I asked.

Justine had told me all about her experiences with Carver's aide.

"He's on a plane back to Washington," Carver replied, his eyes narrowing. "He's going to tell us exactly what he knows and then he's going to face the full force of the law."

I nodded.

"We're starting an operation against the remnants of Propaganda Tre and the Dark Fates," Carver revealed. "I want to find every member and expose them to the light of justice. This isn't just about national security for me, Jack. It's personal. They tried to kill me."

"I understand," I replied. "We'll share everything we have."

"Good. I want to make sure there aren't any other Henry Wilsons working against the US government, hiding some perverse allegiance."

"What about Raymond Chalmont?" I asked.

Carver scoffed. "He skipped the country. Took a private plane to Morocco yesterday morning. We'll find him though. In the meantime, we're going to freeze his assets."

"I don't think he'll cope well with hardship," I remarked.

Carver smiled. "Neither do I."

He patted his thighs.

"Anyway, that can all wait. We're here to have fun. Looks like the race is starting."

He gestured at the big screen to our right, which displayed the starting grid. Twenty beautiful, slick, precision-engineered, super-powered machines lined up in ten pairs, waiting for the lights to give them the go signal.

I turned to Justine and kissed her. She smiled.

The crowd cheered as the race started and the cars roared away.

It was absolutely thrilling to hear them approaching, their engines sounding like savage monsters, making the world tremble and shake. I couldn't help but feel a thrill of excitement as the leaders entered the Louis Chiron chicane, slowed momentarily like tamed beasts, before rediscovering their inner animal and roaring as they shot away in front of us.

I looked at Justine and saw her eyes too shining with excitement.

Life was good.

ACKNOWLEDGMENTS

We'd like to thank Rachel Imrie, Emily Griffin, Lynn Curtis, and the team at Penguin for their excellent work on this book. We'd also like to thank you, the reader, for joining Jack Morgan and the Private team on another adventure, and hope you'll return for the next one.

Adam would like to thank James Patterson for his continued collaboration. Thanks too to his wife Amy and their children, Maya, Elliot and Thomas, for their love and support. He'd also like to express his gratitude to his agent Nicola Barr.

There's no rest for Jack Morgan . . .

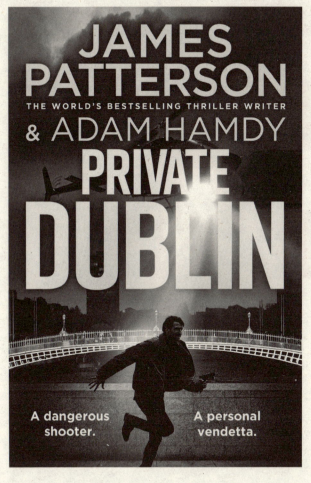

JAMES PATTERSON
THE WORLD'S BESTSELLING THRILLER WRITER
& ADAM HAMDY
PRIVATE DUBLIN

A dangerous shooter. A personal vendetta.

Turn the page for an exclusive extract . . .

CHAPTER 1

THUNDEROUS APPLAUSE FILLED the auditorium, and the filmmakers beamed as though the claps and cheers were dollar bills. I glanced at Justine, who was applauding politely. Even in a theater full of stars, she shone the brightest. Her wavy brown hair fell against the crimson cocktail dress she'd chosen for the premiere. It had a daring slit that showed off her long, tanned legs, and I could hardly take my eyes off her.

"What did you think?" she asked.

"Pretty good," I replied. "Alan will do well from it."

Alan Bloom was a former client, now friend, who was one of four producers of the movie we'd just watched. He was standing near the screen with the director, cast, studio executives and other producers. A *Star Wars* movie is always a big deal, and this, the first in a new trilogy, looked set to dominate the summer box office. The clamor of the crowd was as much a celebration of Hollywood's continued ability to captivate global audiences as it was a response to the movie.

After a standing ovation, people began filing out of Los Angeles's famous Samuel Goldwyn Theater, and Justine and I followed our neighbors into the aisle. Alan caught up to us as we joined the crowd thronging through the nearest exit. He looked wired. Like me, he was in a tuxedo, but he wore his better. Mine felt constrictive, ill suited to my line of work. Alan's fitted like a second skin. Combined with his perfectly coiffed salt-and-pepper hair, tan and dazzling smile, it gave him the appearance of a Bel Air James Bond, buzzing after the completion of a successful mission.

"Jack . . . Justine!" he called over the heads of the people around us. "What did you think?"

"You've got a great movie," I replied. "Congratulations."

"I loved it," Justine said. "I think it's going to be a hit."

Alan's smile broadened. "Thanks. It's always such a relief when a movie plays well."

The crowd swept us through the double doors into the marble lobby of the Academy, more precisely the Academy of Motion Picture Arts and Sciences. It's the headquarters of the organization that runs the Academy Awards and, in many ways, represents the seat of creative power in Hollywood.

The party was in full swing as we entered. Servers distributed drinks and canapes and the room was packed with chattering people abuzz with the energy of success. Deals were being made, careers enhanced, networks strengthened. Alan settled beside me and Justine as we sheltered beside a column.

"These things are always so hectic," he remarked, grabbing a glass of champagne from an agile server. "You want one?"

Justine shook her head. "The atmosphere is intoxicating enough."

"I'm driving," I said.

He nodded and took a gulp. "I need something to settle the nerves."

"Don't feel you have to babysit us," Justine told him. "If you need to work the room, go hustle."

Alan scoffed. "If it didn't look bad, I'd be on my way home to tuck myself up with a good book."

"A producer who reads," I said with a chuckle.

"That's a cheap shot," he replied with feigned hurt. "You guys are my cover. If anyone tries to cut in, just start talking about per diems, catering budgets, or something equally dull. Save me from schmoozing."

Justine and I grinned at Alan, but my smile fell away as soon as I registered a frighteningly familiar sound. The violent staccato of machine gunfire.

I heard screams and peered round the column to see a charge begin. People near the steel-and-glass entrance to the Academy pressed deeper into the lobby, their faces reflecting horror and panic, as a man in a ski mask stalked into the building after them. Behind him I could see a couple of fallen security guards. The paparazzi and fans who'd gathered around the red carpet had dispersed, and people were yelling frantically. I caught cries of "cops," and "ambulance."

"We need to move," I said, an instant before the masked gunman sprayed the room with bullets. "Now!"

The press of people turned into a panicked stampede, and screams joined a chorus of horrified cries as most people tried to flee back into the auditorium. Others attempted to escape through fire exits or doors to the service sections of the building. Some were gunned down as they ran.

I pushed Justine and Alan toward the auditorium, and as we moved, I locked eyes with the gunman. He hesitated for a moment before letting off a volley of bullets in my direction. I ducked into the short tunnel that led to the theater as the walls around me puckered and splintered under the impact of so many bullets.

The shooter was using some kind of machine pistol. I knew if he got into the auditorium there would be an absolute bloodbath, so I crouched against the wall by the doors to the lobby and ignored my thundering heartbeat. Behind me, people were pressing through the short tunnel into the theater.

Justine glanced back, but I gestured for her to follow the crowd to safety. As the shooter's shadow fell into the mouth of the tunnel, I rose, rounded the corner, and grabbed his weapon. A blast of gunfire erupted, spitting flame and lead from the muzzle. The bullets thudded into the wall and ceiling, raining plaster and dust onto us. I drove my shoulder into the shooter's chest, and as he collided with the wall, I caught him with a right hook that dazed him. I grabbed the gun and wrenched it free, but as I was about to turn it on him, I heard a sound that sickened me.

"Jack," Justine said, anguish and pain palpable in her trembling voice.

I glanced over my shoulder to see her in the doorway to the auditorium. Alan was trying to support her as she clutched her stomach. A spreading bloodstain was turning her dress a deeper shade of red. She fell to her knees and looked at me pleadingly.

"Jack," she said, "I'm sorry . . ."

I staggered toward her and barely registered the shooter push past me and run for the exit.

"Save the planet!" he yelled as he sprinted into the street. "Two degrees is extinction . . ."

The words jolted me to my senses and, for a split second, I thought about giving chase, but Justine needed me. I ran to her side and handed Alan the pistol.

"Hold this in case he comes back," I said as I supported Justine.

"I'll call 911." Alan took his phone from his pocket and stepped away to dial.

I registered a few other people around us using their phones, speaking hurriedly to emergency operators, friends or family. I stroked Justine's face. "Stay with me, Justine. Stay with me."

"I'm cold, Jack," she replied weakly. "I'm so cold."

"Someone, help!" I yelled, as her strength gave out and her eyes rolled back in her head.

CHAPTER 2

THE SHOOTING HAD received sensational coverage. The paparazzi, who had been there to cover the premiere, had captured and shared video footage of the masked gunman yelling his environmental creed, and the media had already dubbed him the Ecokiller. Unsure whether he was still armed, security and passersby had kept their distance, and the perp had fled into the night, slipping away in the confusion caused by his onslaught before the cops arrived.

I was in the waiting room at Cedars-Sinai Hospital off Beverly Boulevard, watching the unfolding coverage on my phone, trying to glean any useful pieces of information that might help me identify the shooter, while doctors performed emergency surgery on Justine. The brief ambulance ride from the theater had been the most stressful experience of my life. I could tell from the paramedics' grave expressions and artificially calm voices that she was in serious danger.

I hadn't been allowed into the emergency room. Hours ago a nurse had told me Justine was being taken for emergency abdominal surgery. Since then I'd tried to distract myself with my phone, my hands shaking with fear for her. My heart thudded with anger at the thought of the monster who'd done this, my body flushing hot and cold as I replayed the attack in my mind over and over again. It didn't matter which websites I visited, which news reports I watched, I couldn't shut out the memories of my own failings. I chastised myself for my stupid mistakes. If I'd done things differently, if I'd been better and faster and stronger, Justine would have been at my side now instead of fighting for her life in an operating theater.

"Jack!" a familiar voice called across the crowded room.

Eighteen people had been wounded and four killed in the attack, and most had been brought to Cedars-Sinai, so the place was packed with the victims' family and friends.

I turned to see Maureen Roth, Private's technology guru, entering the room. Known to everyone at Private as "Mo-bot," she was a computer geek extraordinaire. At fifty-something, she was a salutary lesson in the unexpected. Her tattoos and spiky hair suggested a cold, hard rebel, but she had the warmest heart and was thought of by many at Private as their second mom, someone they could go to with their problems. The only thing about her that hinted at a softer side, and spoke to her age, were the bifocals, which I always said looked like they belonged to a

Boca Raton grandmother. She managed a team of six tech specialists in the LA office and oversaw dozens of others in Private's international units. She was followed into the waiting room by Seymour "Sci" Kloppenberg, Private's world-renowned forensics expert. A slight, bookish man, he dressed like a Hells Angel biker, which was where his heart probably lay because he was always restoring old muscle bikes. These two were among my oldest friends and most trusted colleagues and it was comforting to see them.

"How is she?" Sci asked.

"She caught two in the stomach," I replied, scarcely able to believe what I was saying. "She's in surgery still."

"I'm so sorry, Jack," Mo-bot said, and gave me a reassuring hug.

"She's going to be okay," Sci remarked. "Justine's a fighter."

I nodded, but my experiences of losing people in the field told me it didn't matter how strong or determined a person was, a bullet could be the ultimate arbiter of life or death.

"What happened?" Mo-bot asked. "I've seen the news, but how did the guy get in?"

"Looks like he shot door security and then came in and started blasting," I replied.

"Media are saying he was disarmed by a guest. You?" Sci asked.

I nodded. "If I'd been quicker . . ." I trailed off.

"I bet you were as fast as anyone could have been," Sci told me. "You did good, Jack."

I nodded again, but his words rang hollow. It was hard to view my response as anything other than an abject failure when the woman I loved was currently fighting for her life in an operating theater.

"Cops spoken to you yet?" Mo-bot asked.

I shook my head. "I've been told to expect a detective, but I think they're giving me space while I deal with this." I nodded in the direction of the double doors that led to the surgical area. "I don't have much to tell them. The shooter was masked, so I didn't get a look at him. He was about six-one, well built, strong and fast."

"They're calling him the Ecokiller," Sci remarked.

"He yelled a bunch of stuff about the planet as he escaped," I replied. "I want us to find him."

Mo-bot put her hand on my shoulder. "You did well, Jack. If you hadn't been there, who knows how many more might have died. But this isn't on you. Focus on Justine. Let the cops handle this. Sci and I will help."

I looked at Mo-bot and her reassuring smile wilted under the severity of my stare. I wasn't angry with her, but my anger at the man who had put us here shone through. "I can't do that, Mo," I told her. "I need to find this guy and make sure he answers for what he's done."

CHAPTER 3

THAT NIGHT, I dreamed of flames and the screams of those I couldn't save when my Marine Corps CH-46 Sea Knight had been shot down in Afghanistan. I'd been a chopper pilot for the Corps before taking over Private from my old man, and since then had turned his ramshackle outfit into the world's largest private detective agency. I'd faced danger and death more times than I cared to remember. However, the loss of those men, the jarheads I'd served with, hurt most of all. Even though the NCIS investigation had concluded there had been no way to avoid the crash, I'd still felt responsible. It didn't matter what the investigators said, or how many people told me I'd done my best. All that mattered was the blood and honor of the field, and I carried my failure with me. It tormented me still when I was low or troubled. To this day, memories of that crash and the ghosts of those men were guaranteed to make me feel as low as humanly possible, but now my failure to protect Justine had become a new nadir, a low from which I could only recover if she did. In my dream, I fled the scorching heat of the fire, abandoning the bodies burning in the wreckage, but when I turned, I saw Justine kneeling on the rocky ground, clutching the gunshot wounds in her belly, blood spreading across the front of her red dress.

"Mr. Morgan," a voice cut in, and I felt a hand on my shoulder.

I woke with a start to see Dr. Gurdasani, a woman in her mid-thirties, smiling at me gently.

"Mr. Morgan," she repeated, "Ms. Smith is out of surgery and just surfacing from the anesthetic. It's early, but we think she's going to pull through."

"Can I see her?" I asked.

"In a little while," Dr. Gurdasani replied. "Once we've got her comfortable."

A "little while" proved to be ninety of the slowest minutes I've ever experienced. I'd sent Mo-bot and Sci home shortly after 3 a.m. so I messaged them while I was waiting to let them know Justine was out of surgery and recovering. They both wished her well and asked to send them updates. With nothing more to do and my desire to see her filling me with impatience, I tried distracting myself by pacing the now quiet waiting room and checking my phone for updates on the shooting. There wasn't much more to go on, and the sensational stories about the Ecokiller focused mostly on newly released details about the gunman's victims. The four dead were two security guards who'd been on the door, a server who'd been working shifts to help put herself through UCLA, and a junior studio executive who was being hailed as a hero for shielding his colleagues as they escaped through a fire exit. Social media photos accompanied the news pieces, and I felt nothing but sympathy for their loved ones. I tried not to imagine the suffering of such loss, but it was difficult to push past the dark imaginings that had tormented me in that hospital, a place where the line between life and death was at its thinnest.

Finally, when my patience was ragged and frayed, Dr. Gurdasani beckoned me from beyond the ward doors.

"You can see her now," she said, and I didn't bother trying to play it cool but snapped to the medic's side like a faithful dog.

We walked to the recovery ward in silence, passing rooms containing surgery patients wired to monitors and connected to drips. Despite this display of frailty, I wasn't prepared for what greeted me when Dr. Gurdasani led me into Justine's room. Her dark hair was lank and had been tied back from the face that had been so bright and alive only a few hours ago, now pale and clammy. She lay in a bed, a light blanket supported on a frame draped over her bandaged abdomen. I saw she was connected to two drips and guessed one was fluid and the other antibiotics or some sort of medication. A monitor tracked her heart function and a catheter led to a bag hooked to the side of her bed. Her eyes opened as we entered. They were bloodshot and sunken into shadow, and her pupils looked faded. A CPAP oxygen mask covered her nose and mouth, and there was a gentle rush of air with each breath.

"Justine," I said.

Her eyes filled with tears as she registered me moving toward her.

"You can't stay long," Dr. Gurdasani said. She'd hung back by the door. "Justine needs her rest."

I stood by the bed and gently clasped her hand. It was cold and there was hardly any strength in her fingers.

"I'm going to stay right here until I can take you home," I told her.

She closed her eyes and a couple of tears spilled from them and rolled down her sunken cheeks. She shook her head, the gesture so slight as to be almost imperceptible.

I lingered. In the quiet broken only by the humming of the machines surrounding her, I realized Justine was trying to talk. I leaned close to her and she strained to be heard through the oxygen mask she wore.

"Find him." Her voice was a hoarse whisper. "Find the man who did this to me."

Have you read them all?

PRIVATE
(with Maxine Paetro)

Jack Morgan is head of Private, the world's largest investigation company with branches around the globe. When his best friend's wife is murdered, he sets out to track down her killer. But be warned: Jack doesn't play by the rules.

PRIVATE LONDON
(with Mark Pearson)

Hannah Shapiro, a young American student, has fled her country, but can't flee her past. Can Private save Hannah from the terror that has followed her to London?

PRIVATE GAMES
(with Mark Sullivan)

It's July 2012 and excitement is sky high for the Olympic Games in London. But when one of the organisers is found brutally murdered, it soon becomes clear to Private London that everyone involved is under threat.

PRIVATE: NO. 1 SUSPECT
(with Maxine Paetro)

When Jack Morgan's former lover is found murdered in his bed, Jack is instantly the number one suspect, and he quickly realises he is facing his toughest challenge yet.

PRIVATE BERLIN
(with Mark Sullivan)

Mattie Engel, one of Private Berlin's rising stars, is horrified when her former fiancé Chris is murdered. Even more so when she realises that the killer is picking off Chris's friends. Will Mattie be next?

PRIVATE DOWN UNDER
(with Michael White)

Private Sydney's glamorous launch party is cut short by a shocking discovery – the murdered son of one of Australia's richest men. Meanwhile, someone is killing the wealthy wives of the Eastern Suburbs, and the next victim could be someone close to Private.

PRIVATE L.A.
(with Mark Sullivan)

A killer is holding L.A. to ransom. On top of this, Hollywood's golden couple have been kidnapped. Can Private prove themselves once again?

PRIVATE INDIA
(with Ashwin Sanghi)

In Mumbai, someone is murdering seemingly unconnected women in a chilling ritual. As the Private team race to find the killer, an even greater threat emerges . . .

PRIVATE VEGAS
(with Maxine Paetro)

Jack Morgan's client has just confessed to murdering his wife, and his best friend is being held on a trumped-up charge that could see him locked away for a very long time. With Jack pushed to the limit, all bets are off.

PRIVATE SYDNEY
(with Kathryn Fox)

Private Sydney are investigating the disappearance of the CEO of a high-profile research company. He shouldn't be difficult to find, but why has every trace of evidence he ever existed vanished too?

PRIVATE PARIS
(with Mark Sullivan)

When several members of Paris's cultural elite are found dead, the French police turn to the Private Paris team for help tackling one of the biggest threats the city has ever faced.

THE GAMES
(with Mark Sullivan)

The eyes of the world are on Rio for the Olympic Games, and Jack is in Brazil's beautiful capital. But it's not long before he uncovers terrifying evidence that the Games could be the setting for the worst atrocity the world has ever seen.

PRIVATE DELHI
(with Ashwin Sanghi)

Private have opened a new office in Delhi, and it's not long before the agency takes on a case that could make or break them. Human remains have been found in the basement of a house in South Delhi. But this isn't just any house, this property belongs to the state government.

PRIVATE PRINCESS
(with Rees Jones)

Jack Morgan has been invited to meet Princess Caroline, third in line to the British throne, who needs his skills (and discretion) to help find her missing friend. Jack knows there is more to this case than he is being told. What is the Princess hiding?

PRIVATE MOSCOW
(with Adam Hamdy)

Jack Morgan is investigating a murder at the New York Stock Exchange and identifies another killing in Moscow that appears to be linked. So he heads to Russia, and begins to uncover a conspiracy that could have global consequences.

PRIVATE ROGUE
(with Adam Hamdy)

A wealthy businessman approaches Jack Morgan with a desperate plea to track down his daughter and grandchildren, who have disappeared without a trace. As Jack investigates the disappearances, the trail leads towards Afghanistan – where Jack's career as a US Marine ended in catastrophe . . .

PRIVATE BEIJING
(with Adam Hamdy)

After an attack on the Beijing office leaves three agents dead and the head of the team missing, Jack Morgan immediately gets on a plane from LA to investigate. But it's not long before another Private office is attacked and it's clear that the entire organisation is under threat . . .

PRIVATE ROME
(with Adam Hamdy)

A priest is murdered and a Private agent is the number one suspect. But as Jack Morgan strives to prove the man's innocence, he uncovers a much deadlier conspiracy . . .

Also By James Patterson

ALEX CROSS NOVELS

Along Came a Spider • Kiss the Girls • Jack and Jill • Cat and Mouse • Pop Goes the Weasel • Roses are Red • Violets are Blue • Four Blind Mice • The Big Bad Wolf • London Bridges • Mary, Mary • Cross • Double Cross • Cross Country • Alex Cross's Trial (*with Richard DiLallo*) • I, Alex Cross • Cross Fire • Kill Alex Cross • Merry Christmas, Alex Cross • Alex Cross, Run • Cross My Heart • Hope to Die • Cross Justice • Cross the Line • The People vs. Alex Cross • Target: Alex Cross • Criss Cross • Deadly Cross • Fear No Evil • Triple Cross • Alex Cross Must Die • The House of Cross

THE WOMEN'S MURDER CLUB SERIES

1st to Die (*with Andrew Gross*) • 2nd Chance (*with Andrew Gross*) • 3rd Degree (*with Andrew Gross*) • 4th of July (*with Maxine Paetro*) • The 5th Horseman (*with Maxine Paetro*) • The 6th Target (*with Maxine Paetro*) • 7th Heaven (*with Maxine Paetro*) • 8th Confession (*with Maxine Paetro*) • 9th Judgement (*with Maxine Paetro*) • 10th Anniversary (*with Maxine Paetro*) • 11th Hour (*with Maxine Paetro*) • 12th of Never (*with Maxine Paetro*) • Unlucky 13 (*with Maxine Paetro*) • 14th Deadly Sin (*with Maxine Paetro*) • 15th Affair (*with Maxine Paetro*) • 16th Seduction (*with Maxine Paetro*) • 17th Suspect (*with Maxine Paetro*) • 18th Abduction (*with Maxine Paetro*) • 19th Christmas (*with Maxine Paetro*) • 20th Victim (*with Maxine Paetro*) • 21st Birthday (*with Maxine Paetro*) • 22 Seconds (*with Maxine Paetro*) • 23rd Midnight (*with Maxine Paetro*) • The 24th Hour (*with Maxine Paetro*) • 25 Alive (*with Maxine Paetro*)

DETECTIVE MICHAEL BENNETT SERIES

Step on a Crack (*with Michael Ledwidge*) • Run for Your Life (*with Michael Ledwidge*) • Worst Case (*with Michael Ledwidge*) • Tick Tock (*with Michael Ledwidge*) • I, Michael Bennett (*with Michael Ledwidge*) • Gone (*with Michael Ledwidge*) •

Burn (*with Michael Ledwidge*) • Alert (*with Michael Ledwidge*) • Bullseye (*with Michael Ledwidge*) • Haunted (*with James O. Born*) • Ambush (*with James O. Born*) • Blindside (*with James O. Born*) • The Russian (*with James O. Born*) • Shattered (*with James O. Born*) • Obsessed (*with James O. Born*) • Crosshairs (*with James O. Born*) • Paranoia (*with James O. Born*)

PRIVATE NOVELS

Private (*with Maxine Paetro*) • Private London (*with Mark Pearson*) • Private Games (*with Mark Sullivan*) • Private: No. 1 Suspect (*with Maxine Paetro*) • Private Berlin (*with Mark Sullivan*) • Private Down Under (*with Michael White*) • Private L.A. (*with Mark Sullivan*) • Private India (*with Ashwin Sanghi*) • Private Vegas (*with Maxine Paetro*) • Private Sydney (*with Kathryn Fox*) • Private Paris (*with Mark Sullivan*) • The Games (*with Mark Sullivan*) • Private Delhi (*with Ashwin Sanghi*) • Private Princess (*with Rees Jones*) • Private Moscow (*with Adam Hamdy*) • Private Rogue (*with Adam Hamdy*) • Private Beijing (*with Adam Hamdy*) • Private Rome (*with Adam Hamdy*) • Private Monaco (*with Adam Hamdy*)

NYPD RED SERIES

NYPD Red (*with Marshall Karp*) • NYPD Red 2 (*with Marshall Karp*) • NYPD Red 3 (*with Marshall Karp*) • NYPD Red 4 (*with Marshall Karp*) • NYPD Red 5 (*with Marshall Karp*) • NYPD Red 6 (*with Marshall Karp*)

DETECTIVE HARRIET BLUE SERIES

Never Never (*with Candice Fox*) • Fifty Fifty (*with Candice Fox*) • Liar Liar (*with Candice Fox*) • Hush Hush (*with Candice Fox*)

INSTINCT SERIES

Instinct (*with Howard Roughan, previously published as* Murder Games) • Killer Instinct (*with Howard Roughan*) • Steal (*with Howard Roughan*)

THE BLACK BOOK SERIES

The Black Book (*with David Ellis*) • The Red Book
(*with David Ellis*) • Escape (*with David Ellis*)

STAND-ALONE THRILLERS

The Thomas Berryman Number • Hide and Seek • Black
Market • The Midnight Club • Sail (*with Howard Roughan*) •
Swimsuit (*with Maxine Paetro*) • Don't Blink (*with Howard
Roughan*) • Postcard Killers (*with Liza Marklund*) • Toys (*with
Neil McMahon*) • Now You See Her (*with Michael Ledwidge*) •
Kill Me If You Can (*with Marshall Karp*) • Guilty Wives (*with
David Ellis*) • Zoo (*with Michael Ledwidge*) • Second Honeymoon
(*with Howard Roughan*) • Mistress (*with David Ellis*) • Invisible
(*with David Ellis*) • Truth or Die (*with Howard Roughan*) •
Murder House (*with David Ellis*) • The Store (*with Richard
DiLallo*) • Texas Ranger (*with Andrew Bourelle*) • The President
is Missing (*with Bill Clinton*) • Revenge (*with Andrew Holmes*) •
Juror No. 3 (*with Nancy Allen*) • The First Lady (*with Brendan
DuBois*) • The Chef (*with Max DiLallo*) • Out of Sight (*with
Brendan DuBois*) • Unsolved (*with David Ellis*) • The Inn (*with
Candice Fox*) • Lost (*with James O. Born*) • Texas Outlaw (*with
Andrew Bourelle*) • The Summer House (*with Brendan DuBois*) •
1st Case (*with Chris Tebbetts*) • Cajun Justice (*with Tucker
Axum*)• The Midwife Murders (*with Richard DiLallo*) • The
Coast-to-Coast Murders (*with J.D. Barker*) • Three Women
Disappear (*with Shan Serafin*) • The President's Daughter (*with
Bill Clinton*) • The Shadow (*with Brian Sitts*) • The Noise (*with
J.D. Barker*) • 2 Sisters Detective Agency (*with Candice Fox*) •
Jailhouse Lawyer (*with Nancy Allen*) • The Horsewoman (*with
Mike Lupica*) • Run Rose Run (*with Dolly Parton*) • Death of the
Black Widow (*with J.D. Barker*) • The Ninth Month (*with Richard
DiLallo*) • The Girl in the Castle (*with Emily Raymond*) •
Blowback (*with Brendan DuBois*) • The Twelve Topsy-Turvy,
Very Messy Days of Christmas (*with Tad Safran*) • The Perfect
Assassin (*with Brian Sitts*) • House of Wolves (*with Mike
Lupica*) • Countdown (*with Brendan DuBois*) • Cross Down

(with Brendan DuBois) • Circle of Death (with Brian Sitts) • Lion & Lamb (with Duane Swierczynski) • 12 Months to Live (with Mike Lupica) • Holmes, Margaret and Poe (with Brian Sitts) • The No. 1 Lawyer (with Nancy Allen) • The Murder Inn (with Candice Fox) • Confessions of the Dead (with J.D. Barker) • 8 Months Left (with Mike Lupica) • Lies He Told Me (with David Ellis) • Raised by Wolves (with Emily Raymond) • Holmes Is Missing (with Brian Sitts) • The Texas Murders (with Andrew Bourelle) • The Imperfect Murder (with J.D. Barker)

NON-FICTION

Torn Apart (with Hal and Cory Friedman) • The Murder of King Tut (with Martin Dugard) • All-American Murder (with Alex Abramovich and Mike Harvkey) • The Kennedy Curse (with Cynthia Fagen) • The Last Days of John Lennon (with Casey Sherman and Dave Wedge) • Walk in My Combat Boots (with Matt Eversmann and Chris Mooney) • ER Nurses (with Matt Eversmann) • James Patterson by James Patterson: The Stories of My Life • Diana, William and Harry (with Chris Mooney) • American Cops (with Matt Eversmann) • What Really Happens in Vegas (with Mark Seal) • The Secret Lives of Booksellers and Librarians (with Matt Eversmann) • Tiger, Tiger • American Heroes (with Matt Eversmann) • The Last Days of Marilyn Monroe (with Imogen Edwards-Jones)

MURDER IS FOREVER TRUE CRIME

Murder, Interrupted (with Alex Abramovich and Christopher Charles) • Home Sweet Murder (with Andrew Bourelle and Scott Slaven) • Murder Beyond the Grave (with Andrew Bourelle and Christopher Charles) • Murder Thy Neighbour (with Andrew Bourelle and Max DiLallo) • Murder of Innocence (with Max DiLallo and Andrew Bourelle) • Till Murder Do Us Part (with Andrew Bourelle and Max DiLallo)

COLLECTIONS

Triple Threat (*with Max DiLallo and Andrew Bourelle*) • Kill or Be Killed (*with Maxine Paetro, Rees Jones, Shan Serafin and Emily Raymond*) • The Moores are Missing (*with Loren D. Estleman, Sam Hawken and Ed Chatterton*) • The Family Lawyer (*with Robert Rotstein, Christopher Charles and Rachel Howzell Hall*) • Murder in Paradise (*with Doug Allyn, Connor Hyde and Duane Swierczynski*) • The House Next Door (*with Susan DiLallo, Max DiLallo and Brendan DuBois*) • 13-Minute Murder (*with Shan Serafin, Christopher Farnsworth and Scott Slaven*) • The River Murders (*with James O. Born*) • The Palm Beach Murders (*with James O. Born, Duane Swierczynski and Tim Arnold*) • Paris Detective • 3 Days to Live • 23 ½ Lies (*with Maxine Paetro*)

For more information about James Patterson's novels, visit www.penguin.co.uk.